Like us, the Polar Bears

by

TESS MARSET

1 Lone Crow Media

Front cover photography:
© 2020 by Zachary Martzke

Book and cover design:
Vladimir Verano, Vertvolta Design
vertvoltapress.com

ISBN: 978-1-7333609-4-4

PUBLISHED BY

1 Lone Crow Media

www.1LoneCrowMedia.com

To Mo,
my own partner in crime

Like Us, the Polar Bears

CHAPTER ONE

Molly Ohashi

Research Paper

Mr. Schumacher

Per. 3 — Science — Jrs.

4. 26. 2016

<u>The Plight of Polar Bears</u>

Introduction

Time might be running out for the lovable fluffy polar bear. Although a popular figure for soda commercials and winter holiday shows, its charm may not be enough to save this bear from extinction. Climate change, the warming of the ocean, and the melting of ice <u>flows</u> are all speeding up doom for the big white bear. We need to ask ourselves, "Where would the world be without polar bears?" The answer may surprise you. This paper hopes to answer that question.

SP? floes

Good intro, Molly!

"How are you feeling? Is everything okay?"

"Yeah, Mom. I'm … all right. Just kinda tired, that's all."

"Are you sure you're okay, baby?"

"Yeah … No … Actually I guess one thing is kinda bugging me."

"Yeah? What is it, Mol?" my mom asked, sighing.

All she wanted at that moment was to smoke a Pall Mall and sit out under the awning in her resin chair with her feet propped up on the steps to watch the sun go down. I could tell by the tired way her sigh escaped through her nostrils, in a soft huff. More than likely, she'd be out there petting my dad's cat, Foe, who always jumped up on her lap to keep her company, although she acted like she hated him when he hung around begging for his dinner.

"I don't know. It's just weird. But maybe it's me."

"What's weird?"

"I don't get why they called it a 'Celebration of Life,'" I said. "Aren't celebrations supposed to be happy events? Even Melody would have thought the idea was totally messed up and not appropriately named."

It really was, the more I thought about it. Although people had tried to be gracious at the service and remind each other that my friend was in a better place, they were weeping, moaning, and feeling miserable just as they would have for any funeral. There weren't many reasons to celebrate someone's death, unless that person happened to be downright evil, but even that was kinda cold. But maybe that was just me.

"It's like … It's just that …" Mom started to say.

She sounded weary. And with good reason. The day before she had worked a double shift just so I didn't attend today's service by myself. She wouldn't admit it, but I could tell her nerves were frazzled by the way her hand trembled slightly as she tucked back her hair behind her ear. She longed for a drink. Just one. And she probably thought that I was asking one of my ass-busting questions again. I wasn't trying to. She *did* ask me what was wrong, after all.

She stared at floor and rubbed her forehead. I knew she really preferred for me to leave her be to smoke her cigarettes in peace. Then she shook her head and explained, "I don't think the Chastings wanted to call it a funeral. Not for their little girl. I think it was just too hard for them to do. I don't know if I could do it."

"But isn't it somewhat ironic, especially since it was a suicide and all? If Melody had had any intention of celebrating life, she wouldn't have ended hers."

Mom closed her eyes and shook her head slowly, like she did whenever she got fed up. I had gone too far. Again. Unfortunately, whenever my thoughts exited my mouth, I didn't necessarily come out with the wisest of things. Mom was always quick to tell anyone she met that I had been nonstop with asking about this and questioning that since I learned to talk. When I was younger, she would scold me and say, "Why can't you just accept things the way they are and leave it at that?"

This time she said, "Molly Genre, what is wrong with you? Would you stop it already with all of your dang questions? I swear they are going to be the death of *me* one day. This isn't the time or place. Your best friend was buried today. So let's show some respect, okay? I thought you said you were going to take a shower when you got home. Go already. I need a smoke." Then she shook her head again and muttered low under her breath, "Sweet Jesus."

I couldn't understand why she still had the desire to smoke, especially after having just attended a funeral. I remembered telling her specifically that the Centers for Disease Control reported that nearly a half a million deaths were attributed annually to smoking, with more than two hundred thousand of them made up of women alone. You just couldn't ignore those kinds of statistics.

"Is it a good idea to be smoking those things, especially under stress? A new study I just read said—"

"Go!"

Mom didn't intend to be harsh on me; I knew that. But she had no idea how to handle me, either. She never did. Dad did, but he wasn't here. She said that I was an anxious baby and always flipping out over everything and now seventeen years later, she said things hadn't improved much.

I retreated to my room, located toward the rear of our mobile home, and slid the pocket door shut behind me. While I removed my earrings, my half-assed collage of photos taped up on the wall over my desk caught my eye. The photos bore testimony to years of birthday parties, first days of school, summer camping trips with Melody's family, Christmas recitals, junior and senior proms, graduation, selfies—each moment ripped from the "BFF Story of Mel and Mol."

Earlier today, some photos of those very same events had been displayed around Mel's casket. It was hard to imagine one of those goofy girls in that story was sealed in that glossy white box with the silver handles, lying still beneath the bright spray of gladiolas and lilies, with her hands clasped peacefully over her stomach. It couldn't be Mel. She was always laughing, and giggling, and shrieking, and talking. She was the most theatrical, animated person I knew.

Beside the photos, the Chastings had also set out a few of her cherished things, including her North High cheerleader uniform and NSDA debate trophy, along with her clarinet whose sounds had evolved from squeaks to sultry tones sometime between sixth grade and junior year. These items were as familiar to me as if they were my own. But what caught my eye was Ralphie, her favorite plush bunny with replacement button eyes for the ones he'd lost when she was three, looking love worn and tattered from a lifetime of little girl hugs. He was so out of place there in front of the rows of white folding chairs, the pleated gold-lamé drapes, and the sobbing figures dressed in black.

It was Ralphie who had brought us together. When I was little, I was so painfully shy, scared, and homesick, that I had spent the first week of first grade blubbering every day after lunch recess. Melody was outgoing and friendly, and to my good luck, not only did she sit in the desk next to mine, she also felt bad for me. Her mom had let her bring Ralphie to school for the first week. I remember how Melody raised her hand just when my head was feeling fuzzy from crying so much. Mrs. Ozette, our teacher, called on her, and Mel asked if it would be okay to share her bunny with me to make me feel better. Mrs. Ozette thought it was a wonderful idea. So did I. That was the Mel I knew—full of compassion and caring. We remained friends from that day on.

I so wanted to snatch up Ralphie, and Melody's uniform, trophy, and clarinet, and run out screaming and flipping off everyone in that horrible place. But I didn't. Instead, I sat obediently and respectfully in my hard seat. I inwardly kicked myself over my lack of courage. Through the years, there had been many times Mel had bailed me out of socially awkward situations out of sheer loyalty, even when she had outdistanced me in the popularity department. I sorely wished that I could have at least rescued her things.

She wasn't supposed to be there. And why did she leave without telling me?

I plucked a selfie off the wall that was snapped at the Wild Waves amusement park last summer and studied the two friends mugging for the shot. It was the last photo we had taken together. Anyone could tell that we, Mel and Mol, were rarely ever apart. In fact, I was treated like a VIP today, with relatives and friends of the family giving me gentle embraces and gazing upon me with the kind of sympathetic reverence usually reserved for cancer patients or centenarians.

At least I thought we were best friends. I had grown up believing we knew every last detail about each other. Confused, I was now left wondering exactly what *did* I know about her? And about others around me? It reminded me of a time when I was little, and my dad took me to visit his firehouse. I felt privileged, because I got to climb up into the shining, clean fire truck. But I remembered how shocked and disappointed I was when I saw its beat and dingy interior with its torn seats and scuffed walls.

I laid the photo on my desk. Suddenly, I felt exhausted in the clothes I had worn to the "celebration." It was as if rocks had been sewn into the seams, weighing me down. I headed for the shower. With relief, I shed the thrift store black skirt with the hem that was coming undone and the white button-up blouse I had borrowed from my mother. I unclipped the barrette stamped with faded blue flowers that struggled to hold back my unruly hair. I freed myself of the wretched leggings that sagged and itched and the bra that couldn't do anything for my flat chest except pinch an angry red ring around my ribcage with its elastic. Finally, I stepped out of my panties and climbed into the shower.

There, in that small space where my elbows bumped the walls, I ran the water hot to scour myself of the events of this awful day that had started out as a Gray Day. I wanted the streaming water from the broken water-saver showerhead that didn't save any water, to blast away, like a fire hose, this sucking mood mud I was mired in. Against the forceful flow I shut my eyes. Only then did they sting, as hot tears escaped from under my lids and mingled with the water that dropped into the drain below.

I hadn't cried when I heard the news of how Melody had been found in her family's cabin, under her comforter, dead from a self-inflicted gunshot wound to the head. It was hard to explain that it was because it simply couldn't be the same Melody I had known for practically every conscious moment of my life.

I guess the fact that I hadn't shown any signs of grief for my lifelong friend, even at her funeral, really frightened the heck out of my mom. On the way home, she told me that it just wasn't natural. But how could I have told her that I couldn't cry at the *celebration* because Mel wasn't there fearlessly leading me like she always did, when we would scream at the football games, sniffle over chick flicks, or pretend to be rock divas, jumping up and down to the thumping bass rhythms blaring from the speakers in her room?

Now, in the last room of our run-down mobile home, beyond the pocket door and behind the curtain, in my tiny shower with the rusting soap dish and the plastic floor that flexed, my tears fell. The pain in my body felt like my very core was cracking wide open, and all of my guts were falling out. In the very next moment, hacking sobs gripped my throat and made me choke. I vomited. I couldn't stop crying.

I was alone.

"I had this weird dream—"

"You always have weird dreams."

"—that a polar bear was swimming out in the open ocean," I continued, as I spread mixed-berry preserves on the whole-wheat bagels my mother had picked up when she shopped for groceries last Saturday.

A bright sunburst pattern on the label of the preserves shouted: "*CERTIFIED ORGANIC!*" in loud orange letters. I paused for a moment to study it. I have found that you can't necessarily trust that things are organic just because a label yells it at you. Most of the mega food conglomerates claim almost everything is organic anymore, anyway.

And of course that label didn't address how many bits of roaches were cooked into the preserves or baked into the bagels. I had read where there is a satisfactory tolerance level of roach bits that actually complies with food inspection clean limits. Besides, as long as they aren't sprayed with insecticide, roaches are considered organic, aren't they?

My mom gulped down the rest of her black coffee and started scanning the kitchen for her keys and lunch bag. She was getting ready to leave for her job as a fitter at L&M Manufacturing. She assembled parts on a line there for a third-party company that supplied colored, clear-plastic panel covers printed with whatever words anyone wanted on them for things like control boards, dashboards, or cockpits. You know the kind that flash information that is good to know, like, "LOW FUEL" or "FASTEN YOUR SEATBELTS."

I always knew that she wasn't satisfied with what she was doing there—in fact, she was studying to be a nurse when my dad left us, but she dropped out of school. She argued that L&M was steady work with halfway decent pay and benefits, and if she were as smart as I insisted she was, she would be somewhere else at a much better job.

"You going somewhere with this?" she said as she checked the stack of bills that absolutely had to be mailed out today.

Oh yeah—my dream.

"The polar bear kept swimming and swimming, looking for an ice floe or anything to climb out on. Next thing, *I was* the polar bear, and my big paws were pushing the water ahead of me, and I felt my breath huffing out of my mouth as I paddled around.

"The water was freezing, and the only thing there besides me was this little yellow rubber duck. You know the kind you float in bathtubs or use in those races to raise money for charity? Anyway, I thought it would hold me up, so I reached for it. It started to sink, but I was too tired to do anything else.

"But the next thing I know, it blew up to be a huge life raft, but still in the shape of a duck. What I didn't know was that it had a small hole under its wing, so it was slowly deflating."

"Yeah, Poodle. Listen, I got to go or else I'm going to be late again." She stopped to kiss the top of my head like she did every morning before she left. "I hope you have a good first day. What are you—a junior, now?"

"Credit-wise, I'm a sophomore. Correction—a Sea View Community College sophomore, home of the Fighting Artichokes. Go 'Chokes," I said flatly, while wiggling a whoop-de-doo in the air with my finger. I never knew what Sea View Community College had to do with artichokes, anyway. You'd think their mascot would be something more appropriate, like a seagull or a sea star. But instead they chose a vegetable. Go figure. I had really wished my Running Start classes were at the U, where they had a husky for a mascot, but my sucky resident school wasn't a partner school with them. But Sea View or the U, at least it was a chance to get away from my high school, especially since I had completed all my required credits there by my junior year. By taking Running Start classes, I was able to get a head start on what I really wanted: a degree in biology.

"Anyway, you've been hanging around home way too much. I just wanted to tell you that it's good to see that you are getting back into the swing of things. Well, hope you have a great first day today. Oh, before I forget, please don't clean the carpet again. It looks like you're wearing a hole in it again. It's really old, you know. And will you make sure to pick up some more milk on your way home? And some sloppy-joe mix, but no more treats for that stupid cat. I think he's pooping underneath the house. Now where are those dang keys of mine?"

"On the cupboard shelf, second one down, next to the salt shaker. Where they always are."

"No. Where *you* always put them."

I knew what she was getting at. Cleaning and putting things in their place was what I did to blow off steam. Some people ate buckets of ice cream. Others worked out at the gym. Me? I scoured and rearranged things until everything felt right again. Mom grabbed up her keys, blew a kiss to me, and right before she was out the door, paused to ask, "So with you up and about now, any chance of you getting in some hours at the bakery later on this week?"

"I don't know, Mom. I'll check," I said, although I doubted my part-time position working behind the counter at Paradise Bakery was still available.

Her ancient Datsun wagon sputtered off, rolling past the double row of decrepit mobile homes in our trailer park that were arranged in a haphazard U shape like a cheap set of dentures. I always knew how far away she was by the Datsun's alternator-belt squeal bouncing off the trailers and echoing back like sonar until she was out of the park. As I listened to the sound fade away into the distance, I was overcome by that same troubling thought that washed over me anytime my mother said good-bye. The potential hazards and accidents out there in the world, waiting around every corner, were innumerable. So it was entirely possible that I may never see her again.

For example, a semitruck driver might become distracted while texting, forget to brake, and plow into her. Or maybe a disgruntled coworker at L&M might snap and bring a gun to work to mow everybody down. Or maybe the much-anticipated earthquake of all Cascadia subduction-zone earthquakes might strike, and her building or the one I am in might collapse.

It's not that I am some kind of psychopath who *wants* something to happen to my own mother. Not at all. In fact, the thought terrifies me daily. I would be devastated and couldn't go on if anything ever happened to either one of my parents or any of my extended family. That was why in this one instance, although it sounded strange, I was relieved that my father lived more than 1,300 miles away in Golden, Colorado, where he worked as a paramedic. I would be freaked-out if I had to send him off every day, knowing his job was filled with fires, toxic gases, bombs, heights, and accidents.

Ever since I could remember, out of the clear blue and even when things were okay, I worried about all sorts of horrific events that could potentially harm my family or friends. According to Annie Beacon, the psychologist at the County Health Care Clinic where I used to visit every third Thursday of the month when I was in seventh grade and my mom was trying to figure out why I acted the way I did, I suffer from generalized anxiety disorder.

While most normal people find these kinds of thoughts alarming, they happen to me often—almost daily, even. So often, I do my best to force them from my head because, to my immense relief, family and friends do come home safe and sound, eventually. I am reminded then that all is well and nothing ever comes of all the worry. At least most of the time. Anyway, these thoughts are part of the reason why I hate it when people don't say good-bye when they leave. The idea that they could be here one moment and gone the next without any kind of closure, wigs me out.

As for now, Mom was right. It was time for me to get back into things, although I knew it was going to take some effort. After the "celebration," everything took so much more effort that, well basically, I hardly did much of anything outside of cleaning the trailer and sculpting my endangered animals.

My gut feeling told me to stay put on this first day of classes, and that same feeling tried to find a way to finagle out of going. If it weren't for the fact that I was on a timeline to become a marine mammal researcher one day, I probably would've given in. I contemplated staying home and telling my instructors that I had gotten the dates confused, or that I was a late register, or I was sick. Instead, I finished my tea and bagel (including roach bits), scrubbed my teeth, and agonized over what to wear.

The first time at anything, particularly first days of school, was nerve-racking. I examined my face closely in the bathroom mirror to make sure there were no nasty surprises, like a zit or a unibrow forming. Fortunately, there weren't, but what stared back at me didn't lend much hope either. I was a strange mix. The tip of my round Asian nose teetered at the end of a straight Irish bridge like a grape on a tongue depressor. My deep-set eyes were like two brown bears peeking out from slanted caves, my dad's Japanese genes resulting in my epicanthic folds. My mom said that I also have my dad's thin smile and his habit of worrying about things.

I have a flat chest and no hips, like my Grandma Ohashi; our shapes much like the profile of an ironing board. Because of this, I was often the butt of jokes snickered between the jerk-off boys in my high school. Their favorite torments included "Hey, chicken tits," and, "Your bra would probably fit better if you wore it backwards." I didn't even have the benefit of beautiful, shiny Asian hair. Instead my rebellious dull brown mop couldn't decide whether to be straight or wavy, and was tamed only by a number of clips and bobby pins.

I wish I had been born instead with my mother's curvy curves, catlike green eyes, and wavy red hair. However, the only things I inherited from the Afton side of the family were my boxy jawline and a diamond-shaped birthmark on my left elbow.

Grandma Ohashi told me that my "statuesque" height of five foot six must've come from the Afton side. I wouldn't consider myself "statuesque" by any stretch of the imagination, but I guess I couldn't expect much from a tiny woman who stood only four foot eight in her stocking feet.

Continuing my self-inspection and noticing my hands were chapped from the scouring and cleaning around the trailer these few past months, I reached for Melody's half-empty tube of aloe moisturizer. I kept it on my nightstand, between a box of tissues and the stack of books I'm reading on marine life.

I remember she got it at Macy's. She was drawn to anything expensive and had insisted on buying it, saying she loved its jasmine fragrance. A week later, she gave it to me, saying she couldn't stand the smell. As my Grandpa O would say, she was but "a flag in the wind."

The lotion soaked into the palms and backs of my hands, and I couldn't help but ponder how weird it was that her tube of moisturizer was still around, yet she was not. Socks and shoes left by the door, overdue library books, strands of hair caught lingering in a hairbrush—to survivors, there had to be numerous mundane reminders of loved ones who had passed away.

How painful it must have been for poor Mrs. Chastings to have washed the blouses that still smelled like Mel's perfume, or her hoodie that had the french-fry sauce stain on it from when we had gone out to eat three days before she did what she had done. It seems wrong for a scent or a stain to outlast a human being.

I shook the tube to get the lotion to settle down to the end so I could squeeze out what was left. It wouldn't last much longer, getting used up little by little each time until, sooner or later, there would be nothing left.

When I locked the door and knocked on it twice to leave for school, rain dotted the driveway, and gathering clouds loomed ominous to the west. I hoped they weren't thunderheads. Seagulls were lining up on the rooftop of our neighbor's trailer on Lane B. When they headed inland and hunkered down like that, it usually indicated some pretty bad weather was moving in. I remembered an article that stated lightning had killed an average of fifty-seven people each year in the United States over the last thirty years, and injured over five hundred more. *That's a huge risk for me to be riding around in this,* I thought as I peeled back the crinkly blue tarp off my old convertible. Bilbo, our neighbor's useless dog, heard the noise and started barking as usual from inside his trailer. That idiotic dog never shut up. I wondered if dogs ever got struck by lightning and concluded that they surely must.

Unfortunately, my car's ragtop was stuck in the down position, which, in a city known for rain, wasn't very pleasant. Once, I tried driving with an open umbrella duct-taped to my seat back to keep me dry at the stoplights. I reasoned that if I drove slow enough, that it should stay put. It was an epic failure. I'll always remember the umbrella sailing off into the streaming traffic below as I was crossing the I-5 overpass. I heard a few cars braking hard and skidding but was too afraid to find out what had happened.

My Grandpa O had left the rusting car to me because when I was little, I loved riding around in it with the top down. He also liked the way that he and I were the same—always reading, researching, and asking questions. The car was cool when I was young and didn't know much, but now it seemed clunky and outdated. Its mirrors were also too small, so I asked my dad to mount extra-wide truck mirrors to the sides so I could see drivers in my blind spots.

Just as I was removing the last of the bungee cords that held the tarp in place, a gust of wind blew the soggy mess upwards and wrapped it around me, like a burrito. The clothes I had so carefully chosen for my first day of school were now splotched with water that harbored algae, mold spores, and diluted pigeon shit. I had no time to search for another outfit without being late, because while the car warmed up, I would have to check the front door lock two more times again before taking off for school.

In the morning drizzle, I spied a man in his forties standing on the corner and wearing a grungy mattress. He swayed back and forth while jiggling a huge red arrow of a sign that said "BIG MATTRESS BLOWOUT. EVERYTHING 75% OFF." Shivering in my thin rain jacket as I waited at the stoplight, I was hardly better off than the sodden-mattress man in this weather, but at least he was insulated.

"Hey, you in the ragtop! Need a new mattress? Come on over! Big mattress sale! Seventy-five percent off! That's right!" he started calling out to me.

There was no way to describe the feeling of being publicly singled out by a man wearing a mattress when your day hadn't even started yet. My stomach lurched as echoes of "Hey, chicken tits" replayed in my head.

"Yeah, you. I can see you hunkering down in that convertible. Come on over and check out our big mattress sale. Don't tell me that you don't want to save a little money. With the money you save, you can fix that ragtop and not sit in the rain."

Feeling like a bug under a spotlight, my head buzzed. I knew I should have listened to my instincts and stayed home. It was really turning out to be a horrible, horrible day. As he continued to call out and wave to me, I kept my gaze fixed ahead and inched up to the car in front of me, hoping to escape the mattress man's attention and wishing that the excruciatingly long light would change already.

When the light finally turned green, I mashed down on the gas pedal, forcing the old car to get up and go. The man and his mattress grew smaller in my big side mirrors. I heard his voice fading in the distance, "Where are you going? Turn around and come back to the mattress sale …"

As if that wasn't a bad enough start, my Biology 108 class, the one I had anticipated taking since I started Running Start, almost two years ago, wasn't much better. Dr. Pope, the instructor, informed the class that the lab section involved group work. In my experience, group work usually boiled down to other members busy on their phones or visiting with each other while I frantically made sure the work got done correctly, completely, and turned in on time. I always hated group work, even with people I knew, and this time I would team up with a total stranger.

I hadn't noted who was seated closest to me, and within a few minutes of the announcement, most people in the class had paired off already. I wondered if I gave a bad impression with my damp, splotchy clothes. A friendly looking girl who was taking notes in front of me remained, but just when I was about to ask if she wanted to partner up, another girl sitting beside her asked instead. I wasn't fast enough.

Oh well. I was about to settle back and go it alone when Dr. Pope said, "There should be a partner for everyone in this class. If you haven't found one yet, I will come around and find one for you." I groaned inwardly and did a quick head count. Twenty-two people were present. Why did it have to be an even number? That meant that there would be absolutely no chance of working alone.

I sighed with resignation. There wasn't going to be any getting out of this. It appeared that I was the only person in the room without a partner except for a guy I could see out of my peripheral vision to my left, a few chairs over. Grudgingly, I turned in my seat to address him.

He looked twentysomething—older than most of the eighteen- and nineteen-year-olds that filled the room. Tall and lanky, he was so thin his clothes draped on him as if they were hanging on a hanger. His curly dark-brown hair covered his head like a floppy hat. His dozy eyes behind black-framed glasses made him look as if he had just been roused from a cozy nap.

Casually kicked back in his chair, he continued doodling in his notebook, seeming not to care whether anyone chose to partner with him.

I cleared my throat.

He glanced up at the board and then doodled some more. I cleared my throat again, and when he wouldn't respond, was forced to say, "Uh, hey . . . Um, excuse me ... Do you want to be partners?"

The guy glanced up once more, turning first one way and then the other, trying to see who was addressing him, until finally he pivoted in my direction. He slid his hand up under his hair and removed a wireless ear bud that had been concealed under his curls. Then with a bob of his chin, asked, "Are you talking to me?"

"Uh yeah. Do you want to be partners?"

He shrugged. "I guess."

Oh great. This is going to be fun, I thought. *He doesn't want to do this at all.* When he showed no sign of moving, disheartened, I gathered up my things and sat down next to him instead.

We nodded at each other, awkwardness forcing us to avert eye contact and to find something else to focus on. Before we could introduce ourselves, Dr. Pope told us to open our lab workbooks to review the upcoming lab and assignment deadlines for the semester. According to the contents, we would dissect a worm, a sea star, and then a shark, and map out a cross section in a forest patch to count species and create field notes. But first we had to prepare for Lab One's experiment involving bean beetles.

As she lectured, I stole a sideways glance at my new lab partner and wondered if he was paying any attention. From what I could tell, he had returned to doodling again, sketching some kind of complicated war scene featuring snarling, helmet-wearing American cats that were brandishing machine guns at angry Nazi hounds who were driving panzers. It wasn't half bad.

Cautiously, I took a peek at him. I thought he was, just kinda-sorta, a little cute, but I couldn't be 100 percent sure. I wished Melody were here to compare notes on him with me, like we always did with guys, and confirm my observation one way or the other. More than likely, she would have thought he would be more attractive if he weren't so thin and pale, and ditched the glasses, and cut his hair. However, he seemed all right to me.

"This lab will take four weeks to complete and deals with adaptation. Which leads me to say that when you consider adaptation, every plant is a specialist in its own ecosystem, as it is suited to thrive in very specific conditions. In fact, that goes for every living organism, including you. Now, ask yourself—will that specialist survive when you start changing any one of those conditions? Can it thrive? Keeping those questions in mind, you will design an experiment on adaptation using live specimens for the first lab activity tomorrow. The introduction for it can be found in your Peale and Morgan workbooks on pages eight to thirteen. I suggest you read the assignment completely, and be sure to answer all the questions in the exercise.

"Now, for the last fifteen minutes of class today, I would like for you to start collaborating with your partner. Make sure to coordinate and schedule times to come into the lab to care for your specimens and to gather data," Dr. Pope directed as she walked about the room.

I opened up our workbook to Lab One. The experiment was titled, *Alteration of bean beetle adaptation through environmental manipulation.*

Fishing for camaraderie with my newly appointed partner and hoping to break the ice, I threw out sarcastically, "Bean beetles. It had to be bean beetles. Oh boy. I can't wait."

In my experience, I have found if you can get a person to laugh at or hate something with you, you can quickly establish some sort of rapport. In truth, biology was my favorite subject. My dream career was anything biology related, particularly conservation. And the thought of conducting a lab experiment with live creatures, albeit bean beetles, was especially exciting. I preferred to work with something alive on any day, rather than cut apart something that was dead.

"Oh man, I love beans," said my new partner, breaking into a grin as if he were expecting a bowlful to be served to him at any moment.

I waited for him to continue. When he didn't, I assumed that he had misunderstood. I explained carefully, "This lab is about bean *beetles* and how long it takes them to adapt to some other food source."

"Right. I still love beans," he answered.

From what I could tell, he appeared to be functioning okay on a cognitive and emotional level, so that left only one conclusion. *Oh great. He's a weirdo.* I sighed inwardly to myself. It figured I would get stuck with one for a partner.

"I'm Sig," he said, sticking out his hand to shake mine.

"Sig?"

"Like Sigmund Freud, the father of psychoanalysis."

My brow furrowed. *Was Sigmund Freud referred to as Sig?* I wondered.

"You know - The Couch, tell me more about your dream, an Oedipus complex. Any of these ring a bell? Uh, not to be confused with Pavlov, of course."

"So, you're named after Freud?

"No. I'm named after my uncle."

"Wait—" I said, confused.

"Sigmund F. Despain. My parents made sure to get an *F* in there for the middle initial." He held up his hands and shook his head. "That little *F* has caused me so much shit. You have no idea."

I felt sorry for him. It really was a tedious name. Then again, I knew what it was like to be strapped with one just as cumbersome. It was a good segue, so I decided to switch tactics to commiseration.

"Well my full name is Molly Genre Ohashi. My mom's Irish and my father's Japanese, and for some reason they thought it was hysterically brilliant to name me Molly Ohashi. They said if I ever put an apostrophe after the *O* to make it O'Hashi, it would be the perfect blend between them both. They just loved how President Obama celebrated St. Patrick's Day by putting an apostrophe in his last name to make it O'Bama. Get it? *O-Bama?*"

He nodded appreciatively and said, "I'm there."

"But the *Genre* part—that was purely my mother."

"And ... ?" He waited for the punch line.

"*Genre?* You've got to be kidding. It's not even a name. It's a noun. I don't know what drugs my mother was taking when she thought of that."

"So, does she?"

"Does she what?"

"Take drugs?"

"No. No of course not. I was just saying because of my name—"

"Nice! One less thing you have to worry about."

I studied Sig. His confident yet absurd manner was a bit unnerving and unlike anyone I had ever met before. It was like being presented with a plate heaped with random food from an all-you-can-eat buffet. It was a lot to take, hard to identify, and difficult to decide where to start.

Struggling for equilibrium, I tried again, "So, are you a biology major?"

Sig snorted. "Who me? Yeaaah, right. No." He had an unusual way of speaking out of the side of his mouth when he smiled.

"I just thought since this is a biology for majors course that—"

"*It is?* Uh-oh. I thought this was accounting. Time for me to bounce." He rose in his seat as if to leave, and then sat back down. "Nah, just kidding. Actually the biology for nonmajors class was completely full. I have to take a science with a lab credit anyway for general studies, so I figured this would work."

"Oh. So, what's your major then?"

He shrugged. "Don't know, 'cause I have no idea what I want to do, yet. I wouldn't mind being an engineer, but I suck at math. And then I thought being a poet would be kinda cool, but my writing sucks too. Or maybe a barista. Or a baseball player. Anyway, I was going to cruise for a while to find something that hits me along the way. How about you?"

"Me? It's always been biology. I've wanted to be a field biologist ever since I was seven. I always received As in all of my science classes and really loved my junior bio class in high school, because that was where I decided to devote my life to saving another species. I want to study polar bears. Their habitat is drastically shrinking, and they could be extinct by the next century. I want to be part of the conservation effort to save them."

"Right on," Sig nodded. He patted down his jacket pockets and then produced a snack bag from one of them. It was open already, and he extracted an onion ring from it and held it out to me. "Funyun?"

"Uh, no thanks," I said quickly. There were just too many things wrong with that scenario—unsanitized hands, accepting food from a stranger, artificially colored cornmeal extrusion, pocket lint—to feel comfortable.

He shrugged and popped the onion ring into his mouth, followed by three more.

"You must be wondering then, if I really like biology and I've always studied it and this is my major, why I'm still in Bio 108 instead of further along."

"No worries. I wasn't."

"Oh." I was almost sure he would notice I wasn't that much younger than he, and the fact that, technically, I should be in at least a 200-level class by now. I felt compelled to explain. "Well I would've almost been done by now, but my friend died, and I kinda freaked out. I missed a half a quarter."

"Wow, that bites."

His candid response threw me. The conversation screeched to a halt. I expected a more extended response to the heavy news I had just laid on him, but none was forthcoming. Before things grew too awkward, I stammered, "Well how about you? You don't look like a freshman."

"You're right. But it doesn't change the fact that I am."

At another loss for words, I felt unsettled, as if I had just gotten off of one of those playground merry-go-rounds, and I was trying to walk in a straight line but wasn't sure which way was up, because the ground kept tipping in at all angles. However, I had a strange suspicion that there wasn't going to be any chance of regaining my balance now that Sigmund F. Despain was my partner.

Chapter 1.5

Shannon Afton, Fabrication Specialist at L&M Manufacturing and Molly's Mother

I'm not sure what has gotten into Molly now. Ever since she started up with her college classes again, all she's been talking about are beetles, environmental adaptability, and some boy named Sig.

Don't get me wrong. It's a welcome change, especially after those long months following Melody's funeral, when all she did was sleep and walk around like a zombie. First there were the really tough times—two months straight of Gray Days where she hardly got out of bed, let alone past the front door, no matter what I tried whether it was encouragement, threats, or bribes. Whenever I wasn't home, I knew she was just lying there, huddled under her blankets, staring at the walls, with Rob's cat curled up with her. I was really worried about her—I didn't think she was going to pull through. When she finally got out of that bed, she didn't go anywhere for three months more, hardly venturing beyond the patio of our mobile home.

But what really scared me was when she didn't show any of the signs of grief that people typically show, especially when someone they are close to dies, not to mention if they die by something terrible, like suicide. I had read in *O Magazine* that there are five stages of grief: shock and denial, anger, bargaining, depression and detachment, and then finally acceptance. Molly definitely showed the depression and detachment phase, but not any of the others. I thought she might have to unload or go through some kind of angry meltdown, and I asked her if she wanted to talk any. Instead she would either clean, sit and stare at the walls, or spend hours on her computer, not saying a word, just poring over all those articles about studies that she finds. That's why I like to encourage her when she sculpts those little animals out of clay. At least it's something normal.

What happened to her friend was such a tragedy. Melody was always a really sweet kid, ever since she was little. And she came from a good, solid family, too, so what she did came as a real shock.

Her parents were those kind of perfect people that had it all together. Their lifestyle, their house, and, well … *they* were perfect. Straight-laced was more like it. It was hard for Rob and me to relate to Derrick and Debra Chastings when the girls were little, so we really didn't get together with them much.

We tried it once, when the girls were in the third grade. The Chastings had a barbeque at their place and invited us over. The hardest drink they served was iced tea, which, at that time, was a little on the "light side" for Rob and me, if you know what I mean.

Derrick talked about his car dealerships and mutual funds and his gun collection. Debra was one of those super stay-at-home moms, so she kept trying to get me to swap recipes with her and meet up for scrapbooking.

For some reason, we just didn't click. But it didn't matter. We saw enough of each other at the girls' school events and when we dropped Mol off at their place for parties and such, and we also exchanged Christmas cards. That was plenty.

The girls, on the other hand, were inseparable. You hardly ever saw one without the other. Sometimes I felt that Melody was too bossy, but Mol never complained. And that was why—I know it sounds bad because I'm her mother—I was waiting for Molly to fall apart when Melody did what she did.

What surprised me is that Molly never did fall apart. Instead, she went through the whole *celebration* thing with this strange expression on her face: the kind she wore whenever she was thinking hard about something. I kept asking her if she was okay, and she kept saying she was. So there wasn't much more I could do for her.

I even expected her to let loose with those crazy questions of hers—the ones she's been asking ever since she learned to talk. But that didn't happen until after we came home.

By that time, my nerves were shot. Funerals are hard enough, but funerals for children are downright hell. I know I was a little short with her, and I feel horrible about it, but I had had enough, and at that point all I could think about was how good it would be to have a gin and tonic just then. Or two.

The next day I called the psychologist Molly used to see at County for her ongoing depression and anxiety to ask if I should do anything just in case. But Annie told me just to wait and keep an eye on her. Or she could schedule an appointment immediately if I really felt the need to.

I wish I could've taken her up on it, but things are tight even with the child support I get from Rob, and I can't afford the payment at the clinic even with its sliding scale. Although his medical insurance covers her through age twenty-six, it doesn't cover mental health services. Even if it did, it has such a high deductible that we can never meet it before the discount kicks in. And my insurance through L&M is lousy. It barely covers me. I know he would pay for her to be seen if he could out of pocket, but he's hitting on some hard times himself.

At least if he were here, he probably could've gotten her to talk. Not those questions of hers, but I mean *really* talk and open up about her feelings. I was never good at that. I've always had a hard time understanding where she's coming from. Sometimes that is what I hate most about him—the fact that I wish he were still around, especially to help raise Mol.

She's not an easy kid, let me tell you. Don't get me wrong. She is helpful; you should see how she cleans the house. Almost every day, Poodle—that's my pet name for her because when she was a toddler, she got into making little yapping noises just like a poodle—scrubs and vacuums and sweeps. I don't know why. It's not like we make such a huge mess between the two of us. And she always does her schoolwork and gets straight As. In fact, she was able to complete all of her high school credits early despite all the time she missed. She even sculpts these cool little figurines when she has spare time instead of wasting it playing video games like so many of her peers do. I never have to remind her or scold her to do her chores like some people have to with their kids. But she's also a hard one to figure out, and there's always something new that is bugging her.

When Poodle was little, there were other ways she wasn't like other kids. I mean she's as smart as a whip and polite and everything, but she never gave the impression of ever being genuinely happy. You know how it doesn't take much to make a child brighten up? Sometimes it isn't more than a new toy or getting ice cream. But not Mol. She was always quietly moping about, like a sad little ghost.

And if she wasn't doing that, then she was worrying about everything. It could be sunny out, and she'd worry about drought and wildfires. If it was raining, she'd worry about flooding. If it wasn't sunny or raining, she'd worry about earthquakes. It was enough to drive me crazy. Her teenage years haven't been much better. She's just learned to hide her feelings more and doesn't cry as much.

So now when she comes home talking nonstop about beetles and this guy named Sig, who's her lab partner, I can't help but worry myself. I sure hope he is a positive influence on her. The last thing Molly needs right now is another upset in her life.

Chapter Two

The native range of *Ursus maritimus* extends from northern Alaska up to the North Pole in the Arctic Circle. To survive in this harsh climate, polar bears show remarkable adaptations to stay warm including a four-inch thick blubber layer and black skin underneath its dense, pure white fur. Scientists believe its black skin helps to absorb the sun's rays (Cooper 72).

Polar bears stand upwards to 7 feet tall and can weigh approximately 700 to 1000 pounds, although a 2,209-pound male was the largest one ever recorded. They are considered one of the largest in the bear family, coming in second only after the Kodiak bear. By comparison, Kodiaks can weigh 800 to 1400 pounds and stand up to 8 feet tall (79).

I checked first one side of my nose and then the other in the mirror. Next, I scrutinized the small red patch between my eyebrows. It wasn't good to wake up first thing in the morning to feel a sore spot between my eyes that could indicate a zit under construction. And it was centered right over the nasal cavity and entrance to my sinuses … *Wonderful.*

Glancing down at the dog-eared copy of my father's old high school health book that he failed to return after he graduated, I studied the illustration on page seventy-two. The image was of a man's face, his nasal region outlined by three red dashed lines and labeled the "Triangle of Death." The base of the triangle ran across his top lip and the point landed between his eyebrows. The caption warned that the outlined area was where nerves led directly to the brain. And any squeezing or irritating of acne in this area could result in a dangerous and potentially lethal infection to the brain.

How many unsuspecting people out there have died from squeezing zits and infecting their brains, and no one knew any better? And why wasn't this information better known and publicized? As a matter of fact, why wasn't it in my book for health class in sophomore year? I wondered what the symptoms for a brain infection were. My head hurt with worry about how this zit was exactly centered within this hazardous zone.

Making a mental note to research it on the internet when I got a chance, I forced myself to refocus on getting ready for school. I didn't want to be late. I was looking forward to biology class, and if it weren't for this pimple that could infect my brain and potentially kill me, the day would have been off to a great start.

Almost two weeks had passed since Sig and I met, and he was working out to be a much better partner than I had anticipated. Despite his offbeat, laid-back demeanor, he proved reliable and actually knew what he was doing as far as designing and conducting the experiment. In fact, our lab protocol had been voted the best by the rest of the class. When I saw the sloppiness and slack practices of some of the other lab partners I could have been stuck with, I was relieved that things had worked out the way they did.

Even better, my opinion finally counted for something. While I loved Mel more than anything in this world, she always took the lead on things for as long as I could remember. And whenever I had offered some thoughts of my own, she usually won out with her will and vivacity, neither of which I could ever possibly possess.

Sig was different from Mel in that he acknowledged my ideas. He actually listened to my suggestions and feedback, shrugging with that "awright" indifference of his as we carried out my plans.

When I caught up with him in the lab, he was transferring the pea-sized mung beans, one by one, to petri dishes containing the adzuki bean tissue cultures. Each mung bean had been implanted with a single egg laid by a female bean beetle The task was tedious, but he was patient and careful.

"Hey, you're here early. How's it going?" I asked peering at the dishes from around his lanky frame. He stood over a foot taller than me.

"Can't complain," he said. "This is the last one. Then all we have to do is wait."

It would take two more weeks of careful checks on the eggs to catch the larvae as they started to emerge to weigh them. According to the lab, if there was enough total mass between all of our little maggots, we could declare emergence success and demonstrate that the beetles had adapted to a new host, the adzuki plant, and prove our hypothesis of a rapid evolutionary response to an environmental change. If the beetles didn't adapt to the new environment, it could indicate they were less fit to survive and propagate. It was actually a pretty cool experiment.

"That's it. Hopefully, these little bean-munchers get down and make more little bean-munchers," Sig said as he screwed the covers on to the petri dishes. Putting on an awful Austrian accent, he continued, "Then they will be the Arnolds of the beetle world's buff and fitness."

"Make sure the temperature is exactly thirty-degrees Celsius," I added, watching him place them gently into their incubation box.

"Bam. Done."

When he turned around, I held out a bottle of hand sanitizer, flipped open the cap, and prepared to squirt.

"What's that for?"

"To sanitize your hands. You've been handling the beetles."

"They all took their baths. I checked."

I continued to hold it out to him, until finally he conceded to a squirt of gel onto his hands. He rubbed briskly, and then simulated taking a shower, slathering it under his armpits, in his hair, and on his ribcage. I blew it off. There wouldn't be any way I could stomach watching him eat his morning pretzel and peanut butter without sanitizing, knowing that he had handled those beetles.

"There. Happy?" he asked, holding his palms out for me to inspect.

I squirted some into my own hands to sanitize before putting the bottle away. I didn't like to take chances. There were any number of viruses you could pick up off of public areas. It was one of the reasons I gave up biting my nails in the fourth grade.

Sig eyed me curiously. "What are you doing that for? You didn't even handle the beetles."

Ignoring him, I chose to study our subjects. They were so vulnerable and singular as they lay placed on the artificial world we had created, when I was struck with a winsome thought. "I wish something like this could be done for polar bears, when I think about it."

"What? Introducing them to adzuki? Or having them sanitize?"

"No, getting them to rapidly adapt to a new environment. They are struggling to survive, because their world is changing too quickly. It's like what it said in our lab book for this experiment," I said, thumbing through the chapter. "See, here it is—'If individuals of a species have adapted to a particular environment, any change in the environment, such as global climate change, may lead to reduced fitness,'" I read aloud. "It's so sad."

"Yeah. I streamed this doc the other night that showed how polar bears bite the big one because they're swimming way the hell out in open water for miles and miles. There used to be enough pack ice for them to haul out and take a breather before. Now, with the ice caps melting, there is less ice for them to find. The big honking males get exhausted and drown. Forget about the cubs—they're toast. Or, I guess they're ice cubes. Or more like ice cubs, right? Anyway, I was watching that and thinking what they could seriously use is some kind of swim platforms. I remember when I was a kid, there was a lake we used to swim in that had them. They were the bomb to climb up on to warm up and take a snooze."

I was picking at the hangnail on my chapped thumb when his words struck a chord and sunk in. Suddenly it all clicked, and starbursts went off in my head, our digression from the bean beetle experiment nothing short of an epiphany. In fact, it was the exact solution to the problem.

"Oh my Cod—" (I was uncomfortable using God's name in vain due to my quasi-Catholic upbringing. Remember me freaking out about lightning strikes?) "did you say 'swim platforms?' You're brilliant, Sig! That's it! You're fricken' brilliant!" I was so excited it was hard to contain myself, and I started hopping—although feeling a little self-conscious, so it was more like bopping off of my toes.

"Brilliant? O-kaaay, thanks. Um, not really." He blinked at me with those dozy eyes and glanced about suspiciously. He obviously hadn't caught on yet.

"Don't you see? There isn't anything quick that can be done to turn around something as massive as global climate change. So in the meantime what if … what if there *were* giant swim platforms anchored out in the open sea where the ice floes used to be? The polar bears would then find a safe place to haul out and take a rest. They could learn where they were located, and they would pass that knowledge along to their cubs. They would adapt and maybe survive the climate change! Or at least hang in there until us stupid humans figure out how to undo the damage we have done. Anyway, it could buy them some really valuable time."

"Yeah … yeah, I guess," Sig said, nodding as the idea took hold. "But how many swim platforms are you talking about?"

"It depends. Biologists would have to tally the total population of existing polar bears and check where they typically swim—you know, their high-traffic areas. And then they could plant so many platforms per number of bears based on the amount of traffic in each area. It's easy."

Attempting to be serious, Sig cupped his chin, and with his eyebrow arched, his eyes first darted one way and then the other in thought. "Okay, but would the bears be willing to share the platforms with each other? You know, with them being territorial and all? Or would there be splashing and pushing into the water and penguin lifeguards blowing their whistles, threatening to kick them out of the ocean for horseplay?"

"The chances of two or more polar bears swimming out in open water coming upon the same platform at the exact same moment is pretty remote. And if they happened to do just that, they would be so exhausted from swimming, I doubt they would have any energy left to fight each other. Besides it must happen even with the ice floes now. I'm sure they have ways to work things out already."

"Hmmm … I guess it would work."

"I *know* it would work!" I said, but my excitement immediately cooled as reality set in. "But it will never happen. Something like that would cost way too much money."

"I suppose. More importantly, it'll never happen if no one ever goes for it."

"Yeah. Someone's got to pay for it."

"No, I mean someone's got to start it off."

"Yeah, right. But who's going to do it?"

He thought for a moment, and then turned to me and said, "Well if someone's gotta do it, how about you? You're the one jumping up and down. Start a campaign. Spread awareness. Raise money for swim platforms."

I stared at him as if he had sprouted two heads. It wouldn't have been any less bizarre if he had asked me to enter the Olympics for ski jumping. "Me! You're kidding, right?"

"No, I'm not. And what's wrong with you?"

"What? There's no way. I couldn't pull that off."

"Why not? People do it all the time for causes that they care about. They create a Facebook page or a blog about it and BAM— the thing goes viral and everybody's talking about it and chipping in. Next thing you know, mucho dinero amasses."

I don't do social media. Well, at least not anymore. Once, back in my freshman year of high school, I attempted it. But it felt as if every keystroke had at least a million viewers reading it, and that my profile was being spread far and wide to strange places and strange people I didn't even know. The thought of stalkers, hackers, perverts, pedophiles, slave traders, and Big Data tracking my every move eventually overwhelmed me. If it weren't for the fact that I needed to continue my research and stay current on issues, I would've given up the internet all together. Instead, I only used my phone to talk or text to people I know directly, skipped all of the other apps and stuff, and enabled no-tracking on my web searches.

"I don't do any kind of social media."

He laughed. "Yeah, right. You're shitting me, right?"

"No, I'm not joking. I don't do social media."

"Seriously? Are you even human? No wait, you're a cyborg, right?"

"So, let's say I did do it just for this one thing, what exactly am I supposed to do then? How am I going to raise that kind of money?"

"There's crowdfunding for that sort of stuff. Didn't you read about the kid who raised like a hundred thou for making a bowl of potato salad or some dumb shit like that?"

"I could never do that."

"Potato salad isn't all that hard to make."

"You know what I'm talking about."

"I'm not kidding, Mol. Why not?"

"Well, why not *you*?"

"I'm not the one who wants to dedicate my life to saving polar bears. For me, it's preserving something more along the lines of like tube socks or Walkmans."

"Okay, even if I tried, it won't be until after I graduate and find a job in that field."

"No offense, but they'd all be fish food by that time. Why wait so long?"

"It's just that … this is huge. And, well … well, no one is going to listen to me. Why would they?"

"You really don't know that. So far it sounds to me like a bunch of excuses."

I continued to feel doubtful. Clearly Sig didn't know what he was talking about. As I got to know him better during these past two weeks of school, from time to time I noticed that he came up with some ideas that were way out there. Like how he advocated for a fry-your-own-potatoes counter in the cafeteria or wanted to design a gondola that ferried students across campus up over the buildings to cut down on foot traffic below. Me creating a campaign to save polar bears apparently was another one. He must not have noticed that I was nothing but a seventeen-year-old hapa girl living in a mobile home park and attending a community college whose mascot was a vegetable.

"All right, let me put it this way—do you want your grandkids to grow up in a world where there aren't any polar bears?" he said.

"I'm not having any children. There is no way I'm bringing a child into this messed-up world."

"Okay. Then do you want *my* grandkids to grow up in a world where there aren't any polar bears?"

"You're going to have kids? With everything that is going on? Terrorism, global warming, nuclear threats, pandemics? Are you crazy?"

"You're changing the subject. So are you going to do this or what?"

"Never mind. You are crazy. I'm sorry I said anything."

By evening, against my will, the idea seeded itself in the wrinkled crevices of my brain and took root. *Could I actually do this? ... Maybe I could ... . I bet Melody would've tried it.* I fought the sharp sting rising up in my chest. I wished she were here, not only to spearhead this, but for us to share the experience.

I needed to distract myself. After a few minutes of poking around on the internet, I checked a few updates on the polar bears' current status. It was dismal at best. Next, I perused a few other sites that showed genius whiz kids winning top awards in science for things they had invented or discovered or for civic projects they had started.

The list went on and on: a fifteen-year-old in Puducherry, India who perfected an early-detection test for Parkinson's; an eagle scout in Anaconda, Montana who raised money to help save timber wolves; an elementary school in Barre, Vermont that collected enough pennies to save a migratory-bird habitat. Heck, there was even an eight-year-old Brownie who sparked a massive cleanup of a portion of the Schuylkill River in Pennsylvania. The article quoted her saying, "The river was so yucky and polluted, it was gross," and ran a photograph of her in her uniform, with a grin sans two front teeth.

I inhaled and clasped my hands together under my chin, trying not to hyperventilate as my stomach tap-danced. This could very well become one of those pivotal moments, the ones in movies where the highly improbable was about to take place. Like when the loner nerdy kid jumps on her computer to stop a nuclear bomb from detonating, or an outcast homely boy transforms into the most beautiful and gifted dancer in the production.

"Okay. Yeah, okay. I'm going to do this. I can do this," I muttered to myself as I picked up my phone and texted Sig.

> K. You win.

> Sweet! What did I win?

> I'll do it. I'll give it a try.

> Even better. Give what a try?

> The swim platforms for polar bears.

> Wait – You're gonna build one?

> Ur an idiot. Seriously.
> I'm going to start the campaign.

> Far out! ☺

> I mean YOLO. Right?

> YOLO?

> You Only Live Once?

I think so.

Idk if I can do this alone.
Will you help me? You've got to help me!

Yeah. I guess I can get behind this.

Although I couldn't see him, I knew at that precise moment, he was shrugging.

Chapter 2.5

Molly Ohashi, College Student and Campaigner for Polar Bears

My dad's name is Robert Ohashi, but everyone knows him as Rob. These days, he lives in Colorado. Although it's only a twenty-hour drive or a two-and-a-half-hour flight from Denver to here, I saw him last when I was fifteen. And that was only for a weekend. I would like to travel to see him, but statistically, it's too dangerous to be on the road for that many miles, and I'm terrified of the idea of being cooped up with 250 other (potentially sick) people, while flying in an aging, poorly maintained aluminum can. Even so, I wish that he would come to visit more often.

He moved out when I was eleven, going on twelve. Mom said he ran off on us, but I know that's not the real story. He is much more complicated than that. My dad is just too sensitive. I have tons of memories of him and me doing lots of things together. He taught me how to tie my shoes, ride my bike, and bake cookies. He would read to me at night and was the one who used to help me get through my "Gray Days."

In fact, we came up with that name together when I was four and scared of almost everything, like monsters lurking in my closet or strangers we would pass on the street or the rain clouds gathering overhead.

He was also the only one who understood and accepted my need for compulsory routines. Like he knows that before I go to sleep, I take one sip of water before I get into bed and another one after. If I don't do that, I can't go to sleep. And he also knows that I can't sleep in an unmade bed. If it's unmade, I have to make it up before I can climb in. When I leave the trailer in the morning, I check the stove, the coffee maker, and the oven, twice, to make sure they are off. Then I check all the locks on all the windows. Last, I close the front door and lock it, open it one more time to make sure I had locked it, and then close it again. I knock on it twice to set a memory for myself as a kind of cue. In that way, whenever I am away from home and suddenly panicked by the thought of whether or not I've locked the door, I can reassure myself by saying, "Oh yeah, I knocked on it twice. I did lock it." Dad would always let me complete my routine, no matter how rushed we were.

My mom tries to understand these routines, but if we are running late or if she wakes up on the wrong side of the bed, she runs out of patience very quickly. When they say that opposites attract, I can say it's very true with my parents. It's strange how completely different she is from my dad.

They met at a New Year's party thrown by Tommy, Dad's partner from the firehouse. My parents suspected a setup, because they were the only two single people invited to the party. I liked to hear the story about how at midnight, when the ball dropped and everyone was paired up with their significant others, they decided to pair up with each other just to avoid feeling awkward. They had drunk too much champagne by that time, and each thought the other was cute, so they ended up kissing each other at the stroke of twelve. While Grandma Ohashi said it was foolish, to me it sounded just like the plotline to a romantic movie.

After that, they continued to see each other. My mom said he always made her laugh and made the best chicken enchiladas she had ever tasted, even though they were the easy kind that used canned mushroom soup. My dad said that he was crazy about redheads who were talented in remembering numbers and keeping him in line.

They sounded like a fun couple and as a result, were always invited to lots of parties. However, my parents had to put the brakes on their lifestyle once I came along. I was an "Oops-Baby" or at least that's how, when my mom was buzzed one time, she described the fact that I wasn't planned.

Before my parents' divorce, we would visit my grandparents' house. Grandpa O was still alive, then. As I got older, I came to find out that Grandma and Grandpa O weren't all that wild about my mom and dad's marriage, because secretly they would have preferred my dad to marry someone Japanese.

Don't get me wrong—it's not like they ever treated my mom badly. On the contrary, they were always very polite to her. However, it was the kind of polite you would reserve for a neighbor or someone at the store. And it never went further than that.

If they were so hung up on the culture, they would've immersed my dad in it, including the language, wouldn't they? But what was ironic was the fact that my dad was told to speak English only, out of fear that he would not speak either language correctly. I love my Grandma and Grandpa O, but I always thought that was weird.

Since Grandpa O passed away from shellfish poisoning, Grandma has been planning to go back to Japan, since she misses it so much. We even got passports to go visit her when she moves there. Although, I haven't quite figured out how to get around the flying part of that yet. In the meantime, she's always slipping me money on my birthday, Christmas, and every other month to put away for the future wedding she believes, with all her heart, is going to happen for me, eventually.

The thing I worry most about with my dad is that he drinks too much, and what gets me really frustrated is that he can't seem to overcome it. My mom said he always liked to have a few drinks when he got home, just to unwind, but he totally tanked after he went on a run that involved a ten-year-old girl who had been hit by a car. It's a big secret, and I'm not supposed to know anything about it, but she died on the way to the hospital, and he blamed himself for making a mistake while trying to stabilize her at the scene of the accident.

He's a paramedic—and a really good one at that. He's gotten commendations in the past, and he loves what he does. Although there were no charges against him, and the investigation cited faulty equipment, it really messed with him, and he's never forgiven himself for it.

He still works as a paramedic, but he's lost his spirit and his nerve. More importantly, his confidence is gone. He lives under the constant fear of making another huge mistake that might cost another person their life.

Every day I worry that my dad's going to die one way or another from drinking too much. That's what broke my parents up eventually. My mom finally quit when I was about five. She felt she wasn't taking proper care of me, and I was getting old enough to notice that they weren't good role models.

I remember one time waking up and going to the kitchen for breakfast. I was still little enough to wear those one-piece fuzzy pajamas with the feet attached. My parents were sound asleep at the table that was littered with empty bottles. One of their glasses had even tipped over and spilled onto the floor.

The smell in the air was heavy and stung my nose. I stepped in one of the puddles with my pajama feet. I can still remember the cool feel of vodka seeping around my warm toes. It tingled a little bit. I shook my dad to wake him, but he wouldn't move. I shook my mom next. She wouldn't move either. *Why won't they wake up? Why aren't they cooking pancakes?* I wondered.

I continued to shake them, but nothing would rouse either of them. Growing fearful and feeling something was horribly wrong, I started to bawl, and then scream. My mom finally lifted her head, and with her tangled mess of red hair falling across her face asked me in a groggy voice, "Poodle, what are you screaming about?" Then she turned to my dad and said, "Rob, get up. Rob! You're frightening Molly."

There were times I used to wish that my mom and dad were like Melody's parents. Yeah, the Chastings had a big house, the cabin up north, and their cars were always new. Melody also got everything she wanted. But it wasn't that. It was more because her mom and dad acted like the normal people you saw on family shows on TV. There weren't any fights or drinking binges or divorces.

I remember how close Melody had been with her dad, too. When he came home from work, she would drop whatever she was doing and run to meet him. They would tease each other and laugh.

She was always a daddy's girl, even when she got older. I couldn't help but feel a little envious because she still had him around.

I miss my dad. I called him a few days ago, but the guys at the firehouse said he was out on a run. I left a message, but he never called back. Don't get me wrong. It's not like he never returns my calls at all; he does call me from time to time, and sometimes we text, but it's never enough. I needed him so badly the day Melody died and the months following after.

When I think of him, I see his smiling eyes and hear his calm, steady voice. I think of his strong arms I used to hang off of like a monkey when I was small. I think of the simple silly jokes he would tell me, and the way he would hug me and rest his chin on my head.

I miss my dad.

CHAPTER THREE

Polar bears are perfectly adapted for life on the sea ice and don't hibernate. Throughout the winter, the majority of them will stay on ice floes to hunt seals, their favorite food. Seal blubber has an extremely high fat content, making it an excellent source of energy for life in a cold climate. However, whenever opportunity presents itself, other prey includes walruses, orca, beluga whale, arctic foxes, and beached whales make up their diet, although seals are their most important food source (Hawakaya 113). Searching for an easy meal, the big white bears often scavenge through dumps and garbage cans in towns close to bear territory.

Where should we meet?

How about somewhere halfway?

How about Mr. Liu's?

Meet me under the big neon cross on 75th at 12? It's around the block from there.

K. C u there.

Bring your image nation.

Er—okay?

*Imagination. Stupid autocorrect.

We were getting ready to plan our campaign strategy. I had never attempted anything like this before, so I was excited to the point that my stomach twisted and squirmed with worms of nervousness. This seemed like such a huge *grown-up* thing to do; it was overwhelming. And if it succeeded, Sig and I would join the ranks of those so-called high-achieving young adults credited with developing ingenious solutions to world-class problems.

The plight of an entire species could hinge on whether we could pull this off or not. We could turn the tide. We could make scientific history. We might be featured in documentaries, news stories, and websites—perhaps a book or even a movie might be made about our efforts. Maybe our crowdfunding would reach into the millions of dollars. Our names could go viral on social media.

Despite the fact that we were preparing to undertake such a monumental, potentially world-changing endeavor, we were forced to meet at Mr. Liu's Burgers. Mr. Liu's was the kind of dive in which 'Today's Special' was a jalapeño burger with fries, advertised on a wrinkled sheet of copier paper stapled to a sandwich board, getting soaked in the rain.

I would've much rather met somewhere sophisticated like Noveau's, the upscale bar and grill a few blocks south, that was crowded with business people in power suits having power lunches. I imagined Sig and myself among them, comparing our tablets and schedules, teleconferencing to foundations and sponsors over our smartphones, while deciding on appetizers made entirely from locally grown ingredients.

But the reality of the situation was that I was almost out of money and had to save whatever gas I had left in the tank to get back and forth to school for the rest of the week. At least Mr. Liu's was in walking distance for the both of us, and I could eat there without going bankrupt. And surprisingly, it wasn't in last place as far as its score from the health department.

So I waited for Sig, listening to the buzz of the half-lit neon cross of the Church of the Apostolic Faith above my head that spelled out "Jesus is the Light," while checking the soles of my shoes to make sure I hadn't stepped in any dog poop along the way.

The Avenue frightened yet intrigued me at the same time. It covered roughly eight city blocks and had this weird, funky, cool, but scary vibe about it. It was also located two blocks down from the state university that Melody had applied to and I always dreamed of attending. On most days, panhandlers, drug addicts, and pickpockets mingled on the street among the college students, instructors, and researchers who seemed oblivious to this seamy side of things.

In the few times I had been on the Ave by myself, hoping someone would mistake me for a university student, there were at least three shootings. In fact, Mr. Liu's, where I was about to meet Sig, was across the street from an international fast-food chain that always had some kind of sketchy deals going down in the parking lot in broad daylight.

While the diversity of the Avenue could be hazardous, it was also alluring—like the attraction a moth must feel as it continues to bounce against a hot light bulb. The crowded public way was lined with independent eateries and just about every shop imaginable, with no rhyme or reason to their placement: the bong shop next to the fro-yo place; the Asian-import store next to the Goodwill; and the comic-book store juxtaposed with the university's bookstore across the street.

The sidewalks teemed with kids just a little older than me, and all types. Some of the tragically hip enjoyed sitting cross-legged on ratty blankets alongside of the street, clutching their rescue dogs and discussing Kierkegaard while flipping their blond dreadlocks in angst. Others sucked down venti-sized cups of coffee in the corner coffee houses, stressed and studious while pecking away at their laptops. Still others roamed in packs of twos or fours to escape their dorm rooms, meeting each other for study sessions over yakisoba and

Red Bulls or combing through repurposed clothing at the Buffalo Exchange.

One downside to visiting the Ave was having to bleach the soles of my shoes when I got home. The sidewalks were usually filthy with litter, hacked-up phlegm balls, dog crap, and discarded food. I also held my breath whenever I found myself surrounded by large groups of people while waiting to cross at an intersection. There were so many outbreaks of SARS, MRSA, measles, and whooping cough going unreported at the major universities. The only redeeming thing about going to a Podunk community college was its population was lower, so statistically, there was less risk of catching something.

The cars streamed past me on the busy thoroughfare, and I spotted a flattened squirrel in their path. He had fallen short of his goal of reaching the sidewalk by about three feet. Apparently he was the victim of a hit-and-run, suffering the undignified death of having his entrails squeezed out of his hind end like toothpaste from a tube. It was tragic. No living thing in pursuit of a nut should be squashed to the point that its guts come out its butt. I pondered the possibility of being able to save squirrels in some ingenious way in the future as well, and made a mental note to add them to my to-do checklist.

Down the block, Sig's tall frame cleared the corner and came into view. At first I didn't recognize him. The hoodie he wore beneath his coat was pulled up to cover his head, and he wore sunglasses despite the rain. His dark coat was open and flapping about his long legs as he strolled along the Ave like some oversized crow.

It was odd to see the lab geek, who was typically doodling in his notebook and talking to our bean beetle eggs, completely out of the context of school and looking like some street-punk ass instead. As he approached, I saw he had headphones on. Most likely he was listening to his '80s music like he did every morning when he showed up for class. I never understood what he liked about that genre.

Except for a mumbled "Hey" and nods to each other, we continued on to Mr. Liu's without saying much. Inside the small, run-down restaurant that had no potential, I placed my order with the guy behind the counter. He wiped his hands on his pant leg and barely acknowledged me as he handed back my change with a grunt.

"How's it going?" I heard Sig say to him as he stepped up to order, while I went to find us a booth.

The tables located in the middle of a restaurant's floor always creeped me out. I never sat at them if I could help it, because I either felt exposed or in somebody's way. Instead, I always chose a booth seat facing inward to the dining area, where the entrance was in view just in case any deranged or disgruntled shooter types entered, seeking vindication rather than greasy hamburgers. While I waited, I scrubbed the table with hand gel and a napkin, knowing that there were some bussers who wiped tabletops with the same grimy bar rag they used on the seats.

Five more minutes passed. I wondered what had happened to my lab partner. At this point I realized the buzz of conversation I had been hearing turned out to be Sig and the counter guy. They seemed to be discussing something.

When Sig finally sat down across from me, with his drink in one hand and balancing three small paper cups full of ketchup in the other, I couldn't contain my curiosity. "So, you know him?" I asked.

"Who?"

"The guy who took our orders."

"No. I've never met him before. Why?"

"It's like you were talking with him for a while. He barely said two words to me."

"Not really. He asked me what I was listening to, so I told him. Turns out he digs '80s too. I haven't met anyone who truly appreciates Tears for Fears," he shrugged.

I envied Sig and others like him. You know the ones who are so laid back and totally at ease with the world? He could talk to anyone, and everyone wanted to talk to him. Melody was kinda popular like that, too, but in a different way. Always confident, she chatted at everyone even if no one was listening. I remember one time when she led everybody on our bus in a sing-along of *The Sound of Music* on the way home from school. I, on the other hand, couldn't get a person to call 9-1-1 if I was bleeding from my ears let alone hold open a door for me when I was carrying groceries.

43

I suppose I've never been comfortable with people, and they sense that in me. My parents told me that when I was little, I ran around with a poker face and always hid from people. Over the years my classmates reinforced my belief. I became accustomed to being the last one chosen when teams were formed, and I was never invited to get-togethers or to join any groups. It's why I've chosen to dedicate myself to saving animals rather than pursuing a career that involves a lot of interaction with other humans.

By contrast, oftentimes in our biology class a small group of people would gravitate around Sig like little satellites orbiting a planet. Whenever he walked down the hall, people would call out to him by name, or high-five him as they passed. He typically offered them nothing more than a slight nod of the head or a sloppy grin in return, but they readily ate up whatever he had to offer. He didn't necessarily say much to others, but he didn't have to. For some reason people just really dug him for who he was, not for what he did. I came to realize that when partners were being chosen in biology, I had simply lucked out by the fact that he hadn't been paying attention.

After our food came out, I gelled, and then held out the bottle to him. He waved it off. I wished he hadn't, because I know he had been handling money, and then the ketchup pump dispenser that Cod only knows how many hands had touched. Next, he picked up the saltshaker, teeming with even more germs and viruses, and sprinkled a generous helping of salt on the already-salty fries. As my anxiety mounted and my mind raced, I could only focus on the minute cubes of sodium bouncing and sticking to the fried potatoes.

"I tried sea salt instead of table salt," I blurted out. "I really liked the taste of it and would've definitely preferred using it instead of table salt because it's supposed to have less sodium in it, and it's not bleached with chemical cleansers. Except now I'm reading that sea salt has traces of mercury, lead, and other toxins and pollutants. So I'm searching for the stuff that is mined hundreds of feet below the Earth instead, and—"

"Uh-huh. Same with zombies," he said as he dipped his fry into the paper cup to pull out a huge dollop of ketchup, popped the mess into his mouth with satisfaction, and then licked the salt off his long, germ-laden fingers.

I felt faint imagining how many live viruses he had just deposited on his tongue. I could hardly concentrate. "Wait. What … ? What are you talking about?"

"Zombies. I said it was the same."

"Same as what? What do zombies have to do with salt?"

He gobbled down another fry, leaving a smear of ketchup on the side of his mouth. "If they catch you, they eat your brains. Another thing you can eat with salt."

"That's really gross, you know that? And with everything else going on in the real world all you can talk about are zombies?"

"Well … Yeah."

I so wanted to tell him that I thought he was really very weird. Melody probably would have done so by now, but I figured it would be rude. We still had eight more weeks in the quarter to go, and although he wouldn't have any problem finding one—and couldn't care less if he didn't, I didn't want to have to find another lab partner.

Instead, I started pulling out the project supplies from my bag I had brought along for our meeting. Since I didn't own a tablet, and my phone was hardly smart, I went old school and brought paper, pens, page flags, sticky notes, and a carefully prepared binder with colorized sections and storage pockets, complete with a photograph of a polar bear inserted in its clear front cover—everything we needed to begin.

"Far out." Sig chuckled with appreciation as he surveyed the items I laid on the table before him.

"Well, where do you want to start?" I asked with pen poised to jot down notes on the clean, bright page before me. "But first you've got to wipe your mouth off." The ketchup smear was starting to drive me a little loco.

He grabbed up his napkin and dabbed his mouth, then shook his head. "Nah-uh, Boss. Where do *you* want to start? This is your thing, not mine."

"But you said you would help me."

"Operative word here is *help,* not *lead.*" Then he looked me straight in the eye and said, "Come on, Molly. You can do it."

I sighed. It would've been so much better if he had just expounded on his swim-platform concept. In the lab, it was easy for me to come up with ideas. There, we had books for guidance and followed established instructions to prevent our experiments from failing.

Here in the real world, there were no boundaries. I may as well have been cut loose, free-floating without gravity to stick my feet to the floor. I would've been happy to do anything he asked as long as he pointed the way.

But Sig continued to eat his fries and stubbornly refused to pick up a pen. There was no getting around this.

"All right," I conceded. "Let's make a list."

We tossed around the obvious outlets—social media, crowdfunding, bake sales, and car washes; I listed each one with a big checkbox next to it. However, while it was all doable, it was all pretty mundane and hands-off as well. Those whiz kids in the articles got to visit their subjects up close. In many instances, officials or researchers even invited them to locations, while institutions offered access to equipment or research resources, or communities came together to back them. In contrast, all Sig and I had was just the two of us, with no money, no equipment, no support, and stuck doing everything from a distance.

"Wouldn't it be amazing to go to where the polar bears are and actually observe them in person? Or at least before the platforms are installed, so we could get a sense of the location?"

"What? You mean to the North Pole? In the middle of all that ice?"

"Well, the Arctic Circle. There are two villages in Alaska—Kaktovik and Barrow—where you can seriously see polar bears up close, especially during the months between August and October, when there's less ice. I read that September is the best time."

"But I thought I saw on Animal Planet that polar bears spend most of their lives hanging out on sea ice."

"They do, but they are opportunistic and scavenge if there are easier pickings elsewhere. They'll rest up near villages and come in at night to feed on leftover scraps in trash cans or bowhead-whale meat after the seasonal hunts."

"Whoa. You really do know your shit about polar bears."

"Thanks. I had to write a research paper about them in junior year, and I've kept researching more ever since."

Sig lit up. "Hey—what about an epic trip? I've always wanted to do Alaska, and I haven't been anywhere for a while. I can totally dig it." He tapped and scrolled on his phone's screen, and then held up the results for me to see. "It's like, one thousand, six hundred ninety-six miles from Seattle to Kaktovik and an eleven-hour-fifty-minute flight, with tickets starting at … " He tapped and scrolled some more. Suddenly his bright look dimmed. ". . . thirteen hundred bucks. Frick. I don't know about you, but I don't have that kind of dinero."

"Me neither," I sighed. "And I probably won't, not for a long time. Anyway, I don't fly."

"Seriously? Why not?"

"A ton of reasons. Three-hundred-plus passengers sharing microbes from breathing air that's recycled throughout the plane. Seats that make me feel itchy thinking about the bed bugs and body lice that jumped off the last person who sat there. And then there's the fact that most of the planes are flying well beyond their years, with lousy maintenance schedules. All of those things combined just freak me out."

"And you wouldn't fly even if you had a chance to see polar bears?"

"I don't fly even to see my dad in Colorado."

"Oh …" He pondered it for a moment. "So, how do you feel about bake sales and car washes, then?"

A round of milkshakes later, we had a tentative plan worked out. First, we would research any similar projects already under way. Next, we would talk to Dr. Pope to see if she knew of anyone in the field who could tell us whether polar bears would adapt to swim platforms or not. We needed to track down conservation organizations that would possibly endorse us. We also needed to find a reasonably priced engineer to design the platforms. Last, we would have to raise funds to pay for the engineer, and then build and finally ship the platforms to the Arctic Circle, where they would be anchored in place. According to our best estimate, we needed at least $375,000 for the prototype.

Things were taking shape.

Chapter 3.5

Sig Despain, College Student

MY LAB PARTNER, MOLLY, IS CHILL. If I were asked to describe her, I'd say she was this weird mash-up between a dynamo and a brainiac. Like, if you could imagine Taz being super-smart or Madame Curie being a spaz case, it would be like that, although Molly doesn't realize it. She's jumpy too. Nothing bad, but there's times she's wound a little too tight, that's all.

It's not the first time I've been around others like her, who have their springs coiled in knots. Hell, my great-aunt Sophie, who was ninety-two years old, freaked out over any stranger she encountered at the store who was younger than thirty. She thought they wanted her purse and everything in it—her tissues, her stale butterscotch candies that were covered in purse lint, her back pills, and her five bucks (maybe—and mostly in coins). Or my Uncle Jesse—he used to take us to buy fireworks every Fourth of July, and let us buy whatever we wanted, even the biggest, loudest ones. But now he's a combat veteran after doing three tours in Iraq, and can't tolerate any kind of fireworks or loud noises because of his PTSD. Anyway, the point is, both Aunt Sophie and Uncle Jesse are still cool even with their "issues."

But it's all good. Molly asks intelligent questions, which is more than I can say for most people. And when she's not feeling bummed, she's spunky, kinda like a pug puppy, which cracks me up. The only thing I want to know is what's with all the hand gel? Reminds me of the hospital.

CHAPTER FOUR

The polar bear's range stretches from northern Alaska to the edge of the North Pole. It can be found in countries of the Arctic Circle such as United States, Siberia, Canada, and Russia. A male polar bear will roam 700 miles in a year. A female's range is smaller, up to 400 miles a year (Smith and Robeson 119).

Devising our plan and finishing our research generated a list of people we had to talk to, starting with Dr. Pamela Pope. As she was our instructor and the only real scientist we knew, we figured she would be a great choice and hoped that she could point us in the right direction and give us some contacts. By two thirty on the day of our scheduled appointment with her, we waited in the narrow hallway in front of her office, staring at a bulletin board on the wall that was cluttered with carpool posts, student-insurance ads, and flyers for studying abroad in Caracas, Venezuela. I reviewed our notes and images and rearranged them to make sure they were in the right order to present to her. Sig was less engaged and surfed his phone.

She finally showed up, twenty-three minutes late, and bustling into her office holding Starbucks in one hand and a glass container of bean salad in the other, while shouldering a ratty tote bag bulging with papers and books. When we explained our plan, we had expected her to be enthusiastic about the project, because not only it was an ingenious solution to the plight of the polar bear, but also two of her very own students were initiating it. We thought she would be helpful.

She wasn't. Not even a smidge. In fact, when we filled her in on the details, her eyes got squinty and she appeared annoyed. She was so underwhelmed, blinking at us through her bifocals and eating her salad with her mouth open and making chomping noises, we may as well have been telling her about the contents of my medicine cabinet.

When I offered my notes and images to her, she waved them away with a brusque, "Nah-uh. That's okay. I don't need to look at them." And instead of giving us names of individuals, organizations, or foundations to contact, as we had hoped, all she said was that our best bet was to try the internet. When she finally divulged that little nugget after stonewalling us for twenty minutes, all I wanted to ask her at that point was exactly what she had gotten her PhD in—the obvious?

The worst part was her indifference. Leaving her dingy office that was crammed with files, books, and papers, I felt as thoroughly burned as if I had been rejected for a job. I thought that scientists—biologists—would be eager and excited to help each other, especially if it meant the preservation of an endangered species. All in all, we were off to a dismal start.

My frustration boiled over as we marched down the hall. "Well, that went over like a lead balloon. What a total waste of time. I mean, doesn't she give a damn?"

"Apparently not."

"I thought that we were all supposed to be in this together. Shouldn't we be helping each other out? Not only as fellow biologists, or teacher to student, but as fellow human beings and stewards of this planet trying to prevent a species from extinction? I can't believe all she had to say was 'look it up on the internet,'" I said, mimicking Pope with a disgusted sneer.

"It's clear she's not into polar bears, that's for sure. I bet it's bread mold or single-celled organisms that rock her world. For some reason, I have the undeniable feeling that it's probably something very narrow and very small."

"I don't get it. She didn't even try. All I know is, Mr. Schumacher would've listened. Or at least been polite enough to act interested."

"Who's Mr. Schumacher?"

"My biology teacher in junior year. His class was amazing. It was the one in which I knew I wanted biology for a career."

"Well, what about contacting him? Maybe he knows someone. Or at least knows someone who knows someone."

"I can't. He retired last year, and I don't know where to find him. I heard he moved back east somewhere to be with his grandkids." I sighed, "This is a major setback, already."

Sig chuckled and shook his head. "Oh, this isn't a setback. Trust me. Don't give up so easily. You just have a little more work to do, that's all."

"How can you say that? I don't even know where to start."

"How about the internet?" He laughed.

When I glared at him, he laughed even harder.

Out in the parking lot, he came to a complete stop in his tracks when we reached my rusting heap of a car, where it sat in its glory with ragtop down, cracked leather seats puddled up from an earlier rain shower, and its peeling "Stop the War" bumper sticker à la Grandpa O. It was his first time seeing it. Embarrassment heated my cheeks to a rosy glow.

He let out a low whistle as he looked it over. "A '59 Sunbeam Rapier. Seriously? Is this your drop-top? Man, what a sweet ride!"

"Don't be a jerk. It's bad enough that I have to drive this thing. I don't need you to mock it, too. I've had enough mockery for one day."

He rested his hand on the door as he admired my car's interior. "No, I'm not kidding. This really is the shit."

"Uh-huh. You said it."

"Where did you get it?"

"It was my Grandpa O's daily driver. He left it to me when he died. When I was little, I thought it was really cool, because it was a convertible. He used to take me to get ice cream in it. Now the top is stuck down, and I can't get it to go back up. And the whole thing is rusting to hell. On one hand, I love it because it was my grandpa's, and it reminds me of him, but on the other hand, it's not so cool anymore."

"Mind if I take a look?"

I stepped aside, waving him toward the tired little car. He walked around it, peering in and about and appreciating details from its leather gearshift knob to its heavy steel bumpers. Then he examined the folded-up roof that lay across the back end of the car like a large dead bat.

The next thing he did really blew me away. Like a magician, he reached into the left pocket of his long coat and withdrew an adjustable wrench. It was medium-sized, with nicks and scratches in it, apparently from other situations that had required heavy wrenching. Why he was carrying such a tool in his coat pocket, I had no idea. With it, he deftly tightened a few bolts with a few twists of his wrist and with a grunt, broke another loose from rust. From his right pocket he miraculously produced a small can of WD-40, which he sprayed on the hinges. Finally, he swiped the puddle off the back seat with the edge of his hand, climbed in, and knelt on the cushion. Facing the roof, he grabbed it with both hands and jerked it hard to the left a couple of times. It hardly budged.

"Okay, give it a try and see if that works."

I eyed him skeptically for a moment, climbed in, and sighed an "Okay," although I thought the whole thing was futile. Then reaching past him, I gave the roof a tentative tug. For the first time since I have owned it, it lurched up a couple of inches on its hinges.

"Keep going," Sig instructed. "Here, let me help you." We both pulled and tugged as the black cloth top slowly unfolded upward, freeing itself from the accumulated dirt that had settled in its folds and the rust that had stiffened its joints over the years. It teetered above my head, and then came down softly in place, where I locked it down. The sky was now blocked off from the interior of the car. The world was muffled and quiet all of a sudden.

"I have a roof! It's fixed! Oh my Cod. Where did you learn to do that?" I asked excitedly.

He shrugged. "On the internet."

For once I was protected from the elements. I felt sheltered. I wouldn't be freezing or wet or have the wind whip my hair into a tangled mess as I drove. No longer vulnerable, I wouldn't be subject to soggy-mattress men calling me out on street corners. And I could finally hear the old AM radio that still played through the cracked speaker cones.

It was luxurious. It felt as if I had been given a new car, and I almost hugged Sig out of happiness, but at the last minute, feeling shy, I thought otherwise. Instead, I offered him a ride home. It was the least I could do after he had fixed the roof.

"Would you mind if I ask why you carry a wrench and lubricating oil in your coat pockets?" I questioned as we cruised in the Sunbeam through the winding streets filled with falling leaves (without any of them falling into the car, I might add).

"No. I don't mind if you ask me at all," he answered. I waited for him to explain, but he didn't.

He indicated for me to stop at a blue-and-white rambler-style home with a modest yard. A large 4x4-pickup truck crowded the driveway. Its long bed was packed full of cardboard boxes and furniture covered by a tarp, with bungee cords crisscrossed over everything.

Sig suddenly sat up in his seat as he peered out the window, his body tense. I thought I heard him mumble something like "This isn't supposed to be happening today," but I wasn't sure, because the radio was playing, and my mind was chewing on how everyone I knew lived in regular houses except my family.

Then he said, "Thanks for the lift. I gotta go."

With an abruptness that was unfitting of his laid-back image, he hurried inside and shut the front door behind him. It was the fastest I had ever seen him move for anything, and I thought it was strange. But then again, Sig did a lot of strange things without much explanation.

When I arrived home, I studied our old mobile home snoozing in its algae-green spot under a stand of cedars and hemorrhaging streaks of brown-red rust from its screws. Once I had tried scrubbing the grime and rust off of its dingy exterior, but my mom made me stop when she saw I had worn the paint down to bare metal.

Out of curiosity, I had researched our mobile home's make and model when I had nothing better to do. I found an old sales brochure for it that was buried on the manufacturer's website. The ad from the '60s featured our "Solitaire Edition" standing proud and dazzlingly white on a perfectly mown lawn, while a happy, three-point-five-person family enjoyed a barbecue spread on a picnic table under its smart green-and-white-striped awning. Fifty-some years later, the same dilapidated awning yawned a smattering of tattered holes now, and instead of grass, the artificial turf leading up to our front door was balding from too many rainy seasons and trampling feet.

I swept off the leaves and tree needles that had blown onto the turf and picked up my mother's flip-flops from where she always abandoned them at the doorstep. I could never get her to put them in the bin for shoes I kept right outside the door.

She was already home, off early from work. After I hung up my schoolbag and washed my hands, I started setting the table as she prepared dinner.

"Hey Poodle. How was school?" she said over her shoulder, as she pan-fried ground beef burgers mixed with eggs, onions, and stale croutons.

"It was all right." I really didn't feel like sharing the Dr. Pope disaster with her, because either she would be disinterested or fighting mad at my instructor. There was no middle ground. "Why are you home early?"

"We had a fire drill this afternoon, and after everyone finally got back inside and on the line, there wasn't much that was going to be accomplished in the last hour of the day. Besides, I wasn't feeling all that great, so I decided to head home."

"Are you sick?"

"No. Don't worry. I'm not contagious, just crampy."

"Oh. Hey, when you fry my burger will you—"

"Cook it 'til it's well done and drain off all the fat? I know, to kill the E. coli. I remember that from the last time you told me."

"Okay, thanks … . Mom?"

"I'm still right here, honey. This place is only so big, and I haven't moved an inch," she said, as she turned over the sizzling meat that was swelling up like fat greasy pucks in the pan.

"Which is exactly what I was about to ask—did we ever live in a regular house?"

"What do you mean a 'regular' house?"

"A regular house. A *real* house."

"Well, what do you call what we're standing in right now?"

"I dunno. A rolling breadbox or tornado bait. I haven't decided."

"It's a *manufactured* home, smart ass. And yes, this is a real house."

"It's not like a real house. All we have to do is uncover the wheels, screw on taillights and a license plate, and we can move this *manufactured* home anywhere. You can't do that with a real house. A real house doesn't have wheels!"

"Well neither does this one, or haven't you noticed? This one has a concrete floor. No wheels."

"Yeah, but that's how it got here—on wheels. It wasn't like it was built with wood and nails on the spot. Besides we can cut an extra door or window anywhere we want on it with a can opener."

"Watch it, missy. And as a matter of fact, your father and I lived in a 'regular home,' right before you were born. But the landlord raised the rent, and then we had you, and we couldn't make ends meet. So here we are. Now what on earth brought that up?"

"Well, we're about the only people I know who live in a manufactured home in a trailer park. Everyone else has regular, normal houses on regular, normal streets."

Mom started scooting the burgers around in the pan with short agitated motions, as if she were playing offense on a hockey team and advancing toward the goal. "First of all, there's no such thing as 'regular' or 'normal,' no matter what it looks like on the outside. And second, we're not like everyone else. If your father had continued your child support like he promised he would until you were 21, we probably could afford a little house somewhere like everybody else," she grumbled.

Red light. It was in my best interest to change the subject as quickly as possible, before she started going off about my dad's lack of payments again and worse yet, his drinking problem. Both subjects were real drags. Besides, I never liked it when she ran him down like that.

"Hey, Sig and I started our new campaign for the polar bears today."

"You and Sig?"

The rapid scooting around of the burgers slowed. It appeared that I had successfully derailed her thoughts away from Dad.

"You seem to be spending a lot of time with him lately. Is he nice?"

"Not *nice* in the way you think," I said, "He's only my lab partner. Anyway, he fixed the roof on my car, so it closes now, and he's helping me with my polar bear campaign."

"Well if that's not nice, I don't know what is. And if he can fix stuff, he sounds like a keeper already," Mom said, placing down a browned puck, potato chips, and microwaved canned corn on a plate in front of me, and then picking up the ketchup bottle to give it a shake.

The thing was, I didn't want to tell my mom that I thought Sig was kind of cute. It was weird, because he was weird, and he totally was not my type. But I did like his eyes, and the way he talked out of the side of his mouth, and the way that he was so accepting of just about everything.

There was no way I could share that with my mom, though. If I did, she'd make a big deal about it and would want to know every last detail, and then ask me every day about him. The worst part was then she would start nagging me about making myself more attractive, telling me to do something with my hair, stand up straight, or smile more.

I just didn't need that kind of pressure.

"Here it is. I hope we can still find some seats," I said, as we located Mansfield Hall, Room 120. Inside, beyond the double doors, the university's biggest lecture hall buzzed with hundreds of voices.

"Let's sit towards the back so we can leave early," Sig said.

I shot him a glare that had withered others before him.

"I mean if, you know, there's like an emergency." He shrugged.

"We're not leaving early. It's really important that we stay for the entire presentation and hear what he has to say. Come on. It's not going to be any longer than watching a movie."

"Yeah, except there won't be any zombies or explosions to make it interesting," Sig mumbled under his breath.

Inside the hall that held about four hundred people, most of the seats from the front on back were already filled. We found a couple of seats close enough to the rear exits for Sig's comfort.

According to the program the docent had handed us at the door, Dr. Gale Mengalor was the director and founder of Marine Neoteric Options for Wildlife, otherwise known as Marine NOW. He was also an expert on marine mammals, and his talk was going to be about how global warming was impacting them. The program featured photos of him in a sub-zero suit standing next to a gigantic walrus lying on an ice slab; another shot showed him weighing a baby fur seal. But the one that really caught my attention was of him aiming his camera at a polar bear that was not more than twenty feet away from him. I couldn't help but feel a burn of aspiration. *I so want to do that.*

We had learned of his talk from a flyer posted on a message board at our own community college. Of course Sea View's Fighting Artichokes never attracted prestigious speakers like him. Our events mostly consisted of talks on the importance of getting your GED, or recruiters promoting military enlistment or blue-collar positions.

"What's *neoteric*?"

I found Sig with his nose in the program.

"I don't know. Why?"

"It says 'Marine Neoteric Options for Wildlife' ... " He scrolled through the screen on his phone. "Okay. Here it is. 'Neoteric' means 'modern' or 'new in origin.' Well, why didn't they just call it that: 'Marine Modern Options for Wildlife?'"

I shrugged. "I don't know. Maybe because it wouldn't spell *NOW.*"

"What's wrong with just using *new*, then? And what's with all these people? You'd think that Jacques Cousteau was showing up. I mean, they're practically salivating over this guy," he said.

Sig was right. When I listened to the crowd around us, they were talking excitedly about Mengalor, his books, and his published articles. As the houselights dimmed and the host introduced the researcher, a reverent hush went over the auditorium. When he walked onstage, thunderous applause erupted. I couldn't help but wonder what all the fuss was about and hoped that he was as good as what everyone appeared to believe.

The man who took his mark beside the lectern looked about a decade older than the photographs in the program. He had wavy silver hair that he left loose and long, almost to his shoulders. He wore a turtleneck sweater, a corduroy jacket with patches on the elbows, jeans, and moccasin-like shoes. His voice was warm and measured, while his demeanor was relaxed and casual. I could tell he was very used to standing up in front of crowded lecture halls.

"It's easy to love a cuddly white bear that chugs soda, isn't it?" he started off.

His first image on the screen behind him was of the popular TV commercial with the computer-generated bear wearing a huge grin and holding a soda bottle in its paws.

"I mean, what's there not to love? At least one would think so. But obviously just loving them is not enough. In fact, those sodas that he eagerly chugs, and the manufacturing processes used in producing those sodas, coupled with transporting them hundreds of miles to market for us to buy, are causing way more trouble for this big fellow than just empty calories and a tubby waistline," Dr. Mengalor said with a charming smile.

The audience laughed more enthusiastically than I thought was sufficient for the simple joke. I glanced at Sig, who had shifted in his seat and crossed his leg. He wasn't smiling.

I hope this will be good. Otherwise he's going to kill me for wasting his Saturday afternoon, I thought.

However, within a few minutes, Mengalor's talk picked up. The images he showed of polar bears coated with oil from tanker spills, scavenging through landfills, or dead and washed up on arctic shorelines were graphic and disturbing. The audience became captivated, and I along with them.

As he went on, his message began to resonate within me. He said those things so eloquently that I had always wanted to say about polar bears and climate change but couldn't find the words, experience, or the wisdom to do so. After about twenty minutes into his talk, I started to feel a real connection with him, as if we shared a common mission.

"It is imperative that we save this magnificent species from being eradicated by our irresponsible and irreparable behaviors. We must take action now, not tomorrow. There's got to be better ideas and better ways to provide help for the polar bear in the interim, so they, as a species, can hold it together long enough for us to figure out and clean up this colossal mess that we humans have thrust upon the world and its creatures."

At that point, I wanted so badly to stand up, wave my arms, and shout, "We figured it out! Swim platforms!"

In my imagination, I envisioned how everyone, including Dr. Mengalor, turned and stared at me, speechless, while their brains wrapped around Sig's and my idea. After it sunk in what a brilliant solution swim platforms were to the problem at hand, they clapped and welcomed me to the stage, where the doctor shook my hand, and then held it up with his in triumph to a standing ovation.

Turning my attention back to the presentation, I whispered to Sig, "After the talk I want to get a copy of his book. Maybe we could get a chance to tell him about our idea."

"Seriously?"

I shot him another look.

He mumbled, "All right. All right."

After he continued for another hour and a half, the renowned marine mammologist brought down the house with a passionate call to action. The audience was pumped. He bowed to a standing ovation and left the stage. The host came back to the mic to announce that Mengalor would be signing books in the lobby.

I wove quickly through the crowds oozing through the exits. Sig struggled to keep up with me. To my disappointment, there was already a long line in front of the signing table to buy Mengalor's book. I felt anxious that the books would be sold out by the time I got to the front of the line, and if there were no more books, Mengalor and my chance to tell him about the platforms would disappear.

"What's with you anyway?" Sig asked while we stood in the queue.

"What? Didn't you hear a word he said for the last two hours? It's exactly what we're campaigning for. He couldn't have gotten it any closer if he tried."

"It was cool, what he was saying and all, but it's not like he said anything that we didn't know about the problem already."

"No, but he talked about taking action *now* to save them, while scientists and researchers are scrambling to solve the changing climate situation. Don't you get it? We already have the answer."

"Well, I wouldn't go that far …"

"Let's see what he says. I'm sure he will totally understand our idea."

"Wait, you're seriously going to tell him about the platforms?" Sig stared at me, wide-eyed with disbelief.

"Yup."

"I thought you were only joking."

"Nope."

As we approached the table, the sign by the shrinking stack of books said they cost twenty-eight dollars. I dug around in my purse for whatever cash I had and came up with only twenty. In fact, it was the very last of the cash I had stowed away from working at the bakery. I bummed a ten off of Sig, who begrudgingly handed it over.

"Hello, and to whom should I make the inscription?" The researcher greeted us with that same charming smile and a pen poised in hand when our turn came up.

"Dr. Mengalor, it is a great honor to meet you. I really connected with what you were saying," I said eagerly.

"That's wonderful. It's so great that your generation is getting the message and heeding the call to action," he said.

"Oh, we have. I mean, are. In fact, we are raising money right now to build swim platforms for the polar bears for when they are swimming out on open seas," I blurted out.

I waited for that "a-ha" moment to come over him. It never arrived. He simply stared at me, expectantly, like he was waiting for me to start speaking English.

"You know, so they have someplace to haul out on and won't get exhausted and drown. The platforms would be anchored out in deep water, and the polar bears could teach their young where they are," I explained.

Mengalor studied me for a moment more, gave his head a slight nod, and said, "I see. Well, that's a very interesting concept. I wish you the very best of luck with your campaign. Now to whom should I sign this book?"

"Don't you want to know how the platforms are going to be built?" I asked.

"Listen, why don't you visit my website. There's a contact page there where you can email your thoughts about this to me." He appeared a little uncomfortable, like I was preventing him from wrapping things up, and I wondered if he was worried that I was the overenthusiastic type he would have to call security on. I could hear people behind us saying something about hurrying up. "Would you like your book signed?" he said once again.

I surrendered it to him. He opened it, signed his name, and said, "Thank you for coming." Then he handed it to me and waved the next person in line forward.

"Wow. That was a total waste of time," Sig said as we walked toward the exit. "Seems Mengalor's *call to action* was more to persuade people to buy his book than in coming up with actual solutions."

"I don't agree. After all, he did invite us to contact him through his website."

"I bet he says that to everyone, Mol. Especially those fans who are just a little too fanatical. His click-through rate after one of these talks must be phenomenal."

Maybe, I thought. But I also knew that I would be busy tonight drafting a letter to the director. It was worth a shot.

"Oh damn."

"What is it?"

"I just gave you my last ten bucks. Now I can't get any of those mini donuts at the truck outside. God, when they sprinkle cinnamon and cardamom on them, they're fricken' awesome." Sig rubbed his stomach. "Well, I hope you like your book. I made some huge sacrifices today for it," he sniffed.

"Yeah, I can see that," I said as I smacked the small round bulge of his stomach.

Later that evening, I found the Marine NOW website. It was as impressive as Mengalor's talk, although on it I saw much of the same material he had used in the presentation. Nonetheless, that same charge of excitement I had in the auditorium for his call to action sparked within me. I had to make sure I worded it just right, so he would notice that I wasn't just another crazy fan with a crazy idea. Feeling a little shaky from nervousness, I clicked on the contact page and started typing:

Dear Dr. Mengalor,

I really enjoyed your presentation today on how climate change puts marine mammals, such as polar bears, in jeopardy. In answer to your call to action, my friend and I have come up with a great solution to aid the polar bears as the ice floes melt. We propose to build swim platforms and anchor them out in the open water so the bears can haul out on them. We have started a campaign called SPFPB for Swim Platforms for Polar Bears and we are going to |

The cursor stopped, and I couldn't type anymore. A warning popped up on the contact page that I had reached the maximum ninety-word limit in the message. As I skimmed over my letter to see how I could shorten it, I deleted several words, and next a sentence, and then automatically hit the return key out of habit to start a new paragraph. The page flashed, and a new warning displayed: MESSAGE SENT.

"Oh no. No no no no!" I said, as my fingers frantically tapped Ctrl+Z on the keyboard, hoping to correct my mistake. My letter was so full of deletions, it would sound idiotic as it was sent.

I couldn't get the site to cooperate. I tried drafting the letter again, but another warning said that only one message per email user was permitted. Obviously the site was not designed well, or a sneaking suspicion told me that it was programmed to do exactly what it was doing. My mind cranked through alternatives. I could get Sig to email Mengalor, although I knew he probably wouldn't, and then complain more about missing out on his donuts. I could use my mom's email address, but then if Mengalor replied, it would be to her, and she'd probably ignore it or delete it. I could start up another new email address for myself ... but I realized it would look really weird on the other end with the same message and all, and his admins would probably flag me as some kind of lunatic stalker.

Finally, swallowing a sour mix of despair and frustration, I conceded. I knew I had blown my chance of contacting Mengalor and making an awesome first impression. Wearily, I lay down on my bed and cursed technology.

It was a Gray Day.

I didn't talk to anyone. I just couldn't.

Most people didn't understand what my Gray Days were. Instead, they tended to think that I was just feeling discouraged, bitchy, bummed out, or trying to avoid something. This was different. To illustrate, Melody would get sad or angry or discouraged at times when she thought that "everybody was being mean" or if things weren't working out the way she wanted them to. It never lasted more than a few hours. When I was down, often, she would try to tell me jokes or give me suggestions like "why don't you eat some chocolate," or "treat yourself to something fun," or "go watch a funny movie," reasoning that what I was experiencing was so easy to fix that simply eating, shopping, or watching something would snap me out of it. These things usually got her, and most other people, out of their mood.

But anyone who has been through a Gray Day, and I mean *really* been through one, knows it was nothing like that at all. No amount of chocolate or treats or jokes was going to get me out of one.

Unlike Melody's funks, which had a direct source, these came out of nowhere, most of the time, whether I was feeling happy, sad, angry, or calm. There was no telling when, how, or why they occurred. Annie tried to explain hormone studies and chemical changes in the brain due to fluctuating serotonin levels to me, but knowing the facts never helped me to weather them any better. Neither did her prescribing any of the SSRIs, due to me vomiting most of them up and not being able to sleep.

For me, a Gray Day was a physical thing, too. It was coldness cutting through my core, the way trickling water slices through ice, leaving me numb and hollow inside. And when that happened, I had nothing to give to anyone. It was too much effort to talk, much less think. A simple word—almost any word, whether it was well meaning or mundane, from anyone—could reduce me to tears immediately. So it was not like I was very good company anyway. My best friend knew about my Gray Days and even she used to avoid coming over whenever I was experiencing one.

For this Gray Day, I huddled in my blue fleece robe that was covered in polar bears. Grandpa O gave it to me for my birthday right before he died. He knew how much I liked them. The robe was my favorite and comforted me when sad subjects like Melody or Grandpa O memories popped up here and there among the other tragic bits that bobbed around in that dark sea of thoughts flooding my day.

In trying to cope, I reorganized the sheets, towels, and pillow-cases in the linen closet, dusted all the dinnerware in the kitchen cupboards, and added a timber wolf to my endangered animals menagerie. But mostly, I just stared at the walls in my bedroom.

A few days later, when I began to feel somewhat normal again, I went to Sig's house. It was Saturday and he had agreed to give up some of his free time to help me with the campaign in return for having bummed a few rides. I was eager to work on the campaign with him and a little nervous too because, like I said, I was developing a crush on him. When I arrived, he was so engrossed in a show he was streaming that he could hardly look away, a Funyun ring, held hostage in his fingertips and halted midway to his mouth.

On the show, two men dressed in strange baggy suits made of parachute material perched on the ledge of some ludicrously high cliff. They checked the cameras mounted on each other's helmets, and then calmly surveyed the suicidal sheer drop-off at the edge of their toes, thousands of feet below them, while talking with each other as though they were standing in line at the grocery store and comparing the price of tomatoes. Next, the camera zoomed up on one of dudes as he inhaled, paused for a second, and then jumped, followed immediately by the other. Another point of view from the ground showed two tiny figures flinging themselves off of the mountain ledge like lemmings to the sea.

However, the anticipated parachutes popping open, followed by a lazy drift downward never happened. But neither did the anticipated splat. Instead they soared through the sky with their suits spread wide like high-tech flying squirrels. Amazingly, they remained level with their arms swept back, without having to flap or kick or do anything, and rode out the pull of gravity, buoyed aloft on air currents and rising thermals from the valley beneath them. Their helmet cams shot an eagle's view as they rocketed above alpine lakes and through deep canyons, while an onscreen callout clocked them flying at close to two hundred miles an hour.

"Oh my Cod. What is this? What are they doing?" I asked, with my attention riveted on the spectacle. It was incredibly terrifying. I got cold sweats just imagining flying in an airplane, locked in a metal tube 35,000 feet above the ground. It was completely unfathomable what it must feel like to jump off of a mountain cliff in nothing but a flimsy bag made of nylon.

"They're BASE jumpers, flying with wing suits."

The perspective toggled from helmet cams to the ground cameras that captured the flyers as they streaked overhead, each jumper making a roaring sound like a small jet airplane. Dumbfounded, with my mouth agape, I stared at the death-defying aerial maneuvers before me. The flyers skimmed dangerously close across mountain peaks and hilltops, buzzing treetops and meadows. They were even better than Superman, because they were real people.

When the two-minute flight came to an end, the jumpers touched down lightly, as if they had just stepped off of a bus. I blinked a few times, trying to process what I had just witnessed. A piercing pain in the palm of my hand made me realize that I had been clenching my thumb so firmly beneath my fingers that the joint ached from being squeezed tightly, and my nails had dug into my skin.

Sig let out an excited whoop. "That is the shit! I sooo want to do that. It's a dream of mine one day. I already have three hundred and fifty bucks saved up and need only seven hundred more for a suit and the training. That is, if I don't blow my savings on scuba diving or bungee jumping instead."

I couldn't believe what he had just said. Those wing-suit dudes obviously had death wishes, but now Sig did, too? That was when my mouth finally engaged, causing every emotion I had stifled while watching that adrenaline-charged footage to spill out in a torrent. "Are you … you … fricken' *crazy*? Those guys are insane! And you're insane to want to do that! Why would you ever want to throw yourself off a cliff in nothing but a flimsy bag and plummet over trees and rocks at high speeds with absolutely nothing to hold you up or slow you down or catch you should you drop out of the air and *splat*—hit the ground? You'd be obliterated! I mean, if you're that crazy, why not save all the trouble and expense and step out in front of a train or take a bath with a plugged-in hair dryer?"

"I dunno," he shrugged with his gaze still glued to the screen and a half-dreamy smile on his lips. "It looks like fun. And it's not like they are suicidal. They just have unique skills and know how to make the most of them. The way I see it, you only have so many trips around the sun. Better do it while you can." He crunched through his waiting Funyun. "A yellow and orange suit would be the bomb."

I threw my hands up in the air and let out a loud groan. Obviously he wasn't listening. "Don't you get it? It's completely asinine to take chances like that with your life. There are no reset buttons," I scolded. "And it's just plain stupid."

He chewed on that for a moment, and then, fixing those dozy, dark eyes on me said, "You know? I know now what the fundamental difference is between you and me. I mean, aside from the whole me-dude, you-chick, thing, that is."

"Huh … ?" I should have been used to him throwing curveballs by now, but I wasn't. "What are you talking about?"

"It's like, you're going through life, agonizing about all the ways you are going to die. I prefer to go through life, planning all the ways I am going to live," he said simply. "Life is in its experiences. If you can't remember doing it, you didn't experience it. And you don't experience it by watching others."

I racked my brain trying to come up with an argument or at least a scathing comeback, but Sig's perplexing observation gummed up the gears. What was I going to say to that? When I searched my memory for my life's experiences, I realized most of them had been spent spectating others, like Melody, doing things. What had I been doing all of these years? Deflated, I closed my mouth and plunked down on the sofa next to him.

We stared at the TV in front of us.

"Yeah, but aren't you afraid of dying?" I finally asked. "I know I am."

"Not really. Not anymore."

"You aren't?" I had never met anyone who wasn't afraid of dying. I really needed to know what that was like. As ironic as it sounded, even Melody used to say she was afraid of dying. That's why I still couldn't believe she did what she did. In fact, I spent half of my last Gray Day pondering that alone. "Why not?"

"Didn't you come over to work on your campaign?" Sig said, picking up the remote and switching off the set with a sense of finality. "I don't plan on dying any time soon, but there's going to be a lot more polar bears biffing it out there if you don't get moving on this thing."

It was obvious that he wasn't going to answer my question. And I didn't know him well enough to push. Besides, it was true. I had only about an hour before I had to go home to write an expository essay for my English class, and then deep clean the oven. I took out my notebook and opened it to the page I had marked with one of those little sticky flags. "Okay, what do you think of this campaign slogan I came up with: 'Swim Platforms for Polar Bears' or 'SPFPB' for short?"

"'SPSPFV?' Wha—?"

"No, 'SPFPB.'"

"Wait. 'SPSPB?'"

"'Swim Platforms for Polar Bears—*S P F P B*.' It's not that hard. What's the problem?"

"I don't know. It's kind of a tongue twister. And it sounds like swim platforms are some kind of constituent group voting for polar bears. What about 'PBNSP' for 'Polar Bears Need Swim Platforms?'"

"'PBNSP.' Yeah, I guess," I conceded.

Sig watched me carefully. "Hey, if you really want 'SPSPF,' it's your campaign. Actually, it's kind of catchy, once you get used to it."

"Do you really think so?"

"Yeah. It rolls right off the tongue: 'SPSPF.'"

"It's 'SPFPB.'"

"Right."

Chapter 4.5

Dr. Pamela Pope, PhD, Biology Instructor at Sea View College

THAT'S ONE OF THE MAJOR PROBLEMS with kids today. Lack of true, deep-seated conviction. I see it with my students all the time. Sure, this sort of nonsense before might have been regarded as romanticism—back in the nineteenth century. And even then, the human race was so jaded, there was hardly anything to be *enlightened* about.

But in the hard-core realism of the twenty-first century, what with everything going on in the world today—terrorism, addiction, sex scandals, mass shootings, weapons in schools—there is no other word for it than pure delusion. And it's not for lack of information or education, either. More than at any other time in history, we live, breathe, and are immersed in the Information Age, where everything we need to know about anything is virtually at our fingertips.

In fact, a Harvard sociologist and a prominent juvenile-behavior psychologist were discussing this exact thing on NPR the other day. Bored, middle-class kids clue in to something new and exciting that is different from their sheltered, cushy lives outside of formulaic sitcoms, video games, and mindless dance remixes. And when this *something* is novel to them, it elicits a strong emotive response.

Suddenly, this response awakens some deep call to action that in the long forgotten past would've resulted in rites of passage, but now, instead, develops into a crusade to *save this* or to *end that*. Next, up go the card tables with the hastily made poster boards and the jars to collect donations. They create a catch phrase, slap it on some idiotic meme, and *challenge* others to participate in their cause, hoping it will grow viral through tweets and posts.

And God forbid if you don't *like* the damned thing or follow their page. That alone evokes protest, shaming, and individual *meltdowns*. But when the going gets tough, or the results aren't instantly gratifying, or it just flat out takes too much effort and chews away at their oh-so-important social-media time, they readily dump their precious cause like last week's Cronut. With it go all the passion and fervor that was supposed to save the world by pinning ribbons on your lapel or walking a 6k or sharing videos on YouTube. And despite the sincerest pleas and the very best intentions, albeit temporary, it all amounts to nothing more than a passing fancy or theme of the week, if you will.

You won't find these kids standing up to a tank in Tiananmen Square, taking on the National Guard at a Kent State, sitting defiantly at a lunch counter in the Deep South during race wars, or chaining themselves to cattle guards to protect spotted owls. They are not *committed* to the cause. They merely protest or become martyrs for the cause as long as the cause is trending. At the first sign of trouble, they stress out, fold, and retreat back to Mommy and Daddy and their First-World lives. No, these kids are a bunch of wimps, wannabes, and pretenders.

Take, for example, those two that came into my office the other day with that totally ludicrous campaign to save polar bears. I had really expected something far more from Molly and Sigmund. They have produced some of the best lab reports ever out of my Bio 108 class. But boy, was I disappointed when they pitched that far-fetched scheme to build floating contraptions anchored out in the middle of the Arctic Ocean and Bering Sea for polar bears to haul themselves out on in open water. It was utterly absurd.

And if that wasn't bad enough, they expected me to take time out of my suffocating schedule to round up the names and numbers of field contacts and affiliates! I didn't know whether to laugh out loud or toss them out of my office on their delusional asses. They must have been blind or totally oblivious to the stacks of grading and grant applications sitting on my desk. Besides, I wouldn't embarrass myself with that nonsense.

It was clearly evident that they had not been paying attention to my lectures on fitness of species or natural selection. If polar bears are dying off because of factors produced by something as big as climate change, then there is nothing some hunk of plastic anchored out in the ocean is going to do to stop it. They will die regardless. Period.

These little morons should know how the real world works by now. All I can say is they had better wake up and smell the proverbial coffee, or they're not going to make it out there. I'd like to know what they'd do if all the safety nets that continue to enable them were pulled out from under their feet. I remember how hard it was for me to complete my doctoral thesis: "Implications of coral-reef die-off upon the wall permeability in *Valonia ventricosa*" after someone had stolen my notes and data and published it as their own.

Or how I clawed my way up, down, and sideways on the fucking food chain to become science department head—the first female to accomplish this, mind you—here in this Podunk community college, after the post promised to me at "Swartmouth" was handed over instead to some jerk who was—surprise! A male. Talk about conviction? I'm the only one more stupid, slaving away at this thankless job teaching imbeciles who would rather waste everybody's precious time on theatrical causes for drama's sake than contributing productively to society.

Then again, I don't know why I am wasting *my time* getting worked up over this. If the universe is still on course, as I am sure it is, Ms. Ohashi and Mr. Despain will most likely get distracted by their shiny phones with Snapchat and Instagram and whatever the new flavor of the week is, and with any luck at all, they will forget the whole damn thing.

CHAPTER FIVE

As with many animals, polar bears mate in the spring. When females reach the ages from ~~6 to 8,~~ * they are usually ready to mate. In the vast expanses of the arctic, it still remains a mystery how males who are sexually mature are able to locate females who are ready to mate. Female brown bears leave scent trails for males to find them. Scientists believe this could also be the case with polar bears (Cooper 47).

* Write out all numbers under ten

I love Sig. I love the way he had the freedom to do whatever he wanted, whenever he wanted, no matter where he was, or who was watching. It was like he had no cares at all. Me, on the other hand, couldn't shake the persistent feelings that either: A) an earthquake, home invasion, drone attack, massive car accident, or something else equally horrible was about to strike at any second; B) I'd contracted some rare and deadly, yet undetected for the time being, virus that was incubating within me; or C) something much worse that would encompass or eclipse both *A* and *B* combined.

Sig, on the other hand, took risks without a second thought of consequences or ramifications. I guess life had just been that good to him. Case in point—an incident that happened when he gave me a ride to school, since my car was out of gas: his parents finally helped him get a reliable, yet beat-up, little import to drive (aka "Mr. Chips," but more on that later). There we were, driving along and discussing the merits of '80s music. He, of course, couldn't say enough about it. It was his absolute, all-time favorite genre. I, on the other hand, wasn't convinced. It was still morning, and hearing Stevie Nicks sounding like a mosquito with a head cold on the tinny speakers in Sig's car wasn't making the argument for him.

Anyway, not more than a mile or so from my house, he noticed two guys on the side of the road working on their car that had its hood up. These guys were pretty rough—you know the kind with grizzled stubble, shabby clothes, scars, and scowls? And they seemed very unhappy with their situation—as if their murderous crime spree had been interrupted by the breakdown, and the police were closing in.

So what did Sig go and do? To my absolute horror and without any word to me, he pulled over in front of them and stopped the car.

"What are you doing?" I said.

"Seeing if they could use a hand. It looks like they're having trouble with their car."

"What! Do you know them? Besides we don't have time. We'll be late to school."

"We're fine. It'll only take a minute," he said, as he hopped out faster than I could tell him he was making a really bad choice.

I watched him through the rear window, agonizing over whether I should get out and join him, run away, or stay put in the car. I decided the latter was best. In that way, should those men decide to beat Sig with a tire iron, rob him, or throw him into oncoming traffic for recognizing them from an FBI most-wanted poster or something, I could dial 9-1-1 and lock myself in until the police arrived. Someone had to have enough sense to be ready to call the cops if necessary.

His back was toward me, so I couldn't tell if he was okay. My chest felt as if a woodpecker had been trapped inside of it. I wished I could have heard what was going on, as my ears strained to catch any escalating voices of anger or threats. Instead, I only heard the bang of the car hood as they slammed it shut. The next thing I know, all three of them started walking *straight toward me.* Blood pulsed in my head, as fear gripped my throat. The two men still seemed very unhappy. *Maybe they have Sig at gunpoint and were forcing him back to the car so they could take both of us hostage, since we could identify them and tell the cops their last known location,* I surmised.

I had all but stopped breathing as Sig climbed in behind the wheel and the two men got into the back seat of the small car. I stared at Sig, my startled expression trying to convey the message that this was a very, very bad idea. Instead, he scanned the rearview mirror and asked, "So where did you need me to take you?"

"The nearest gas station would be fine," the older guy said, his voice gruff. His heavy brow jutted out like a shelf above his smallish eyes, making him look exceptionally stern. The smell of gasoline and exhaust from the freeway, brought in on his and his companion's clothes, filled the car.

I glanced over my shoulder at the pair and hoped they wouldn't sense my nervousness. They returned my stare without saying a word, the younger one with the shaggy beard tilting his head in a slight nod to me.

Trying not to appear obvious, I glanced at their laps for concealed guns or clubs in their pockets that they would use to overtake us at the next opportunity. When the older guy cleared his throat, I turned around quickly and faced forward. Anxiety gnawed at me as I waited to feel the bullet pierce my back through the seat or a cold garrote slip around my throat. In the meantime, my unsuspecting lab partner, who had unwittingly dropped us into the hands of serial killers, drummed his thumbs on the steering wheel in time to a song on the radio.

After agonizing minutes that were more like hours, we finally pulled into the nearest gas station. The younger guy said, "This is great. Thanks man! We really appreciate it."

"No problem," answered Sig.

"Can we pay you something?" said the older guy.

"Nah. I'm good."

"Hey dude, we got to give you something for bailing us out. We would've been stuck there all morning if you hadn't stopped."

Sig thought for a moment. "My lab partner here is starting a fund to save polar bears from extinction. She hopes to raise enough money to have swim platforms built before the remaining ice floes melt from global warming and all of the polar bears drown. If you're down with that, a donation would be sweet."

"Is that right?" Older Guy asked, sizing me up and down.

"Uh, yes. Yes, sir," I stammered, feeling my cheeks flush.

"Far out," he nodded. "I always liked those pop commercials with the polar bears in them." He dug into his back pocket, extracted his wallet, and pulled out a twenty. "Here, hope you can save them in time," he said, handing the bill to me.

"Yeah, good luck," Younger Guy said, handing me a five.

"Well, thanks again," Older Guy said as they got out of the car.

"Sure. No prob. And thanks for the donations," Sig said.

I was still in shock as he waved good-bye to them and we drove away. "How could you do that?" I squeaked when I finally found my voice.

"Do what? We still got time to make it. We're not going to be late. Besides, that was pretty dope that they contributed to 'The Cause.' Twenty-five bucks. And you didn't even have to give them your SBFPB shtick."

"*SPFPB*. No—I'm talking about picking up total strangers! Are you nuts? What if they had killed you and raped me?"

"They could've raped me and killed you just as easily," he answered.

"You know what I mean. We could've been in serious trouble back there."

"Then we wouldn't be having this conversation, right?"

I shook my head in disbelief. "It's not fair. It's just not fair."

"Huh? What's not fair? Were you hoping for serious trouble? Don't tell me you're an adrenaline junkie."

"How is it that you can just come out and do anything you please with no repercussions?"

Sig gaped at me and blinked. "Wha—? What do you mean? If I could do anything I please—which I can't—I'd be out robbing banks or stealing hot cars right now. No repercussions? Yeah, right. You have no idea."

"No, it's true. What you are able to pull off is only reserved for a very select few people in life. Melody was one of them. You're another. You can be as outspoken and as unorthodox as you want and not worry about consequences. Just like that guy who moons the morning commuter train to Seattle every day. He's another one.

Why hasn't he been arrested already? Everyone knows exactly where and when he's going to do it every morning. Average people, such as myself, are not permitted to be like you or Melody or that guy who moons the train. No matter how much we would like to, or how much we try. There are always consequences."

"Maybe you've just never tried hard enough. Or maybe you really should go ahead and moon a train if that's what lights your bulb."

"Me, moon a train? Huh, right. It's never going to happen," I snorted. "Besides, I'd probably end up being jailed for like fifteen years with no chance of parole."

"Not likely. Probably there's more of a chance that you'd meet with disapproval. That's the part you're really afraid of."

I glanced at him out the corner of my eye. He was right, of course, but only partially right. Being ignored was worse than disapproval in my book.

"There's a solid ninety-seven-percent chance that none of those things you fear will ever happen to you if decided to cut loose," he said.

"Ninety-seven percent? Where's that from, the Bureau of Justice crime statistics?" It was a website I frequented, but I couldn't recall any study specifically on what he was talking about.

"No." He shrugged. "Ninety-seven percent just sounded like enough."

"Well, three percent sounds like enough for me to not even attempt it."

If we were going to get anywhere raising money, it was time to try direct solicitation. I checked into crowdfunding, but most sites required some kind of video of me explaining the idea. Even though Sig strongly recommended that I do it, the notion nauseated me. There were two problems with this: 1) I hated the way I looked and sounded on video, and 2) my aversion to social media. Besides, I'd probably commit a major gaffe without realizing it, and the whole thing could go viral for all the wrong reasons, which was shaping up to be a pretty solid number three.

At any rate, he reminded me that if I was totally serious about saving the bears, some kind of solicitation to raise funds was absolutely necessary. From what I had read about those little genius whiz kids, most of them had to go through this step. It was all part of the effort. Sig, on the other hand, had a quiz in art history that he couldn't miss, so he had a good excuse to not make a fool of himself.

I decided to take the lesser of two evils and go out among would-be contributors. Not that this was any less nauseating. The idea of approaching anyone for anything, especially strangers and especially for money was particularly onerous to me, but at least it wouldn't be recorded for eternity on the internet with the possibility of hearing my voice played back.

After class, I set up a table in the courtyard outside of the student union, next to the smokers' shack. I put out my quick-oats container, repurposed as a donation can, and labeled it in dark-Sharpie letters, "DONATE TO SPFPB—Save our Polar Bears, PLEASE!" along with a stack of flyers I had photocopied in the library, outlining our effort. Last, I set out the trifold poster board we had collaborated on over the weekend that featured irresistible photographs of polar bears and cubs that I had ripped off the web, an awesome illustration of the swim-platform prototype that Sig had sketched up, and a graph the shape of a thermometer showing our goal.

We decided that if we posted the three-hundred-seventy-five-thousand dollar figure we needed to fund the entire project, it would make us seem really delusional, so instead we set the bar at five grand just to get things rolling. Still, it was a very long way up to the top. With a red marker, I barely shaded in the bottom curve of the thermometer indicating the first twenty-five dollars we had raised so far.

Once everything was set to receive people, my nerves electrified my stomach, making it feel both charged and queasy at the same time. I tried (*hard*, as Sig suggested) to act nonchalant and confident, hoping to Cod that no one would notice my awkwardness. The only thing that could've been worse than this was if I had tried to collect donations at my high school. There, everyone made a fricken' mockery about everything, even when you were trying to be serious. At least fund raising wasn't a foreign concept on a community college campus. And, at least here, I could count on the student body being mature enough to get behind such an important issue. I forced a smile as people passed, but after a while, it felt more like I was grimacing.

However, as the afternoon wore on, I eventually started to wish that someone, anyone, would notice me. Most people walked by without ever glancing my way, like I was invisible. I was just beginning to wonder if, in reality, I was actually trapped in some kind of parallel universe, unseen in this world, when a few students from the smokers' shack stopped to check out the photos and query what it was all about. A couple of them threw what pocket change they had into the donation can. I'm pretty sure another one stuffed something else into the can as well.

After an hour more, I grew restless and counted what I had collected so far: $3.72, and a coupon for a free small soft drink at Taco Bell. Things were pretty dismal. It was then I thought about Sig's earlier challenge to me. *I could moon that train*—metaphorically speaking, of course. If he could do it, and Melody could do it, I could do it. I had to break free from my prison of introversion. My voice deserved to be heard just as much as anybody else's, damn it.

I cleared my throat. "Help polar bears survive global warming. Donate to 'SPFPB!'" I said loudly.

For all the response I got, I may as well have been yelling beside a waterfall. I squared my shoulders, lifted my head higher, and gave it another try, but this time a little louder. "Please give to 'Swim Platforms for Polar Bears!' Polar bears need your help!"

Not one person stopped. In fact, a few gave my table a wider berth as they passed.

"Swim Platforms for Polar Bears!! Help save them!"

From across the courtyard, some guy throwing a Frisbee to his friend yelled back, "Hey, why don't you take a swim yourself!" Of course, he and his friend thought this was hilarious and broke out in loud guffaws at my expense. Next they started mocking me by yelling to each other in high, quavery voices, "Heellpp meee! Heellllp meee!" which of course they, and nearby bystanders, thought was incredibly funny.

Yup. Three percent was more than enough for me.

🐻

I couldn't wait. I reread the text message one more time just to make sure:

> Will be there on Tuesday

My dad was coming to visit. It had been over a year since we were last together. And he would stay as long as Thursday evening, because he had to be back to work on Friday. After he had moved to Colorado, there was always one reason or another in any or all of our schedules—mine, his, my mother's, even my grandmother's (because he stayed with her whenever he was in town)—that kept us apart. And Colorado had been bone dry from a really bad drought for the last five years or more, so he and the rest of his department were kept very busy.

My mom, of course, was less than enthused by his message. I could tell by the curt way she muttered, "Oh," when she learned that he was coming, and how she immediately changed the subject to the amount of bleach I was adding to the whites whenever I washed our underwear. Later, she fell into a distracted, crabby mood, complaining about the electric bill going up and Foe's constant mooching of food.

Although she wouldn't come out and say it, she preferred Dad not to stay with us at all while he was in town. But I had begged him to spend at least one night with us at our trailer, instead of at Grandma O's. Usually, whenever he visited, I would stay at Grandma's place to be with him. But most of her things had been packed up for her move back to Japan. In fact, it was the real reason Dad was in town. She needed him to make the arrangements and oversee the shipment of her stuff, because she insisted that the shipping company wouldn't take directions from an old woman.

For the night he would stay over, Dad would have to sleep on our sofa. I flipped the cushions and fluffed them, freshened them with baking soda, vacuumed twice—getting deep into all of the crevices and seams, and then spritzed them with rubbing alcohol to kill germs. I worried about the sunken depressions where everyone sat and wondered how his back would hold up to it. Last, I made up the sofa as a bed and then covered it with an additional sheet to keep it clean and dust free, making sure to keep Foe off of it.

"What's all of this?" my mom asked when she came home from work and spied the sheet. She started tugging at one of its corners to pull it off.

"No, don't," I said. "I'm trying to keep the sofa clean for Dad. Please don't sit down on it."

"Well, where are we supposed to sit then?" she said. I could hear the irritation creeping into her voice. One of her favorite spots after dinner was chilling on the sofa to watch TV or read her *O* magazines.

"You can have the armchair and I'll sit on the floor or use a kitchen chair. Really, I'm perfectly fine with it."

"Poodle, don't you think you're going overboard with this? He's only here for one night. And he's used to sleeping … well, just about anywhere. Trust me." Sarcasm tightened her smile.

"I just want him to be comfortable, that's all."

"Whatever. It's a good thing he's not staying for a week, otherwise, you'd probably cellophane-wrap the entire house."

I ignored her crack and said, "So, do you think he still loves enchiladas?"

She rolled her eyes and went to her room.

When I arrived at Grandma O's condo, I hopped out of my car. My feet glided over the ground as I ran up the walkway. Expecting a hug, my grandmother opened the door to greet me with happy, outstretched arms. I spied him standing right beyond the door, but Grandma O dominated and wouldn't step aside, insisting instead on going through all of her typical questions about my health and school. Out of respect, I answered her, trying to be patient.

Finally, Dad cut her off. "Hey Ma, I'd like to see my daughter, too!" he laughed and broke in with a hug of his own. "Mol," was all he said as we wrapped our arms around each other. I savored the moment to take in the smell of his shirt and let him rest his chin on my head like he always did.

When we stepped back, I took a better look at him. Although his eyes were smiling like they always did, his hair was a little grayer, his face more lined, and he was thinner than when I had seen him last. Suddenly, an unexpected shyness sprung up between us from unshared moments that were long past and now crammed into this tiny space of time. It was an odd feeling, because when he used to live with us, we did so much together.

That awkwardness was frightening, and I grew anxious. Maybe we couldn't relate to each other anymore. It pained me deeply to know that any time spent in each other's company could be strained.

He must've noticed it, too, because he asked, "How are you? And how's school? How's your mother?" all a little too quickly.

"I'm fine, and school is great," I answered, which was only partly true, but how could I unload all that had happened in the past year alone right there and then in my grandmother's foyer?

"What are you, a college freshman, now?"

"I'm still in Running Start, but technically, a sophomore, Dad. Don't you remember I messaged you that?"

"Oh right. And how's your mother?" he asked again.

Abruptly Grandma O interrupted, "Molly, unless you want something to eat, we must continue with the packing. We're starting to run out of time." Grandma O hardly ever mentioned my mother since the divorce, and it seemed like she wasn't going to permit it now. "You both can talk while you pack."

I followed my dad to the living room, where he apparently was in the middle of boxing all of my Grandpa O's books. "Ma, how about getting rid of some of Dad's books? He's got like a thousand of them here. Do you seriously want to ship all of these? It's going to cost you a fortune," he called out.

Grandma O poked her head in from around the doorway. "Those books go with me. Unless, of course, Molly wants any of them. Molly, help yourself to Grandpa's books. He was waiting for you to get old enough to read them. And I guess that time is here."

I scanned the covers—there were ones on philosophy, cars, advanced physics, astrology, geology, dogs, sailing—he had his own mini library. "There's just so many here," I said.

Dad picked up one and read the spine before carefully putting it in the box. "Yeah, Dad sure loved his books. Always learning, just like you. I can't do that. I haven't read anything for pleasure in years."

"I don't know which ones to take. There's so many to choose from." I selected one on mammals and another on weather.

"You might as well take what you want. He would've liked that. You're more like him than I could ever be."

"It's true," Grandma O piped in quietly as she passed through the room. She had the ears of a bat, and apparently she had been eavesdropping. I really wished she hadn't been.

"No, Dad. I'm hardly like him at all. I wish I could be as gutsy as he was. One time, weren't you telling me about some of the close calls he's had in his life? What were they, again?"

"Well, I remember him saying that once he had been struck by lightning when he was a kid. He was out playing baseball when a storm moved in. It left a scar here where it entered," he touched the top of his shoulder, "And it exited out his big toe. The lightning even blew a hole through his shoe."

"Wow, that's crazy," I said.

"He had also been hit by a car and broke his pelvis when he was in his teens. And another time in his thirties he fell off a roof and busted his back."

"Don't forget the internment," Grandma O included, as she crossed through again from the opposite direction.

"Right. He had also been interned at Manzanar when he was a child during the Second World War. When I think about it, after everything that had happened to him in his life, it's kinda ironic that eating one bad shellfish took him out." Dad raised his eyebrows in thought.

"Well, you're definitely like him, being an emergency responder and all. It takes a lot of guts to keep going, especially when you know it's dangerous."

"Nah, it's my job. I'm not so gutsy as you think."

"It's true." Grandma O couldn't help but pitch that one in. I love her, but sometimes she could be really annoying, so although I knew I'd miss her when she moved to Japan, this wasn't one of those times.

"You are, Dad. In fact, you're my hero."

"Me! You poor kid. Maybe I should buy you some more comic books."

Although it was late, I wanted my dad to stay up and visit. Instead, he turned in by nine thirty, saying that he had a headache and had to get up early the next morning. I knew it was more because of the disagreement he had had with my mom.

It happened after we all were back at the trailer. With his help, I had made his chicken enchiladas for him and also invited Grandma O over for one last dinner with us. Mom, of course, wasn't thrilled about this either, but I figured it would be a while before we were all together again.

While we ate, Grandma O tried to persuade my parents again to let her take me to Japan with her. She insisted that I would have a much better life and upbringing there. Mostly, I knew she was worried that I wouldn't find a guy, get married, and produce grand-children for her. Although I thought it would be cool to visit Japan and stay for maybe a month or two to travel around to tour, I didn't want to live there, permanently.

At first, Mom and Dad joined forces and resisted her suggestion, like they had been doing since my grandmother decided to move back to her homeland and first came up with the idea several months ago. However, once they thwarted her, they turned on each other. I could hear the snips and digs they fired back and forth about stupid little details that shouldn't have amounted to anything, like the best way to store the leftovers or whether Foe needed his shots. They continued this long after Grandma O went home and until my dad turned in for the night.

I had a sinking feeling. My parents loved each other once. And from what I could tell, they still did. What I didn't understand was why they just couldn't work things out between them. Whereas facultative symbiosis would have been awesome—where they would choose to live together—I would even settle on just obligate symbiosis—where they couldn't survive without each other.

It was Sig's turn to give me a lift home, as I was out of gas, again. His 'new' car was a boxy little hatchback that once was used as a media tool for some now-defunct organic potato chip company. The interior smelled like potted meat and stale cigarette smoke. Its headliner was stained from soda spray, and the dashboard was cracked from too many road trips to vendor conventions, distributors, and spring fling events. It had over 257,000 miles on it already. The most bizarre thing about it was the photos of floating potato chips screened onto its windows and body panels. I asked him when was he going to remove them, but he said the floating chips were the best part.

He loved "Mr. Chips," as he promptly dubbed it, explaining that it was much better than walking any day. Whenever he had a chance, he was always turning a wrench, cleaning, or tacking something up on it.

Mom had dropped me off at school in the morning, so the afternoon found Sig and me pulling up in front of our hemorrhagic trailer (Oops! I mean our *normal* home) in Mr. Chips. It was the first time my lab partner would see where I lived. Heavy with shame and anxiety squirming inside of me like a pool of eels, I went into panic mode.

Although I had vacuumed the living room and deep-cleaned the bathroom the day before, I blanked on if any clothes were left out this morning. I also couldn't recall if my mom put her coffee cup in the dishwasher. Most of the time she left it on the counter, and I would put it away for her. And I hoped Sig wouldn't notice the fraying, artificial turf with the black bald spots worn in it as we neared the door.

Inside, he looked even taller under our low ceiling, as he slipped off his shoes and placed them by the door beside mine. "This is nice. Wow, it's so clean," he said, surveying our living room and kitchen from his place by the door, although I couldn't tell if he was just being polite. "Whoa, what are these?" he asked, drawn immediately to the collection on the wall shelf.

I had forgotten all about my clay figures that my mother insisted on displaying. I never intended on anyone outside of the family seeing them. Blushing, I stammered, "They're nothing. Just ... well, it's something I goof around with when I'm really bored and have nothing better to do." I didn't want to tell him it was mostly on my Gray Days, when I couldn't bring myself to do much of anything else, except clean.

Pleased, he held up the Siberian tiger and studied it closely. "So, you made these?"

I fidgeted a shrug. "Yeah. They're not very good. I can never get the ears right, and trying to get the fur to look natural is infuriating."

"Far out," he said, admiring my orca and next, my Kitti's hognosed bat. "These are, like, blowing my mind. *Pssshhkk!*" He made a mini-explosive sound while fanning his fingers out from the side of his head. "Seriously. They are friggin' awesome."

Blushing more, I mumbled, "Thanks."

"Wait, what kind of bird is this?"

"A passenger pigeon. All of the things I sculpt are—"

"Extinct or endangered. Yeah, I totally got it. Pretty impressive. Uh-huh, you even got our platform buddy here," he said, holding up the polar bear.

"He was one of my first."

"Cool. Are you going to paint any of them? Or just leave them like this?" he asked, referring to their bone color.

"I haven't had a chance to paint them. I'm trying to assemble all the endangered species together in sort of a 3-D album before they disappear off the Earth. Eventually I'll get around to painting them, when I get them all complete. Or maybe I won't. I haven't decided."

"A 3-D album ... I see that humans made your list too? That's pretty prophetic," he said as he examined the figurine of a man that he had swapped for the timber wolf and kiwi.

He couldn't know that it was the likeness of my father. I had made it one time when I was missing him terribly. "Yeah, well at least some do."

Just then the door opened, and my mom came in carrying the cat, followed by my grandmother. "Mol, you're really going to have to do something with this cat. Mr. Martino said he caught him hanging around his doorstep. His prowling around makes Bilbo go berserk, and I don't want him bugging the neighbors," my mother said, holding out Foe for me to take.

"I doubt it's Foe. Bilbo goes berserk over his own shadow."

"Molly Dolly! How are you, honey?" Noni said as she hugged me and laughed. The only way to describe my maternal grandmother was to picture a pear with a laugh like a frantic turkey. She quickly scanned me, like she always did, trying to find something to compliment me on or nag me about. Sometimes she could really drive me up the wall with her mindless chatter, but she was very sweet when she wanted to be, and her intentions were usually kind. "And who is this?" she asked, studying Sig up and down with an eager expression. I hoped she wouldn't say anything to him that would embarrass him or me.

"Mom, Noni, this is my lab partner, Sig. Sig, this is my mother, Shannon, and my grandmother, Irene."

Mom brightened upon meeting him, and I could see her give him the once-over while she shook his hand. Not that Sig noticed. My friends never do. My mom was much more covert than her mother was in taking in people. She had such a subtle way of gulping up a person's entire appearance in one blink of her large eyes; the subject of her scrutiny was never the wiser. I, however, spotted it immediately. Next, I waited for the follow up gesture—her almost imperceptible nod to her mother. It became painfully obvious, at least to me, that they had been discussing my relationship with Sig.

"Molly has talked so much about you, I feel I know you already," she said to him.

Mortified by her remark, I could've throttled her. He must've thought that all I did was gossip about him the minute I got home.

"I told her about our lab experiment and our campaign, that's all," I tried to explain to him while my cheeks glowed red.

"Yes, your mom tells me that you and Sig are trying to save bears?" my grandmother asked me. "I never knew there was anything wrong with them. What is it? Not enough food? Hunters?"

"Well, not all bears, Noni, although the grizzly's numbers are down to only fifteen hundred in the lower forty-eight. Just the polar bears, and it's because of climate change. Our polar ice caps are melting, and there are hardly any ice floes left for them to haul out on when they swim in open water. They drown from exhaustion."

"If you are going to save bears, you should start with Yogi. He's my favorite. Have you ever heard of Yogi Bear, Sig?" Noni twinkled and laughed as she gazed up at my lab partner. She always liked tall men. He stood about a foot-and-a-half taller than her cotton-top head. And apparently, my spiel on polar bears had sailed right over it as well, like most of my conversations with her.

"No, ma'am, I haven't," Sig answered.

"You haven't heard of Yogi Bear! He and Boo Boo were always after the picnic baskets, and the ranger had to try all sorts of things to stop them. I can't believe you haven't heard of Yogi Bear. Did you know he was named after the baseball player Yogi Berra, who played for the Yankees and—"

"Yogi Bear is a cartoon. It's polar bears we're saving," I said, trying to steer her back on topic. Once she latched on to something, it was hard to break her from it, although in this case, at least it diverted the attention away from her and my mother implying that I had been talking about Sig.

"They lived in Yellowstone … no, Jellystone Park. I remember one time when the ranger was rounding up Yogi and Boo Boo and … now what was the name of the ranger again?"

"Are you staying for dinner, Sig?" my mother asked.

"Huh? No, I can't, Mrs. Ohashi—"

"It's Ms. Afton. But, please, call me Shannon."

"Eh, okay, Shannon. It's my turn to cook dinner tonight. But thanks anyway."

"You cook? That's awesome! Boy, wouldn't that be a nice skill for someone I know to learn," she said as she cast a sidelong glance at me.

There was only one question I had at that exact moment: *Did mothers earn some kind of points for harassing and humiliating their children in front of friends, or was it simply a bragging right?*

"A boy who cooks?" Noni said. "You know, some of the best chefs in the world are men. Who knows? Maybe you'll become one, too, if you keep cooking. They make really good money. My uncle Charlie was a cook at a five-star restaurant in New York City back in the thirties. Now, what was the name of that restaurant again? The Portergé? The Porter? Something like that. Anyway, he was no lima bean. He used to have to get up at four in the morning just to prepare—"

"Noni, Sig's got to get going now," I cut in before she started winding up again. I practically pushed him out the door as he said his good-byes to my mother and grandmother.

"I'm really sorry about that," I said, as I followed him to his car, hoping he didn't think that I was a total freak from a freak-a-zoid family.

"Sorry about what?" He paused with the door open before getting into his car.

"My mom and grandmother. Sometimes they ask the strangest questions."

"They're cool. It's better than them not asking any at all."

"Actually, I'd prefer that."

"Okay, I have one for you. What did your grandmother mean when she said 'he was no lima bean'?"

"She meant, 'lazy as a lima bean.' It was a line she heard on a show once, and she just won't let it go. It doesn't make much sense out of context, especially for anyone who hasn't watched the show. I know I haven't, and it took me a long time to get what she meant."

"Huh." He shrugged. "You know how much I like beans, but I have to admit, that one kinda threw me."

How could I have known that we would end up kissing?

The morning together had been nearly perfect. On an impulse, we decided to go to the arboretum. I'd been wanting to go for a while, but nobody I knew personally thought that trees, plants, and gardens were all that interesting. Oftentimes, I longed to explore other places around Washington, but could never get myself to go, feeling uncomfortable about being out there all alone. But when Sig heard me mention this, without a second's hesitation we were on our way. It had been years since I had been on a hike, and even though we were in a city park, I didn't realize how much I had missed it.

Next, we stopped at my favorite restaurant, where we impulsively splurged on grinders that cost about a-half-a-gas-tank's worth of funds. Finally back at his house after lunch, I figured the surprises were over once Sig had to do chores. I offered him a hand, so we could get to some more campaign planning and then studying for our biology midterm exam.

"Sheets are my favorite clothes to fold, especially the fitted ones," he said, as he hauled out the basketload of clean laundry and set it down.

"You're like the *only* person I know who actually enjoys folding clothes. And sheets are the worst, *especially* the fitted ones, because they never come out right."

"That's exactly why they're my favorite, because no matter how unruly they are, you could always make a neat square out of them," he said with satisfaction.

"Neat from unruly? Huh. I'd like to see how that is done."

"Seriously? It's friggin' easy. I can't believe you aren't showing me this. You start by nesting one corner into the opposing one and repeat with the other two. Next, you fold the sheet hot-dog style, side-to-side, and then smooth out the wrinkles."

"Hot-dog style?"

"Lengthwise. Don't you know hot-dog style? I thought everyone knew hot-dog style. Last, fold it over onto itself, twice, into a tidy square. And if you do it this way," Sig said, holding up a uniform fabric bundle for me to inspect, "everything works its way out, and nobody ever knows the mess you started with. Bam."

"You're weird, you know that?" I said to him.

He grinned and agreed, "'Yeah."

He hoisted up another a king-sized fitted sheet, this one was printed with bright yellow daisies, and held it out for me to take an end. Deftly, he tucked one rounded corner into the other. Next, as serious as a color guard, we formed one long rectangle, and then another. Following his orders, I approached him with my end, and as we joined the corners, we came together. Our stares locked.

He had this warm, honey-in-sunshine look on his face, with that funny, sideways grin that tugged up at the left corner of his mouth. Suddenly, it felt like butterflies had been released in my stomach and had fluttered up my esophagus. It was an oddly compelling moment, and there was nothing more I wanted to do than to kiss him just then. I'm guessing that he must have felt the same way, because the next thing I knew, our lips came together, and it wasn't like I had jumped him or anything like that.

I had never kissed anyone, nor been kissed, before, so I didn't know what to expect. Melody, having been kissed—a lot—had clued me in on a few things about it. I remembered her describing it feeling like melting inside, being hard to catch her breath, lighting up her crotch, and wanting more. When I was fourteen, I practiced kissing the inside crook of my bare arm, imagining it should be a reasonable facsimile to a guy's lips. It wasn't.

As for my sudden animal attraction to Sig, nothing prepared me for what it actually was like. I thought our kiss would be just like the ones in the movies, starting out as a tentative touch, and then erupting into a full, passionate embrace, with the world and everybody around us fading away, and the king-sized sheet with the daisy print dropping in slow-mo to the floor by our feet.

Instead it was mushy. And slimy, too—like kissing a warm slug. Either way, there weren't any Hollywood sparks or crotches lighting up or even a smidge of lingering animal lust. Everything came to an abrupt stop.

"Did you find that as weird as I did?" I asked, the moment we broke away from our kiss. We searched each other's eyes for any contradictions or perhaps more to see if the other would flinch, stunned by our initial attraction, and then unintentional lip-lock that turned uncomfortable.

Sig's eyebrows knitted together in thought. "I don't know whether it was so much weird as awkward. Or maybe a little of both," he answered analytically, as if he were observing our mung-beetle larvae and taking notes. "It felt like I could be kissing my sister."

"I don't have a brother, but yeah, I agree. Like some kind of relative."

I reasoned the kiss was simply a matter of one thing leading to another, like a Rube Goldberg machine that used twine and rolling balls to swing shoes and move kitchen spatulas to catch a rubber mouse or make a piece of toast. We had had a good time together this morning at the arboretum, and then a satisfying lunch. Next, that dopey grin of his that always gets to me, and if I checked my calendar, there probably were some monthly hormones working against me too.

He asked, "So, should we continue with this?"

Reading each other's minds, we both shook our heads and agreed almost simultaneously, "No."

By this time, I could feel Sig's saliva drying on my mouth. With panic rising, I imagined it contained traces of his bratwurst grinder and the sour-cream-and-chive potato chips we had been eating, in addition to all the viruses and bacteria he had been exposed to at the restaurant that lie incubating in the moist environment behind his lips.

"We don't have to discuss what just happened, do we?" I asked. As my lips dried, they felt tight and shrunken. I didn't want to close my mouth in fear of ingesting something.

"No, I'm good," he said. "How about you? You good? Do you need to talk about it?"

"Yes. Yes, I'm good. And no, I don't need to talk about it."

He studied me closely, and then grinning, shook a finger at me. "Ah, I know what's bugging you. You want to go wash out your mouth now, don't you?"

"Well, I ..."

"Sure you do. You're freaking out about all the cooties I just gave you, right?"

"No offense?" I asked.

"None taken. Go on and get out of here. You know where the bathroom is."

Did I tell you that I love Sig?

Chapter 5.5

Yuna Ohashi, Housewife, Widow, and Molly's Grandmother

MY GRANDDAUGHTER, MOLLY, IS ONE of the true blessings my only son, Robert, has in his life, but he doesn't realize it. She is bright, smart, and very capable. Robert, himself, was the same when he was young. So much promise. His future lay before him, waiting for the taking. He could've been a doctor and heal the sick, but instead he rides around in a fire truck. *Neko ni koban*—like giving gold coins to a cat. He squandered his talent and youth on drink, until his father and I grew greatly disappointed in him. I also knew his marriage to that redheaded American was going to be trouble, for how often does a man in love mistake a pimple for a dimple?

Molly, instead, is more like her grandfather. Yuki always had his nose in a book. He was always questioning. If the sun was shining, he wanted to know how far away it was from the Earth. If we were admiring a beautiful canyon, he wanted to know deep it was.

And like his granddaughter, Yuki was a dreamer, dreaming of great things but never reality. Like buying that convertible car in a city that is known for rain. I would tell him to keep his feet on the ground, but he would scold me and say, "A frog in a well cannot conceive of the ocean." All of his foolish dreaming and mulishness … I begged for him to arrange for his ashes to be placed with his ancestors in Kyoto, but he refused. He said the United States was his home, and that was where he would be buried. Big dreams got him nowhere. He will now spend eternity beside a chain-link fence bordering a storage facility, because when he bought the plot, he didn't have the sense to question the undeveloped land next to the cemetery.

I wanted Molly to return with me, to Osaka. She is now a young woman and in much need of developing poise and grace. She would receive a better education in Japan and a better life. And she would learn to appreciate her culture. Instead, she is marooned here with only her dreams, just like her grandfather. Except her dreams involve crazy things like bears and cold, far away oceans—nothing that is going to help her achieve success and happiness in life. What is worse, both her father and her mother refuse to let her go. Yet they do nothing to develop her. For them, giving birth to a baby is easier than worrying about it. So it is with a heavy spirit that I must leave without her.

Robert told me what has happened to that blonde friend of hers. Very tragic. My granddaughter is stronger than that. She will have to be.

I send Molly money every few months, for her to use toward schooling and proper training to become a successful secretary instead of that other business with bears. She will eventually discover that following foolish dreams will only lead you to rest beside a chain-link fence for an eternity. Maybe she will come to her senses and work in one of the tall, shining buildings downtown for a powerful executive as—what is it they call them these days?—an administrative assistant. At least until she finds a husband.

Molly has the same straight body as me, strong, like a tree. Except she is very tall, like a man. When I have the *uchikake* sewn for her wedding reception, I will order additional material to accommodate her tallness. She gets her height from her American mother's side. That won't help her in finding a husband too quickly, so maybe I still have time.

CHAPTER SIX

Female polar bears mate only every few years, so males must compete with each other for mating rights. When male bears fight over females, it is a fierce fight with lowering heads, <u>bearing</u> teeth, putting back ears, **sp 'baring'** opening mouths wide, and roaring to mean business. Although the fight seems very frightening and loud at the time, if the loser is injured, he will usually back off. Polar bears don't typically fight to the death for mating rights (Sokolov 88). After the male bear wins the female over, the couple will only stay together for about a week to mate before going their separate ways. Polar bears are not monogamous; a dominant male might mate and impregnate several females within one season.

My room is not much of a room. No matter how much my mom wants to call what we live in a house, essentially, my room is nothing more than the rear end of a trailer. Its only view to the outside world is through two small, square windows covered by louvers. The louvers' cranks have long since broken, so I can't rotate them open anymore to look out or open the window. When I was younger, I used to open the windows and louvers, especially during the warm days in August and September, to let the rich, woodsy scent drift in from the only cedar tree of the three trees in the trailer park that stood across the way from us. This cedar was scraggly and undersized compared to ones you find in the forest, but at least it offered shade in the morning and smelled like life.

On weekdays, with my mom and pretty much everyone else in the trailer park at work, the silence in the trailer is total. I am isolated in this white box. The only noises come from my own movements, such as the snap of the elastic on my panties as I pull them up or the tick-tick of my keyboard as I surf the internet for articles. If I listen close enough, I can even hear the sound of my vertebrate grinding together whenever I rotate my back. Maybe that's why Mr. Martino let Bilbo bark so much—anything to fill the silence.

On Gray Days, I hole up in my small room, in the rear end of our trailer, and stay in bed longer than I should, studying the thin wood paneling turned orange with age. Sometimes, I count the black stripes that mark each board and contemplate their alternating pattern of wide and narrow spacing, along with the chips, stains, and nail holes inflicted from years of occupation. Sometimes, I make out human features in the wood-grain patterns. Other times, I wonder who designed the faux wood—envisioning some forgotten artist, toiling for hours hunched over a drafting table covered in sprawling pages of wavering lines, swirls, and knots.

My bed is nothing more than a twin-sized mattress with a headboard that has a decal of a princess on it, the same bed I've slept in since I was little. For thirteen years, the princess has loitered there on that headboard, in a field of pink and yellow flowers, petting a unicorn that rests its head in her lap. When I was around four or five, I used to make my dad tell me a different story about those two every night. In retrospect, it was impressive how many princess–unicorn adventures he was able to invent without ever repeating. Eventually, the pair faded and scuffed from all the bed making, linen changes, and times I pretended to be afloat on an ark with my stuffed animals.

When I outgrew that bed, Mom promised me a matching bedroom set. But that idea pretty much went out the window when Noni found an old chest of drawers and bought it for me. It is French provincial and has antique crackling and bowed legs that squat on curled toes. One of its fancy drawer pulls is missing, and another has lost its screw, allowing it to swing like a pendulum across the front of the drawer, etching a perfect arch in the paint. If I had had any choice, which I didn't, I would have gone for something more contemporary, like IKEA, instead.

Rapping its top with her arthritic knuckles, Noni proudly told me the chest was an expensive piece of furniture, built from solid wood, and that she had gotten it for only twenty-five bucks at Good-will. She credited her find to her shopping prowess and discerning eye for quality.

I didn't want to break the news to her that twenty-five dollars was too much to pay for veneer, water-stained pressed wood, and missing staples. I mean, while it is totally cool to reuse old furniture and all, this one is beyond beat. I have to be careful how much I stuff in its drawers, otherwise I'll accidentally push out its warped cardboard backing.

The only piece of furniture in my room that I care about is my dad's old high school computer desk. I am comforted by the thought of him sitting there, just like I do now. When I slide out its keyboard drawer, I enjoy the rainbow peace sign he inked in Sharpie. He told me he drew it one night when he was studying civil rights for American History.

Over the desk, the only bright spot of color in my room is my Mel-and-Mol photo collage. Correction—at least it was, until Melody did what she did. These days I can hardly look at those photos of us together. But I can't bear to take them down either.

I focus instead on the mung bean plant sitting on my dresser near the window. It was left over from Sig's and my experiment. The larvae had hatched and successfully switched to the adzuki beans; their evolutionary response in adapting to a new local host plant was rapid, as Sig and I had predicted. Following lab protocol, Dr. Pope made us exterminate all of the adult beetles after the experiment, to prevent them from getting loose and becoming invasive agricultural pests. She wanted us to get rid of the plants too. I spotted the tiny sprout on one of the beans and sneaked it out. It was sad enough having to freeze-kill our beetles, I didn't think it was necessary for the little sprout. Now, the mung bean plant is nothing more than a scraggly stalk with large oval leaves. I know it will eventually outgrow its pot, and we have no yard to plant it in, but for now, it is a tiny, green oasis against the wasteland of orangey-wood paneling and alternating black stripes in the rear end of a trailer.

The light glowed intensely blue. The sun shimmered in a rippling canopy, but its rays couldn't penetrate the depths where I hung suspended. All was silent, except for the occasional sound of escaping bubbles rushing upwards.

My skin, guarded by dense white fur and a layer of blubber, was unaffected by the icy arctic water. Overhead, I spotted the flat underside of the yellow rubber duck, bobbing upon the surface, but I couldn't reach it. My paws, tipped with black claws, frantically dug at the water. They pushed like paddles, trying to propel me skyward, but no matter what, I continued to sink. The fight to reach where air awaited me became desperate. Exhausted, I gave up the struggle for the surface as I descended deeper and deeper into the endless ocean abyss …

I awoke to the smallness of my room. It was the second time I had had that dream. Half asleep and groggy, I was wondering what to make of it, when a sharp rap against my window woke me up fully. It was then I noticed the wind howling outside.

I hated nights like this. The windstorms in our area were so severe. Oftentimes they caused mass power outages and broke off huge branches from trees. Anyone could get crushed at any min—

It sounded like a small explosion went off at the same time our trailer jumped on its foundation. I screamed. Within moments, my mom was at my door, dressed only in her nightgown, her flaming red hair standing on end. "It's an earthquake, Molly! Get up!" According to my earthquake evacuation plan, we were supposed to leave the trailer, shut off the gas, and head out to our trailer park's empty swimming pool that had been drained and closed years ago because of liability issues.

I scrambled to find Foe, who had hunkered way under the sofa while my mother searched for a flashlight. The cat pinned back his ears and yowled with fright. When I reached in to pull him out, his nails clung to the carpet.

"Molly! Come on! We have to get out of here," my mom ordered.

I didn't want to die, but I didn't want to leave Foe, either.

"Please Foe. Come here, kitty. Please! We've got to get out of here," I pleaded with him. He finally relented at the last minute and let me scoop him up.

Outside the trailer, gusting winds peppered us with tree needles and rain. Josh Rosier from Lane A, the next lane over to us, came running past with his flashlight.

"Is it an earthquake?" my mother called out to him.

He turned to her, confused at first. "Earthquake? No. It's a tree—the whole thing came right down." He shined his light's beam away from our yard to the trailer next door. "The top of it nearly took out our home."

When I glanced across the darkness of our driveway, letting my gaze follow the path of light, something was wrong. There appeared to be an unnaturally large presence blocking our way. A few seconds later, our brains registered exactly what we were staring at.

From what we could make out in the dancing beam of Josh's flashlight, the cedar tree had come down, apparently toppled over by the wind and uprooted from its soil bed. What we thought was an earthquake was actually it crashing down. Suddenly, we became aware of a strange quiet beyond the howling wind. Bilbo wasn't barking. As our sight grew accustomed to the dark, they traced a horizontal trunk line to where a horrible realization came over us. The tree had fallen on top of Mr. Martino's mobile home.

A few shouts later, other neighbors came out of their homes. Josh was already on the phone to the fire department that was only a block away. My mom found out from some of the others that there weren't any other trailers hit. The fire truck showed up within minutes, and the crew told us all to return to our homes so they had room to work in the tight area. The buzz of chainsaws and voices of emergency personnel continued for the rest of the night.

The morning light revealed that the tree had narrowly missed our trailer. The length of its trunk looked like a hot dog with a trailer for a bun. Whereas the tree used to look scraggly when it was standing, lying horizontally—it looked massive. Piles of cut branches, from the firefighters' work to extract Mr. Martino, had been thrown off to the side of the lane. One of the branches had scraped the side of my mom's car. Luckily, my car had its roof up this time for the storm, otherwise, the seats would have been filled with tree branches and tiny cones.

I walked over to where the tree used to stand firm against the sky but had since come undone and lost its mooring in the soft earth, its exposed roots, gnarled and tangled in the sun, never having seen the light of day until now. It saddened me to see the death of any tree, but particularly mature ones, and especially the ones I saw on a daily basis that had somehow became part of my life. I could only wonder what it must've been feeling as it lay there, vulnerable, with its limbs cut off, after so many years of quiet existence. My hand grazed and patted its rough trunk. "You poor tree," I told it quietly. I was going to miss that cedar.

When I returned, my mother was standing on our Astroturf in her bare feet, shielding her eyes from the rising sun that found the front of our trailer now that the tree didn't shade us anymore. She looked worried as she surveyed the scene next door. "I hope Mr. Martino is okay," she said.

"Yeah, me too. But I kinda hope that Bilbo isn't." The words squeaked past my lips before I could stop them.

"Molly Genre, that's not nice. You know that dog is the only thing he has."

"I know, but couldn't he have kept something a little less yappy, like a hamster? I feel worse for the poor tree."

Just then, our neighbor pulled up in his old Lincoln. Mr. Martino was a retired, single man in his early seventies, who walked with an unusual gimp. He got out, viewed his flattened trailer, and noticing us standing there, approached us, which in itself was odd, because we typically never conversed. I considered him one of our "hi-bye" neighbors—the kind where the only interaction you ever have with them was when you saw them, you waved "hi" or "bye," but that was it. My mom said as long as a neighbor was considerate and quiet, that was all that mattered.

"Is your cat okay? Was he inside with you?" he asked.

"Forget about the cat, he's fine. How about you—were you in there last night? We thought it was an earthquake when that thing came crashing down," my mom said.

"I was sleeping in my bedroom up by the front. It missed me by about ten feet. You know, my hearing's not so good anymore. And last night with all the wind rocking the trailer, I took a few sleeping pills to help me get to sleep. So, to tell you the truth, I didn't notice a thing. Sound asleep. The only thing that woke me up was the fire department breaking down my door."

"Is that right?" my mom said, contemplating him as if he were superhuman or something. "Well, it's nothing short of a miracle that you survived. And where's Bilbo? Is he all right? Was he in the trailer with you? We haven't heard him since yesterday morning."

"No, he's fine. He's at the vet. They put him under to clean his teeth, and he wasn't doing too well after he woke up, so he stayed overnight so they could monitor him. Luckily he was there instead of in the trailer with me."

"Yeah. Lucky." I hoped my disappointment wasn't obvious. "How did you get through all of that? You seem so calm."

He shrugged. "If I was to lose it every time something happened to me in my life, I'd be in the nut house by now. Nah. I'll save my worry for the big stuff."

His words stuck in my ear as I studied him. If a tree crushing his home wasn't big stuff, I was afraid to ask him what he thought the big stuff might be.

"It's been two days. Why haven't you answered your phone or the texts I sent you?" Sig asked as we walked from class to the parking lot.

How could I explain to him what a Gray Day was like? I placed my bet that he, like all the others, wouldn't understand.

"Our next-door-neighbor's trailer was crushed by a tree."

"Seriously?"

"Yeah, it came down in the middle of the night."

"Did it, like, crush your neighbor or anything?"

"No, he slept right through it."

"Whoa. So how about you guys? Did it do anything to your trailer?"

"No. Luckily, it missed us completely."

"Right on. But that still doesn't answer my first question."

I remained quiet.

He continued, "We dissected sea stars yesterday. Since you weren't there, Dr. Pope made me work with another group. You know those two girls who are always getting grossed out about everything? Yeah. Them."

"Was the sea star still alive when you started dissecting?"

"Yeah. Why?"

"Well, I'm glad I missed it then."

He studied me carefully. "Are you going to tell me what's up?"

I weighed his question carefully. Could I consider him a good-enough friend? Good enough to trust that he wouldn't think I was some kind of mental case if I explained my episodes of depression and anxiety to him?

To me, a friendship is a lot like an avocado. The avocado's thin skin reminds me a lot of casual friendships, where very little is divulged between me and the other person. These external relationships don't mean much and can be peeled away and thrown out, sometimes pretty quickly.

Next, the yellowy meat: although most people would consider it the best part of the fruit, it is either eaten or grows mushy, rots, or dries up. It never lasts. These friendships taste good at the time, but are only temporary, for whatever reason. While they are definitely an improvement from being just a peel, they don't account for much when things get tough.

But close friends are like the hard, solid pit. They are durable, like a rock. I can share anything with them, including intimate secrets, stupid jokes, and embarrassing habits. I can rely on them. The unfortunate truth is that, just the same way the pit is the smallest part of an avocado, the number of friends I consider close is somewhat small too. And with Melody gone, that amount is now even smaller. Basically zero, in fact. Although it makes me wonder—Melody had withheld important, life-altering information from me. Could I have trusted her anymore if she were still here? And had she thought of me as only mushy, yellow meat?

As I tried to keep up with Sig's lanky stride, I realized that he was hardly just a peel anymore. And I really, really couldn't imagine him getting mushy, dried-up, or eaten. Like so very few people I had encountered in my life thus far, he had true pit potential. I decided to test it.

"Have you ever noticed there's nothing that's purely good in the world? Things which you always thought were right always end up having some kind of hidden flaw? I find it downright dismal," I ventured. I thought I'd ease in with a philosophical approach.

"Huh. Like what, per se?"

"Well, take for example the cedar tree that came down. Here I thought it was healthy all of these years, but an arborist came out to investigate for the insurance company, and she suspected it had had wood decay all along from some hidden injury. Probably sustained it from when the trailer park was built around it."

He waved it off. "That's just nature. Everyone knows nature can be a bitch sometimes."

"Oh yeah, speaking of which, how about the grade Dr. Pope gave our beetle lab? Our larvae successfully hatched and adapted to the adzuki just as we had predicted, and our hypothesis was spot on. *And* we had the best lab methodology in the class. Yet all we get is a B+?"

Dr. Pope's reasoning was this: though we did A+ work, the best grade she would ever assign for a lab was a B+. Her justification, she explained, was that nothing in life was perfect. A lab involving living things would have inherent flaws and errors no matter how precise your calculations or measurements, because life itself wasn't perfect. And she felt her students had better get used to this fact.

"Well, it only proves that Dr. Pope is probably overdue for her distemper shot," Sig said bluntly. "I bet she's still pissed off at us for interrupting her chow time."

"Okay, the world is full of more examples. Like, snowflakes are beautiful, right? At least until you find out they are formed around specks of dirt or bacteria. Or … how about people? Like when you've sent Save the Seals your last twenty bucks and later hear that its COO has been pocketing the majority of the donation money and giving only pennies towards the seals. Or, things that flat out don't make sense, like finding out that Heinrich Harrer, who was a personal friend and mentor to the Dalai Lama, was also a former storm trooper."

"Yeah," Sig nodded. "I get it. So is that what's been bugging you?"

"I mean, how can you trust anything or anyone if you're going to eventually discover an ugly, hidden secret behind it? There's always some kind of blemish or deception that brings things down. It's discouraging. Like no matter what it is, who it is, or where you go, nothing or no one is going to be one hundred percent."

"Okay. I admit I've had athlete's foot fungus once, no, twice. And I also have been known to break some serious wind at times. I mean peeling-paint-offa-walls kinda wind. But it's only if I eat more than three eggs at a time. I'm sorry. Those are my ugly little secrets. They're out. But let's just keep this between you and me, okay?" he said in a hushed voice.

I stopped and glowered at him. "Can you be serious for at least one moment in your life?"

Sig laughed and held up his hands. "Okay, okay. So you were saying that nothing and no one meets the bar."

"Well, yeah. You just proved it perfectly."

"Therein lies your problem. It's impossible for anything or anyone to be pure good or pure evil in any case. Why should they be? Take me being an asshole just now, for example. Or the president of Zimbabwe. Or the UPS guy. Not that they're assholes. Well, maybe they are. Anyway, life is too complicated with too many details and too many variables. It isn't just black-and-white certainty. There can't be perfection. That's the point Dr. Pope was driving at, but she sucked at getting there." His dark curls flowed about his neck with each step he took. "So therein is yet another case in point. Even she isn't perfectly evil."

"That's what I'm talking about. I mean, doesn't that make you crazy?"

"Well, I guess, if I let it. But things are what they are, and there's no changing that."

"And that's it? You just call it good with a tired old cliché?"

"Not necessarily. I've learned to work around it. Like, if I was freaked-out about the bacteria thing like you are, I'd make sure that catching snowflakes on my tongue would be a pretty big no-no. Or if I got a snowball to the face and ended up eating some snow, I'd remind myself that my own gnarly mouth bacterium and my immune system would tag team to eradicate any of the snow's bacteria. Or if Pope gave us a B+, and that was the best anyone was going to get, I can take pride in knowing we shredded the top score among the biology class minions."

"But shouldn't there be at least one thing on this planet that we can totally count on?"

"Well, you probably can trust that there will be a speck of dirt or bacteria inside a snowflake, right?"

His answer wasn't enough. Something as simple as germs in snowflakes wouldn't suffice for complicated *serious* issues, like our friendship. I needed to know where we stood. I waded in a little further.

"Well, take my friend Melody. She was the happiest, most cheerful person I knew. She had a very stable homelife. She had everything she wanted. Her life wasn't filled with downer things like divorce, abuse, poverty, domestic violence—you know—adversity. Her parents loved her. Her sister loved her. She had a very normal, functional family. In fact, I never told anyone, but I was envious of her because they were so normal. She even had lots of friends. I really don't know why she hung out with a loser like me, but it probably was because we had known each other most of our lives. But then one day, without anyone suspecting anything, including *me*, her best friend, she ups and ends her life. Just like that."

"That's exactly what I'm saying. Too many unknown variables," Sig said.

"But there should be at least *one* stinking thing in life that we can count on, right? We need something other than ... than ... *God* that we can trust in, right? No matter what?"

"I don't know about that. Seems to me, God smoked quite a few individuals in the Old Testament whenever he was pissed. And in the New Testament, he's pretty much hands-off when it comes to solving any of mankind's problems."

"So wait, you don't even trust God?"

"Eh ... No."

"Really?"

"Uh, nope. In fact, when I hear *religion*, the first thing that comes to mind is a Black Friday sale at one of those craft stores. A herd of people crowding the aisles, acting uncivil, and pushing carts full of fabric, rubber grapes, and crosses with the dead Jesuses on them."

"You mean crucifixes?"

"Yeah, those."

"What does that have to do with religion? Or Black Friday?"

"They're pretty much the same to me—a bunch of people doing the same thing at the same time, simply because they feel they are supposed to do it."

"Then do you consider yourself an atheist?"

"Nah, atheism doesn't do it for me, either. In my opinion, religion, atheism, and cell phone service providers are pretty much the same. They all claim that they will be the one to give you the clearest signal, but in reality, they share the same towers. Worse yet, they all have hidden fees and drop your calls when you need them most, leaving you in the lurch."

"Uh-huh. There's that trust issue again. Our neighbor could've been crushed to death while he was sleeping in his own bed. That tree had been standing there for hundreds of years. Why did it decide to come down just then? Another twenty feet over, and it would have been me and my mom who were crushed. Every time I hear the wind blow now, it wakes me up and I can't sleep from knowing how close we were to checking out of this world. Anyway, it's just too confusing."

"Hell, there are lots of things I'm confused about with no discernable answers."

"Really? I thought you had everything figured out. So, like what?"

"Like, I don't get how our neighbors force their dog to be quiet and obedient, but they allow their children to be screaming, bratty ankle biters. Their dog is only an animal. It doesn't have to worry about what other dogs feel about it. But kids have to be part of a civilized society, and they can't always have their way. And why are there mattress inspection labels that are checked by mattress inspectors, yet there aren't enough food inspectors checking the food we eat? And, if our planet is covered in seventy-five percent water, why are we polluting it with plastic shit? I don't understand any of these things, and trusting God or religion or pure good or pure evil or phone service providers just adds to the confusion, especially if none of it provides any answers."

It *was* a lot to ponder. I sighed heavily. There was a lot more to Sig than I'd previously thought. "Maybe that's the point Melody came to when she did what she did," I said miserably.

We sat quiet for a moment. Across the parking lot a garbage-truck driver on break was parked at a hamburger stand. As if to emphasize my point, when he finished his lunch, he rolled down his window, dumped his wrappers out, and drove off. I sighed again.

Then out of nowhere, Sig suddenly asked, "What would you be doing today if you didn't know it was your last day alive?"

"What? You mean what would I be doing today if I *knew* it was my last day alive?" I answered.

"No, if you *didn't* know. Would you do anything different than what you are doing now?"

"Well, it's not my last day. At least I don't believe it is … Anyway, why would I? I wouldn't know any different. I wouldn't have any clue that I was going to be dead tomorrow. I just don't get what you mean."

"That's it—you don't get it. You don't know if today is your last day or not. See what I mean? Most of us really don't know when we're going to die, do we? If we were handed an exact time, like, 'Hmm, it says here that I'm going to die at nine seventeen in the evening on September twenty-second,' then suddenly we would start making plans like, 'I would do this,' or 'I'd make sure I'd do that.' And that difference in knowing versus not knowing is what makes people want to act better to others or do things that they always wished they could. And it really shouldn't."

"Oh yeah? What would you do different if *you* didn't know today was your last day?"

"Nothing different. I'm already doing it. Being here with you."

No one had ever been so straightforward and honest with me. Not Melody, not my parents, not even my grandparents. It was then and there that I realized I could trust at least one thing in this world. In one giant leap, Sig graduated from yellowy meat to firmly embedded pit.

I now knew I could be honest with him in return. "Want to know why you couldn't reach me for the past couple of days? My dad and I used to call them my Gray Days … ."

When we arrived at Sig's house, my stomach flip-flopped when I saw all the cars parked in the driveway and along the street. He had told me that his mom was throwing a *small* get-together. Given the amount of vehicles present, and the sounds of music and conversation emanating from his house, I pictured a crowd of relatives, friends, and neighbors inside, filling the living room and kitchen and spilling out into the backyard. It was becoming apparent that his mom's sense of *small* was relative to a pro football game.

"Uh, I thought you said this was going to be a small get-together?"

"It is. There's only maybe three cousins coming. Maybe four. You should see what it's like when all of my extended family shows up. Why? Don't you have a lot of family?"

"No. It's basically me. Oh, and my older cousin once removed, Denny, who's married already and has a baby. He lives back east, so it's been awhile since we've seen him."

As we drew nearer, I could hear voices through the open windows. My breath caught in my throat and jitters electrified my stomach. Sig would be the only person I knew there, and if he started talking with any of them and forgot about me, or went to the bathroom and was in there for a long time, or even worse, when he got out, I couldn't find him, I would be sunk. I really, REALLY sucked at making small talk with total strangers, and this would be even worse, because they were his family and friends. I didn't want to embarrass him by acting like some kind of tongue-tied idiot.

With my armpits stinging and turning clammy, I racked my brain for something quick to dodge out of attending. Maybe I could tell him that I wasn't feeling well. But he would know that I was just freaking out and say there was nothing wrong with me except a case of the nerves. Or maybe I could trip right here on the sidewalk and do a face-plant. With the resulting concussion, scrapes, and broken nose, he couldn't expect me to attend. I tried to figure out how I could pull it off, but considering that sidewalk, I was afraid I'd really hurt myself. There have been numerous individuals who suffered broken necks leading to paralysis, or even death, from a wrong fall.

It wasn't fair. It was very easy for him to meet all two of my family members—Mom and Noni. With Dad in Colorado, Grandma now in Japan, and Grandpa O in heaven, there wasn't anybody else. Not that it would have made a difference to Sig anyway. I could have had ten siblings and dozens of extended-family members and he probably would've bonded with each and every one of them.

We were getting closer to the door. Laughter leaked out of the packed house. They would be discussing shared family intimacies and inside jokes that I had no clue about. I knew it was a bad idea to come and didn't know why I had ever accepted his invitation. Mostly, I didn't want to disappoint him.

However, I couldn't take one more step. I decided I'd rather break my neck than meet all those strangers. It was worth the agony of awkwardness. Cuts and bruises eventually healed. A squashed self-esteem took much longer, if ever. Stubbing my toe against the edge of the sidewalk, I pitched forward and braced myself for the painful impact that was coming up shortly when I made contact with the cement.

"Whoa, Mol," Sig said as he grabbed my arm and steadied me upright. "Watch out. You don't want to do a face-plant." With a few more steps, he opened the door and led me in.

"Sig!" everyone cried out in happy unison when they saw us. There wasn't any chance of fading into the woodwork now. I scanned the room. There must've been ten people right there alone. I could hear even more in the kitchen. He pointed to each of them while quickly rattling off their names, and then introduced me to the group. "Hi Molly," they all said in unison again. My lips parted in an attempt to smile. Breaking into a sweat, I croaked, "H-hello."

While everyone resumed their conversations, I slipped off my shoes and placed them off to the side by the door, but when I stood up, I noticed that everyone still had their shoes on. I didn't want to add to the pathogens they had already tracked in off the street and into the house on their shoes, but I didn't want to seem out of place either.

By then, my socks felt warm from being contaminated by the germs and viruses that were most likely crawling all over the floor. Trying to act as natural as possible while wrestling my germophobic tendencies, I slipped my shoes back on while making a mental note to put my socks directly into the laundry the minute I got home, and spray the insides of my shoes with alcohol.

When I stood up, Sig was gone. Immediately, I was torn between trying to locate him and staying put. Things were beginning to feel extremely awkward standing by the door by myself. No one paid any attention to me at all, too busy balancing plates of food on their thighs and filling each other in on the latest. I tried to tune into the conversations to find some way to join in. However, they weren't talking about anything I could add to—mostly something about someone's baby and a Christmas that took place eleven years ago at an aunt's house. Besides, being socially inept, I had never been good at hopping right into conversations, let alone ones carried on by total strangers.

Trying to refocus in effort to calm myself, I considered getting some food, reasoning that it might convince the others that I belonged at this get-together if I were eating something like everybody else. I attempted a casual stroll over to the dining room table, where an appetizing buffet was laid out and a few ten-year-old-more-or-less boys buzzed about like flies. Apparently, from what I could gather from their chatter, they had been playing a Wii Zelda game in the basement and were surfacing only for a food break.

Suddenly, to my horror, I caught the skinny one poking his finger into the veggie dip, sucking it off, and then dipping it back in for another helping. The freckled one, who still clutched the sweaty control stick, dug through the bowl of potato chips with his free hand. Yet another rummaged through the cookies, handling each one until he found the one with the most chocolate chips. The one with curly hair like Sig's sneezed on the macaroni salad, swiped his nose with the palm of his hand, and then fingered the cheese wedges. Feeling nauseated, I placed my plate back down.

"What's the matter? Don't recognize American food?"

I located the voice. It was coming from some grumbly old guy in a wrinkled suit, sitting off to the side of the table and watching me.

Now how was I supposed to answer that? "Uh, no. I'm good. I ... er, I'll wait to eat with Sig," I lied.

He sized me up and down. "If you don't mind me asking, what kind of 'ese' are you, exactly?"

"*Excuse* me?" He was really odd.

"I said what kind of 'ese' are you? You know—Chinese, Japanese, Vietnamese? I fought the tail end of the Korean War and the nose end of the war in 'Nam. So I can tell you have some kind of 'ese,' in you." He studied me carefully, with one eye larger than the other, and his stare as unforgiving as a stone wall.

Surprisingly, it wasn't the first time I had been asked this question. Problem was, I never knew how to answer it. I was as estranged from Japanese culture as I could possibly be. I didn't know how to use chopsticks, sushi made me gag, and I totally didn't get anime. The only words I knew in Japanese were *domo arigato*, and I learned them from the Styx song, "Mr. Roboto." Hell, even my father didn't speak the language.

I had had my biracial-ness questioned for as long as I could remember. Sometimes people asked out of pure curiosity—they couldn't contain themselves and had a burning desire to know what I was, as if knowing made some kind of difference. But other times, rude or racial overtones lurked behind the questions. And this appeared to be one of those times. In preparation, I had always imagined responding to the latter by being flippant with extra bravado by saying something absurd like, "Actually, none of the above. I'm tra*peze* or *summer breeze*," just to confuse and throw them off. But that was when I was safe in my room in the rear of the trailer. Facing off with an antagonist in the world away from home was another story.

"I—I'm American. My father is Japanese American. My mother is Irish American." I hated the way my voice faltered and quavered under this man's scrutiny. Why should I feel so defensive?

"My father fought the Japs in the Pacific in World War Two," he said matter-of-factly. "But I served right alongside of Koreans. Now *those* were some honorable people."

"Oh."

"The Japs. They weren't."

"Uh, right."

I waited for him to continue, but apparently he had nothing else to say to me. My cheeks burned, and I could have sworn the room was shrinking. *Had anyone else heard the exchange?* I thought with embarrassment. Queasy, first from being grossed out by the boys' disgusting table habits, and then from the old man's unexpected inquisition, I abandoned the dining room entirely.

Desperate to find Sig, I found my way into the crowded kitchen, where another dozen adults engaged in several loud conversations at once. A few gave me cursory glances, but that was all, and I wondered if any of them were his parents. I was just about to go out the back door to find a corner of the yard where I could dig a hole and bury myself, when I heard the only familiar voice in the room say, "Mol—over here."

My savior. I turned to Sig. "Where did you go?" I asked him, trying to temper the complaint in my voice.

"Yeah, sorry about that," he apologized. "When we got in, my Aunt Bennie grabbed me to show me my new baby cousin. I thought you were right behind me. After that, I got caught by my Uncle Rasto, who wanted to tell me about his torn cruciate ligament. Why?"

How could I explain that I had been wandering about his house, among his family and friends like a stray dog? And that there were some vector-spreading children in the dining room sifting through the food? And that a racist old man grilled me when he couldn't figure out what kind of *ese* I was?

"Oh nothing."

"Did you at least get something to eat?"

"I am not hungry. I'm fine."

"Hey Sig, honey." A tall woman with wavy, gray hair pulled back into a messy bun approached us. Bringing in an empty chip bowl and beer bottles, she had just entered from the backyard where more friends and family amassed for cool air and a smoke. "And you must be Molly. Sig told me that you were coming." She grasped my hand and shook it warmly with a jangle from the many silver bracelets she wore on her slender arm. "My name's Janice. It's so nice to finally meet you. I've heard a lot of great things about you."

"Yeah, I told her that you're a genius," Sig added.

I blushed and fumbled, "A genius? Who me? No way."

"He also told me about your campaign to save polar bears. That's really admirable." She was only a couple of inches shorter than her son, and her voice was warmed by the same calm timbre as his.

"Thanks, I just—"

"Sigmund! Wow, you are looking great. How are you feeling?" A cheery, middle-aged woman broke into our circle, interrupting me. She hugged my lab partner and then stood back to scan him from head to toe with a bright, expectant expression, as if she were waiting for something. It reminded me of the attention Foe paid me anytime I opened a can of tuna.

"I'm good. Better. Thank you," he answered haltingly. It was the first time I had ever noticed him uncomfortable with someone.

"He's doing great," Janice beamed. "He just has to eat more."

"You have dropped a lot of weight. Now let me see ... I haven't seen you since you—"

"Hey, this is my friend Molly. Molly, this is our neighbor, Barbara Watts. She lives two doors down."

It was weird, what had just happened. If I wasn't mistaken, he had rudely cut her off.

"Nice to meet you," I said.

But before I could give his strange behavior a second thought, Sig continued, "Molly was just telling Mom about her campaign to save polar bears. She's raising funds for it."

"Oh, I love polar bears! Especially those funny ones on the commercials. What do you mean, save them? What's going on?" Barbara queried, looking like a bobblehead, toggling her stare back and forth between us.

"Polar bears use ice floes to haul out on to rest when they are swimming across open water. With climate change, the ice floes are melting in the warming arctic waters and as a result, the bears don't have anything to haul out on. For the adults, swimming the extra distance is exhausting, and some don't make it; for the cubs, it's a sure death sentence. They tragically perish from drowning. So we are trying to raise money to help build some artificial ice floes, or swim platforms, for them. In that way, they could at least rest up before having to swim for miles more," I spoke with confidence for the first time since I had arrived at Sig's house. He was right. Giving the spiel was getting easier.

"All of that climate-change hullabaloo is a bunch of happy horseshit to get people to pay more taxes. Want to know what the polar bears' biggest problem is? I'll tell you—it's getting indigestion from eating the garbage out of people's trash cans. I know, because I use to live in Alaska and witnessed them doing it myself. They're nothing but oversized rats in fur coats and goddamn pests." It was that strange old man from the dining room, and it seemed his disposition and opinions hadn't improved any.

"They're drowning, Grandpa. And just because people bury their heads in the sand and don't believe climate change is happening doesn't make it any less real," Sig intervened.

My mouth almost dropped open in surprise. The old man was Sig's grandfather! The grandson couldn't have been any more different than this belligerent, stocky man standing before us.

"Sig came up with the idea to build the platforms. And it was absolutely brilliant," I blurted out, before I lost my nerve. I was sure his grandfather would at least appreciate his grandson's ingenuity. And I didn't want to give him the chance to run me down again.

"It sounds like a waste of time and good money to me. You can count me out. I'd get more pleasure flushing my wallet down the toilet."

Grandpa Despain's words hung thick in the air, like toxic gas. I caught Sig and his mother rolling their eyes and exchanging looks of exasperation and embarrassment.

"Well, I'm with Molly. It's a fabulous idea! Here's something towards the cause," said Barbara, handing over a couple of bills to me that she had extracted from her purse. "I hope you can save those poor polar bears. And Sig, it's so good to see that you're back to your old self and up and around again."

"Ha! There's another thing all that worrying about this and worrying about that gets you. The kid was perfectly healthy until his mother insisted on running him to the doctor for every little thing. And that's exactly what happened. The doctor dug around until he found something wrong with my grandson. That's why I won't go to any doctor if I can help it. They will always find something wrong with you. It's called job security. Well, I'm not helping any doctor finance his yacht or vacation time-share," Grandpa Despain said with finality.

"Now wait just a minute, Art," Janice protested. "That's totally absurd. Of course I took him to the doctor! Do you ever stop to wonder what would've happened if I hadn't? He was not perfectly healthy by a long shot."

I was about to thank Barbara for the contribution, but Sig abruptly cut in and said, "Right. Hey Mol, I'm heading out to the store to pick up some more beer. Let's get out of here." He practically ushered me out of the kitchen, as his mother and grandfather continued their tense exchange. In a way, I was curious to know what they and Barbara were referring to. Had Sig been sick recently? For the last couple of months I had known him, he hadn't missed a day of school.

As we tore around the corner in Mr. Chips, I ventured to say, "I just realized that your neighbor gave me forty dollars! That was really nice of her to donate money towards our campaign, but forty dollars?"

"Barbara's a widow who doesn't know what to spend her money on now that her husband is gone. And she's crazy about any animal cause. She practically could've bought the ASPCA with the amounts she's donated to them."

"I feel bad, because I didn't get a chance to thank her properly. I hope she's there when we get back."

"Yeah, well," was all he said. It was uncharacteristic of him to be so quiet and distracted. Something was definitely getting to him.

We drove for another half mile or so before I finally asked, "So what were your mother and grandfather arguing about?"

"I hope my grandfather didn't say anything rude or offensive to you. And if he did, I apologize. He's really hard to keep an eye on, and he can be one crotchety, opinionated son of a bitch sometimes. In fact, most of the time."

"No, it's okay. But what did they mean about the doctor?" I knew I was prying, but I had disclosed my Gray Days to Sig. It was his turn to give up some of his secrets if he was to continue being one of my pit friends.

The streetlights streaked overhead in that quiet little car. Then he answered simply, "I have ALL. Acute lymphoblastic leukemia.

It's basically cancer of my blood and bone marrow. I've had it since I was fifteen."

The news socked me like a rock-hard fist to the stomach. *No ... Not Sig. It couldn't be.* A million questions were set into motion all at once in my head, swirling like a funnel cloud, but only dribbled out my mouth in meager spurts. "Wait. Wha—? You? Do you still have it?"

"I received treatment for almost five years. Spent a year and a half in the hospital. I had it all—chemo, radiation, enough drugs to choke a freakin' hippo. Seriously. I never want to swallow another pill again. They even tried a bone marrow transplant."

I was almost afraid to ask, "Did it ... work?"

"My counts have been consistently normal for almost two years, already. I got my hair back, and I'm putting on weight. As far as they're concerned, I'm in remission. So they're calling it good for now."

"So wait a minute, you said that they are calling it good *for now*. What do you mean?"

"There's a very slim chance that I could have a relapse. Very slim. Almost nil," Sig said assuredly.

I, on the other hand, had to swallow hard and remember to breath. I didn't know anyone who had cancer. *What if Sig ...* I couldn't complete the thought. Aside from Melody, Grandpa O was the only other person I knew personally who had died.

"And if that happens ... ?"

"Well, it could result in things like a brain tumor or even losing one of my nuts if it spreads. But that's not going to happen."

"What makes you so sure?"

"Hey, the docs said I'm cured. I'm going with that."

My brain tried to absorb what he had just said, but was resisting. He could do anything he wanted. He could figure out anything. He was the coolest, calmest, most fearless person I knew. However, when I studied him now, illuminated with the passing streetlights in flashing tones of dull yellow light, I felt as if he were fragile enough to shatter into a million pieces at any moment. I lost Melody already. I couldn't lose him, too.

"Should we be doing this then?"

"Doing what?"

"Going out for more beer?"

Quite unexpectedly, he forced Mr. Chips hard into a tight U-turn, making its tires squeal loudly as the little car rolled into the turn. I gripped the armrest and the dash in front of me, bracing for a rollover, and squeezed my eyes shut. When we pivoted in the opposite direction, Sig mashed on the accelerator and sped up the street.

"Oh my God! What are you doing?"

"Taking you home if you are going to talk like that."

"No! Wait. I'm sorry. I just didn't know if—"

He pulled the car over to the side of the road, slammed on the brakes, and confronted me. "Listen, I'm not going to catch pneumonia, or explode, or dissolve into some quivering mass of protoplasm just because I had cancer. I'm okay, or otherwise I wouldn't be here. Trust me, my mother would have me back at the hospital with a mess of tubes running in and out of me, and with nurses, doctors, and therapists telling me all of what I can and can't do, and when I should be drinking, eating, shitting, or breathing.

"So I will tell you right now, and I'm only going to tell you once—if you're going to hang with me, don't be like all the rest. I thought you were cool. You are the only person I knew who was only worried about yourself. Now I know that sounds totally messed up, and don't take it wrong. But that is exactly what I need—a person who lets me worry about myself and minds her own life instead of getting all up in mine."

"Okay. I'm sorry, Sig. Really, I am. I just don't want to lose ..."

"What? Another friend?"

"Yeah. I'm sorry."

"Don't be. And you won't. I don't plan on going anytime soon."

Without any further discussion, he put the car in gear and turned it around again, headed for the store. I glanced at him out of the corner of my eye, and then redirected my gaze straight ahead out of fear that he would feel I was analyzing him. Just then, it occurred to me: I hoped Sig considered *me* pit worthy and not some yellow mushy meat.

Chapter 6.5

Irene Afton, Retired JC Penney's Sales Clerk and Molly's Grandmother

My Molly Dolly was the prettiest Japanese baby with all of her long, dark hair, big cheeks, and slanty eyes. Just like a doll baby. That's why I called her my Molly Dolly. When she was still a toddler, I told Shans that she should've written the toy companies and sent them a picture of Molly for them to use as a model for a Japanese doll baby. I don't know why, but she got after me for it.

"Mom, you've got to quit saying that," she said. "Molly is only half Japanese. And besides, toy companies don't work like that. They already have in mind who they are going to make dolls of, and they usually don't choose biracial kids."

My daughter can be stubborn, and sometimes, a real know-it-all. So every so often, I like to get back at her by saying, "Well then, if she's half, it's obvious which side she gets all her prettiness from."

Anyway, I always worry about my Molly Dolly. She's such a sweet little girl. I used to really worry about her when Shannon and Robert were still with all of their drinking and partying all the time. It was no way to raise a child. All I could do was pray for them.

I was glad that Shans pulled herself out of that nosedive of a marriage. Not that I am happy they divorced. On the contrary. I miss Robert. He made me laugh. I only wish that he could have controlled the drink. And it's just a shame what becomes of so many of these young couples who think they are in love and that their marriage is going to last forever. Nothing lasts. And then they leave behind kids in these half-family situations.

Jerry and I divorced when Shannon was sixteen, and I thought that was bad enough at the time. But I couldn't live with Jerry once I found out that he had cheated on me with the cashier at the QFC. It wasn't like we had any knockdown, dragged-out fights about it. We just went our separate ways. Neither Shannon nor I have heard from him since. He never was much of a talker.

Now, that boy, Sig, seems nice. He's tall and has a cute grin. The way that Molly looks at him, she must like him. Although I sure hope he doesn't get her pregnant. You know how boys are these days. They give the girls a line and flash their little dimples, and these girls are so stupid to fall for all of that. Next thing they end up with a bellyful, and the boys are off flashing their dimples again and impregnating some other stupid girl.

I have to admit, though, my granddaughter has a head on her shoulders. And if she can keep herself from getting pregnant and bogged down with babies, like I was at her age, she can be anything she wants to be. I always wanted to travel the world. I really should have become a stewardess like I had wanted, and set off on those international flights to places like Paris and Rome. It would have been so glamorous.

In a way, I envy these kids. They have the freedom to go off and do all sorts of interesting things. The world is at their fingertips. Like the way Molly wants to help polar bears. Now, we would have never imagined doing something like that back in the day. We might have done a scrap-metal drive or the March of Dimes. But here they are accomplishing big things. And different, too. It's amazing how easy it is for anyone to do anything they want nowadays and find out everything they need to know from those computers and fancy phones.

But I guess I can help in my own simple way. I've been known to stitch a thing or two. And it's something that Molly wouldn't know how to do herself, and I know that Shans would never do for her. In fact, I'm going to make my Molly Dolly something special and surprise her.

CHAPTER SEVEN

In late fall, as she prepares to give birth, the pregnant female polar bear digs a cave out of snow that is typically located on the sea ice or very close to sea ice on a mountainside. This den provides a secure place, protected from the frigid wind. <u>The female and her cubs</u> remain in the den for four to eight months. During 'denning,' <u>they</u> are largely immobile without eating or drinking and must live off their fat reserves, although this is not considered a true hibernation. For some reasons unknown, <u>they</u> do not lose bone mass or suffer from lack of water (Hayakawa 68). While scientists still are not sure of how that happens they believe understanding polar bears may hold clues to treating many diseases.

Watch overuse of pronouns. Alternate w. nouns

What kinds of diseases? Give examples.

Noni meant well; I know she was only thinking about me. But it was a complete disaster as I stood before the mirror and watched the faux fur sag and droop like the hide of some decrepit animal. The polar bear costume she had made for me was easily two to three sizes too big.

Noni's brow furrowed as she stepped back and surveyed the situation, with her hand cupping her chin in thought. "I knew there was something up with that pattern. It said a size eight on it, but when I was cutting it, I could see all along that it was much bigger than that," she explained in self-defense.

I knew it was probably because she had bought the pattern for fifty cents at Goodwill, and chances were that it was some kind of factory second to begin with, although I didn't understand why she would buy it at all if she saw that the pattern was bigger than a size six from the get-go. I have told her over and over again that I was a size five. For some reason, she had it in her head that I was much larger than that. Any other person would have halted production when they started cutting and noticed the problem. But not my Noni.

Pulling and tucking the excess fur in around my middle, as if she had finally solved the puzzle, she suddenly proclaimed, "Unless ... Wait—you've lost weight, haven't you?"

"No," I replied miserably, "I haven't."

"You must have. I measured this perfectly. The way this hangs on you, it's obvious you did."

No matter what, Noni refused to own up to her mistake. I sighed. There was no arguing with her.

"Oh, well, you can still wear it. All you have to do is pad it a little, and it will be perfect."

"And what am I supposed to pad it with, a mattress?"

"You'd wear a bucket on your head, but you won't wear a costume that is the teensiest big on you?" She also had a way of picking some kind of irrelevant fact from the past and meshing it into her defense.

If I knew her at all, she was about to launch into the dog-eared story about when I was a toddler and ran around with a bucket on my head, crashing into everything. It was one of her favorites, and I had heard her retell it almost every year for as long as I could remember.

Noni laughed in her way that always reminded me of a gobbling turkey, and then started rolling the "Moments from Molly's Childhood" tapes. "I remember when you were about two, running around the house with that red plastic mop bucket on your head. You could barely see a thing, but you wouldn't let us take it off, saying it was your helmet to protect you from the rain and the clouds. You wore that and crashed into walls and doors and us. Funny how you thought it was perfectly fine, but you won't wear this. And after all the work I put into making it."

And there it was. Apparently, she had no intention of making alterations. The hideous, oversized polar bear costume was here to stay. You think that my mother would've stepped in and said something to help me out. I mean, compared to Noni, there was nothing wrong with her vision or judgment. But she didn't help me out one iota. On the contrary—she made it official by promptly taking out her cell phone, photographing me in the damn thing, and then immediately posting it to Facebook for everyone to comment on. "You look so darn cute, Poodle!" was all she managed to say while choking on her own laughter. "Is Sig coming over? I can't wait to see the look on his face when he sees you in this."

I was beginning to wonder if she secretly hated me.

Summoning up as much patience as I could, I understood that my family was trying (sort of) to be helpful by supporting my campaign whichever way they could, and I should be appreciative and grateful. However, their help didn't dismiss the fact that the costume looked more like a symbol for polar bear mortality. Its stuffed head was caved in on one side. When I put it on, the eyeholes weren't even, so when I stared straight ahead, its expression was that of some kind of demented killer in a slasher flick. I also recognized the freakishly oversized black nose had been cut from one of Noni's old Naugahyde purses.

For the mouth, my grandmother showed a rare innovative streak by dismantling a necklace of plastic shark teeth that happened to be left over from a luau event at the local Lodge #249 that she attended every other Thursday night for bingo. She made sure to tell me how she hot glued each individual tooth from the necklace onto the jaws. Since there was no rigid structure for a mouth, the teeth gapped in some places and clustered in others.

As a result, the bear's overall expression wasn't one of passive friendliness, as I would have preferred. Even ferociousness would have been better. Instead it was a mix of idiotic derangement, like a saggy, white Goofy with rabies.

Perhaps the weirdest part, at least to me, was that she had run out of white thread, and instead of buying more to complete the costume, she used a scarlet-red one that she had on hand. "It was only to fill the bobbin. Really, Molly, you carry on too much. It's fine. The sewing thread is still white," she said, perturbed at my fussing.

Maybe I did make a big stink about it, but the area in question happened to run down the middle of my chest. The brilliant-red track embedded in the white fur looked like the bear had undergone some kind of crude open-heart surgery.

When I put the costume on to show Sig later that afternoon, he could only gape and stare with one eyebrow sharply arched, trying to make heads or tails of it.

"And what exactly did she intend for you to do with this?" he asked.

"I really don't know. Join a freak show to collect money? Go knocking door to door or stand out in front of stores with a can in my hand? I have no idea."

"I see." He nodded slowly. "So are you going to deep six it?"

"Yeah, right." I sighed. "Nice thought, but you know it took her, like, two weeks to sew this. I can't just throw it away. She would ask me about it and then I would have to either tell her the truth or make up something about where it was, and I don't like lying to my grandmother. And I can't give it back. That would hurt her feelings. But she won't alter it so it fits me properly, either. In fact, she dug in her heels and said that I should eat more and that all polar bears naturally have loose folds of skin just like Shar-Peis."

"They do?"

"No, they don't. Where she got that information, I don't know. When she knows she screwed up, she seriously makes up stuff to cover her butt, or at least she tries to convince you that she read it somewhere."

"You look like you just crawled out from under that crushed trailer next door. Or maybe more like a polar bear who swore off seal meat and went vegan ... you're just a little bit, what's the word? Emaciated."

"Tell me about it. Actually, it would fit you a lot better—Hey! You could wear—"

"Nuh-uh and *hell* no. Don't even ask," Sig cut me off, flashing me the palm of his hand.

"Aww, come on. Why not? I mean, look at this," I whined, holding out my arms and letting the paws dangle down at ninety-degree angles.

"I said I would *help* you, but that doesn't mean that I'm wearing that thing. This is still your campaign. Not mine. Maybe you could use it for the Kickstarter video? No one would ever recognize that it's you in it. In fact, you'll bring more attention to the plight of the polar bears, like it was artistically intentional, and you wanted to illustrate the effects of climate change. You could act like you are swimming until exhaustion overtakes you and you can't haul yourself out," he said, serious and solemn, until a snicker sneaked out. "Or better yet, why not just cut to the chase and say that you've already drowned? You could just lie there on the floor and pretend that you've washed up on shore." He cleared his throat and tried to wrestle away his smirk, but his stomach shook with concealed laughter spasms.

"Fine. Thanks for nothing." When I nodded, the stuffed head shifted forward and down, blocking my vision. As I grappled with my floppy, useless paws to right it, I could hear Sig laughing his ass off.

The Earth Day Festival, downtown in a week and a half, would be my inaugural appearance in the bear suit. Themed, "Go Green or Go Home," it was a huge event and only growing bigger, providing the perfect venue to get some traction on our campaign. If we could hand out enough flyers and put the can out, we could really make a dent in our donations. Better yet, maybe some well-known conservation groups would be there and take an interest in our idea.

Running through the upcoming scenario in my head, I pictured myself behind a table, waving to kids while their parents picked up the flyers and read our cardboard display. What I didn't know was that I was supposed to have registered months in advance for the table. There were none left at such late notice (besides the fact that it would have cost $175 for three days), so we wouldn't have a formal booth.

However, understanding that we could use a break, the registration-coordinator person explained that the Seashore Alliance people typically had someone walking around in a sea star outfit every year. Since they weren't able to attend and so had to cancel, she thought it would be great if I wandered around the festival grounds in my bear suit instead. I could collect donations and hand out my information while shaking hands with children, and even better—she wouldn't charge us anything to get in.

With the festival deadline looming near, I was in the kitchen performing cosmetic surgery on the costume when my mom walked in carrying groceries.

"Hey Poodle. Did you see there's some guys surveying the tree and Mr. Martino's trailer?"

"I heard a truck pull up this morning. I was wondering what they were doing."

"I stopped to ask them if they were here to remove it. But they said they were from the insurance company. One's the agent and the other is in training. So, it's going to be awhile longer before anything actually gets done with it."

"Ugh. So we're going to have to keep looking at that squashed thing?"

"Sure seems like it." She eyed my thread and needle. "Something happen to the costume?"

"I'm just trying to alter it so it's, well, less demented-looking. I'm adding a hat and a scarf to it to make it a little friendlier. Do you think they work? And I want to shrink down this gaping eyehole to match with the other, and cover up this red stitching on the chest somehow. I'm also going to use the stuffing from a couple of old pillows to help pad."

"That should help. Hey listen, baby, Debra called earlier while you were at Sig's and asked if you would stop by sometime today. She said she had something to ask you."

At the mention of Debra Chastings' name, it felt as if an electrical shock had coursed through me, and my pulse started thumping. With a twinge of guilt, I realized I hadn't thought much about Melody since we got busy with the campaign. I couldn't figure out what Mrs. Chastings would want to talk about. It had been ten months since we last spoke, right after the *celebration*, and I seriously thought that would have been the last time we would see each other.

"Did she say what it was about?"

"No. She didn't say."

"Oh."

"Maybe she has something that she needs to ask you. Or maybe she just wants to know how you are doing and reconnect. After all, she's known you since you both were six."

I sighed. "I know."

I stood there, waiting for my mom to say what I hoped she would say. When she didn't, I asked in a small voice, "Uh, do you think you could come with me?"

"I kind of have a hair appointment in about forty-five minutes," she said, wincing. "But I can cancel it if you really need me to."

By her expression, I could tell that she was as uncomfortable about the whole matter as I was. "No. It's okay," I muttered. "I can do this."

"Are you sure, Mol? I mean, it's only a hair appoint—"

"Yeah. I'm sure. I'll be okay."

I lost count of how many times I had walked up those three concrete steps that led to their yellow front door. During the long months of summer, when we were little, Melody and I used to play with our Barbies on those steps. I remembered the time when Jackie, her older sister, was leaving for a date, and we decided to surprise her by spraying her with the hose, and how angry she was as she stormed off, soaking wet, back into the house to change. Or when the warm days of spring arrived, we'd shed the layers that covered us up all winter like cocoons and sit there in our shorts and tank tops, painting our teenage toes in the sun and talking about boys.

It felt more like ten years rather than ten months since I had last stood there facing the wicker wreath that hung on that yellow front door. Debra Chastings loved seasonal decorating, and the wreath with the gingham bow tied around the spray of silk cornflowers and lily of the valley had been last summer's theme. The Chastings' household always stocked artsy-craftsy stuff like specialty scissors, bottles of craft glue, and drawers filled with sequins, buttons, raffia, and felt. They could make just about anything they found on Pinterest. And this wreath was the very last one mother and daughter had made together.

When I was in the fourth grade, I so wanted my mom to be like Melody's mom. I would try to get her to go to the hobby stores, but excuses usually kept us from going. Or if I asked her for help with a school project, she was always too busy. Eventually, I must've nagged and whined enough, because she broke down once and bought some frozen cookie dough at the grocery store. For that December afternoon, our house radiated hominess with cinnamon and brown sugar. She hadn't done it again, since.

The faded bow drooped in a frown. Before, the wreath would've been changed out at least three times with other wreaths that coordinated with the seasons by now. But there it stayed, nailed to the door and forgotten. When I glanced about the front yard, everything was neglected. The hedges were a little less even. The grass was taller. There was a noticeable patch on the side of the house by the door where the paint had flaked off. The impeccable home I knew from all the years I had visited, ate, and slept over, was not so perfect anymore. Jackie had fled to Vancouver to live with her boyfriend, almost immediately after the *celebration*. And my mom told me about the story she had caught on the nightly news not too long ago about Mr. Chastings being arrested for buying painkillers from an undercover cop. This was a man who, according to Mel, barely took aspirin. The story said he admitted his addiction started with taking an old opioid prescription Mrs. Chastings had had after a surgery. Facing criminal charges, he was on the verge of losing his five citywide dealerships.

I almost didn't want to ring the doorbell. When Debra opened the door, she too, looked about ten years older. A chipper, God-fearing woman, with a rounded body that never was frumpy or unkempt in her mom jeans and pastel-colored tops, she was the most positive person I knew. Her optimism used to drive my best friend crazy. "My mom's delusional," Mel would say to me. "There's no way in hell that someone could not say anything bad about someone else at least once in a while. It's not natural. She's seriously overdue for a reality check." In contrast, I thought her mother's cheery demeanor was kind of nice, since my own mother seldom had good things to say about much of anything. An upbeat spirit had often shaped Mrs. Chastings' bright smile. Melody had that same smile, but learned to used it instead on teachers whenever she forgot her homework or on boys whenever she wanted something from them.

Although Debra lit up momentarily when she saw me, that smile never emerged from beneath the downward-turned corners of her mouth. Neither of us knew what to say, so we reached out to hug. She held me tighter than I expected, and then as if she caught herself, suddenly released me and took a step back.

"Molly, thank you for coming," she said, blinking away the water welling up in her eyes and attempting to smile. "How are you doing? It's so good to see you again."

"It's good to see you, too," I said, although the words tasted strange on my tongue.

"Your mom tells me that you are attending Sea View now through Running Start?"

"Yes, I'm majoring in biology."

"Oh, that's super. You were always good in science."

"Yeah …"

"Is it my imagination or has your hair gotten longer?"

"It's grown out." Self-consciously, I touched my braid. "I've got to get it cut."

"Well, it's very pretty. Would you like something to drink? I just made some iced tea."

"No, I'm okay. But thanks."

The small talk had run its course, and the space between us was growing noticeably awkward.

Debra grew somber again. "Molly, I asked you to come over because I wanted to show you something. It's something of Mel's, and I didn't know if you knew anything about it." She turned and started out of the foyer.

I stopped breathing, the air suspended in my lungs. I didn't want to go into the rest of the house. In the past months, I had purposefully blocked it all from my mind. But when Mrs. Chastings glanced over her shoulder at me, waiting, I reluctantly followed.

We crossed their living room that I knew as well as my own, although Melody's was the home I had always dreamed of—cozy, yet sophisticated. A large fireplace flanked the long wall of the room and opposite it, French doors led out to the backyard patio, lined with potted plants with bright flowers. The furniture coordinated in light wood and floral pattern upholstery, complete with matching throw pillows. And typically, delicious aromas of homemade cookies or pot roast baking in the oven filled the Chastings' home, while Debra hot glued or stamped away at her craft table.

The Chastings were the only family I knew that owned an actual china cabinet, stocked with family-heirloom porcelain china, in a formal dining room where a mahogany table and eight matching chairs stood on an imported rug they had bought while on vacation to Morocco. I had had the privilege of actually eating off of that dinnerware with the fine gold trim whenever I was invited for special occasions. It was so much more elegant that the jar glasses, plastic tumblers, and unbreakable melamine plates we had at home.

My favorite item of all in the house, though, was a Black Forest cuckoo clock that hung by the gun cabinet in the family room. It was massive, ornate, and hand-carved with impossible detail. Derrick had picked up the clock in Bavaria when he was stationed in Germany while in the army. I never tired of watching the little bird pop out of the door on the hour with its classic, "cuckoo!" while below the bright painted figures in dirndls and lederhosen whirled about to light, musical chimes playing "Edelweiss."

As we proceeded to her room, Melody grinned back at me from the various photos that were displayed on the piano and walls. I knew which grade she was in for each of them. I almost expected her to come walking out at any moment, pulling her silky blonde hair up into a ponytail, and then flopping down on the sofa, the way that she always did, to brief me on the plans she made for our day.

Instead, the house was silent. The only scent I smelled was laundry detergent. The craft table was clear and appeared untouched. Debra continued down the darkened hallway to Melody's room. A sharp pang flared up deep in the center of my chest. I realized then how much I had willed what had happened to her behind me. I wanted to—no, *needed to*—keep it away. Now it all came crashing together, like when the giant ice floes collide in the open ocean. I didn't want to go into Mel's room, but I knew Mrs. Chastings expected me to.

It was exactly the same since the last time I had seen it. Well, almost exactly. There weren't any clothes or shoes strewn about the floor anymore, and her bed was made up perfectly, with her stuffed animals, throw pillows, and dolls positioned just so, with Ralphie in the middle of it all, his tired head slumped to the side. Her desk was tidied up, papers put away, jewelry stored in their boxes. There were none of the celebrity magazines that she had loved, lying open to the pages showing trendy outfits and heartthrobs with circles drawn around them in her favorite purple marker. It was Mel's room, but then again, it was not Mel's room. It was more like a set for a movie about Mel. It was staged with all the right props, waiting for the central character to come walking in on cue to open the scene when the director called "action."

"I asked you to come over today because I needed to talk to you about something, Molly. Something very important," Debra posed this carefully to me, as if I were six-years-old again.

I simply nodded in response.

"Did Melody ever share this with you?" She reached into the top drawer of the desk and removed a small notebook with neon smiley faces on its cover. I recognized it instantly.

"That's Mel's journal," I said. "But she never let me read it. She only read parts of it to me."

Debra opened up to a page toward the middle of the journal that was bookmarked with a sticky note. "She wrote here that she was seeing a boy named Cole. Then a few entries later, a month before last Christmas , she wrote that he was her boyfriend. Did you know anything about that?"

It was all news to me. After we finished sophomore year, the frequency with which we hung out grew less and less. It got so that I had to schedule any meet up with her at least a couple of weeks in advance, even if it was just for lunch or coffee. I remembered her liking Cole. He was in our English comp class, and they flirted with each other in those stupid cat-and-mouse ways with a lot of in-nuendoes, raised eyebrows, and playful slaps, but I had no idea that they were going out. Worse yet, I had no idea why she didn't tell me anything about it. Or was I just that dense and failed to recognize it? I shook my head, "No. Not at all. Cole was a boy in English, but I didn't realize they were seeing each other."

"Are you sure, Molly?"

"Yes, I'm sure. She never told me about it."

"She was going back and forth with this Cole on her phone and online. Some of the messages she received even had indecent and lewd pictures of him in them—that sexting or whatever that is you kids call it—and there were a few of her, as well … ." Debra's voice trailed off momentarily. Then she continued, "The police are investigating and piecing things together. It appears she was lead-ing an entirely different life virtually. And she even used a fictitious name—Nooky Bunny or Nooky Buns—something like that."

My memory flashed back to the times last year when Mel's phone would vibrate, and she would take it out immediately to look at it. Next she would start giggling and turning red. When I asked her what was so funny, she would quickly put her phone away with a dis-missive, "Oh, nothing. Just something stupid. It's nothing." But she would never tell me what it was, no matter how much I questioned.

"They checked Mel's phone records, and according to her texts, found out that they had had some kind of fight, and she broke up with him. But Cole wouldn't let her off so easily, so … so first he stalked her, and when she wouldn't respond, he started harassing her," she said. Tears started to roll down her cheeks, and she lowered her gaze. "The photos she had sent him of herself that were supposed to be private, he posted online for everyone to see, with disgusting and obscene comments attached to them. The records show that he called or texted her continuously every day with these things—once, over two hundred times within one day. He also told her terrible, degrading things that he wanted to do to her and threatened to expose her ... Are you sure that Melody didn't tell you about any of this? You've been her best friend since grade school. I know she told you everything. It's important that we know all the details. The police are building a case against him. It seems he has stalked other girls before, and one of them may be missing."

Her words shook me, turning me inside out. Mel had adeptly kept all of this from me. I couldn't believe it. Racking my memory, I could not recall a single action or conversation between us that would have tipped me off to her predicament. Maybe if I were like everyone else and used social media, I might have caught something along the way. "No, Mrs. Chastings. I'm sorry, but she didn't tell me about any of this. And I never saw anything online or otherwise I would've said something. I'm telling you the truth. I'm as much in the dark about all of this as you."

"And you didn't hear anything around school? None of your other friends mentioned this to you? Talked about it?"

I was too embarrassed to tell her that I hardly ever talked to anyone there, because they all treated me like I was some kind of loner loser. Melody was really the only person I hung out with there. And she only did it because we had known each other for such a long time. "No. After I started going to Sea View, that was the last I knew about Cole or any of the rest of them. And with Melody volunteering at the playhouse and applying to universities, we hardly had time to hang with each other like we used to."

"There were over two thousand and seventy-eight messages filled with the depraved filth he spread about her! And you didn't see one of them or hear about any of it?"

"No. I thought she would've talked to me. Or to you or to someone ... Anyone." A hard knot constricted my throat, and hot tears stung as they threatened to fall.

"Oh how could she have kept this all to herself? We could've helped her ..." Debra Chastings broke down weeping. "He called

Melody a slut and a whore. He accused her of all sorts of disgusting acts. But she was my little girl … she was my baby … he called my baby a *fucking whore*," she whispered. "I hate him. I hate him with all of my heart, and I hope he burns in hell."

Reeling and unable to bear witness to her anguish, I took in Mel's rock-diva posters on the wall, showing the performers we sung along to and the bottles of brightly colored nail polish lined along the top of the chest of drawers and her trophies she had won for baton twirling back in seventh grade. They were childish and strangely irrelevant now, things from a forgotten era long ago.

Circling my arms around Debra, I held on to the woman whose daughter had accused of not facing reality. The two of us broke down and cried openly, swiping at our runny noses, and standing in the center of Mel's room like two forlorn children. We so desperately wanted the daughter and friend to return to us with that bright smile and that cocky bounce to her step, asking us "What are all the sniffles about?" like she used to say, but knowing that she never would, ever again.

As Mrs. Chastings clung to me, through my tears I contemplated a photo on the dresser. It was taken on a Chastings last family trip to Disneyland. I had seen that shot of the four of them more times than I can remember, but this was the first time I realized that Mel wasn't mugging directly at the camera. At the very last moment before the shutter went off, something must have distracted her. It would've been perfect, if she hadn't looked away.

The cuckoo clock in the family room announced the time. I knew the dirndl-and-lederhosen figures were performing their cheery hourly routine under the little bird who popped out from behind the door, four, no five times. Wrung out and spent, we collected ourselves and hugged once more. Debra patted my arm and whispered, "Thank you for coming over, Molly. And please, if you recall anything, anything at all, I'd appreciate it if you'd call me."

"I will."

She shut the door to Melody's room behind us, and we tottered out to the foyer. There we hugged one more time. She must've caught the feeling that we'd most likely never see each other again. She tried to summon up one last act of optimism, if not for me, then for herself. "And please, come back and visit us anytime, okay? We'd love to see you."

"Okay," I nodded, but I knew I wouldn't be back.

I couldn't move. Everything she had said was all horribly true. After my visit with Deb Chastings, I logged back into my Facebook account that had lain dormant for the past three years. In the search bar, first I entered the name, "Nooky Bunny." I got no hits. Next, I tried "Nooky Buns," but still nothing. I was relieved, but I knew I had to press on. When I typed in "Nookie Bunny," there was Melody, staring back at me. She had 376 friends, and the photos were a dizzy myriad of partying, posing, grinding, Frenching, and flirting. Cole was wrapped around her in most of the shots. When I compared their unadulterated behavior to my own guarded actions, my singular sloppy kiss with Sig seemed childishly naive.

The totality of what I had learned over the last three hours sunk deep into my bones, replacing marrow with cold, gray cement. I picked up another photo of us and studied it as I lay on my back upon my bed, where water spilled out from the corners of my eyes and puddled in my ears.

In the selfie, the two wide-eyed idiots with smudgy-chocolate grins stared back. On that day Mel and I had ditched sixth and seventh period after lunch and went to the mall instead. We were only thirteen and went to the movies to watch *Before the Midnight Comes*, the first R-rated movie that we paid for on our own. Trying to look like seventeen-year-olds, we put on lipstick, stuffed our bras with toilet paper, and talked out loud about attending college classes. We thought we were all that, even though the bored sales associate behind the ticket counter couldn't care less if we were under seventeen anyway. The movie was a drama that was billed as a sexy romance. Mostly it was about a married couple discussing their differences and arguing.

So we decided to ditch the rest of the movie to go to The Parlour for some super-sized buckets of ice cream with all the toppings. We dared each other to finish all of the contents in our quart-sized buckets the fastest. Mel, of course, finished first. She always had a way of going big on everything.

I studied her clear-blue eyes in the photo and that pearly-toothed grin, confident with family, home, and friendship. I wondered now what secrets had she kept hidden all along behind that sunny personality. What was her reason to cover up the desperate situation she was in, one in which she felt the only escape was to take her own life?

Why Mel? Why didn't you tell me? I thought we could depend on each other. Damn. Damn damn damn damn … .

Before I knew it, torn bits of paper were scattered across my neck, chest, and pillow, like fallen snow. I was shocked by what I had done—I'd never get that photo back.

I'd never get my best friend back.

And then I cried, as I had never cried before, racking, panicky sobs that made my chest heave, burn, and gulp for air. I wanted to throw up. I wanted to smash something. I wanted to scream, but with my mouth opened wide, all that came out were choking coughs and hissing and spit and swallowed tears. I had never cried like that before … except for the time my dad moved out.

Chapter 7.5

Robert Ohashi, Paramedic and Molly's Father

MOLLY'S A GREAT KID. SHE'S THE BEST DAUGHTER a father could ever have. She always has been. And smart too—most of the time, she runs rings around Shannon and me. We had such a hard time keeping up with her when she was little, because she was always getting into everything.

Ever since she was tiny, she's always asked a ton of questions—she has so much curiosity bottled up inside of her. And boy, was she happy when she learned to read, and we showed her how to find the answers to her questions on the internet. It's just too bad that she can't get all of her questions answered, no matter where she looks.

But she's got a good head on her shoulders and does well in all of her school subjects. She has always taken her studies seriously. That's half the battle right there. I remember reading a research paper she wrote on polar bears last year. It was actually pretty good, and she got an A- on it.

I know she's going to make something of herself one day. Once she sets a goal in mind, there is no stopping her. She must not get it from me, because I wish I had that kind of determination.

Here at the firehouse, my partner, Joe, is always bragging about his kid being on the honor roll and all, but that's because he's never met Mol. In fact, most of the guys are sure that I'm playing her up, but it's only because they haven't had a chance to meet her yet.

Only a few have seen the picture I keep of her and Shans in my bunk. Joe likes to rib me, calling them my fantasy family, because he's never met them, although he knows darn right well that they live in Washington. Some of the other guys say with me being Asian that it's no big stretch for me to produce a genius kid, but how the hell did I score a knockout redhead for a wife?

Don't get me wrong; we're always poking fun at each other. It's one of the things we do to fight stress after calls or the monotony of the constant maintenance of the trucks, gear, and firehouse. I guess there are times when some of the ribbing gets to me, especially the racial stuff, but I just blow it off. I don't complain, because then HR would start snooping around for discrimination violations, and that's a fast way to get you blacklisted in the department. Anyway, it's all good—like I said, they don't mean anything by it.

At least the guys are pretty decent about minding their own business and have never pried into my time at my old unit. Joe and Captain Stanley are the only ones who know about the incident regarding the child I lost, and they have assured me that information is safe with them.

In fact, they told me they are there for me anytime I need to talk. My problem is, I can't talk about it. I don't know if I ever could. That little girl was only a few years younger than my Molly. Coincidentally, she and Mol even shared the same birthday. Weird, huh?

Molly always looked up to me, like I was her hero or something. Some hero, all right. I pray that she never learns that I killed someone. A child. I feel so guilty and ashamed; I couldn't face my daughter if I ever found out she knew about this. She wouldn't be able to handle it anyway, with all the anxieties she has about everything. I've never known a kid that worried so much. She's like a little old lady.

She did a lot of strange things whenever she got anxious. I remember when she was two and a half, and her Noni was over and telling us that she had caught a cold. Well, Molly heard her and insisted on searching both of her grandmother's hands. She kept saying, "Noni, where's the cold? Where did you put the cold? I want to see it."

Next thing we knew, she had emptied every last bandage from the box and stuck them all over herself. I found her in the bathroom, covered from head to toe in them. She knew that bandages protected cuts. So she said they would keep her from catching Noni's cold, thinking that colds were some kind of invisible bugs that jumped from one person to the next, like cooties.

Another time in our old house, when she was about four, our elderly neighbor came over to borrow some sugar and told Shans that she'd take "a cup of Molly, too, because she was so sweet." We ended up hunting high and low for nearly two hours for the munchkin and were about to call the police to search the neighborhood, when we found her.

She had crammed herself as far as she could under her bed and covered up with all of her stuffed animals and blankets. When we asked her why she was hiding under there, she told us she was afraid that the neighbor was going to take her home with her and bake her in the oven like in *Hansel and Gretel*. She's always been a quirky kid, now that I think of it.

But her Gray Days were the worst. They were hell for her, making her morose and depressed for days. Shans would complain that she drove her up the wall with all the crazy questions she asked, so I use to talk with Molly for hours whenever I was home, trying anything to get her to come around. Personally, I know all too well what those Gray Days are like, and let me tell you—they're hard enough for a grown man to get through, let alone a kid.

I only hope to God that she has outgrown them by now.

CHAPTER EIGHT

Polar bears may be one of the first large mammal species lost in a world that is only growing warmer. These symbols of the Arctic are facing threats not experienced by them ever before as a warming climate and loss of their sea ice habitat make it difficult for the bears to hunt prey, find dens for their cubs, and haul out on ice floes in open water. While denning up or hunting, polar bears can survive off of their fat and go for long periods of time without eating. However, many perish if they are pushed beyond their limits. Even minor fluctuations in the climate could possibly wipe out the species since polar bears have evolved specialized adaptations to live in the extreme frigid conditions of the Arctic (Cooper 201).

ragraph
eak here?

"Hey Mol? Are you in there? Are you coming up for air anytime soon?" Sig called from the other side of my pocket door. *What was he doing here?* I decided to stay quiet, hoping that he would grow bored or discouraged and go away.

His knuckle rapped lightly on the door. "Come on, Mol. You said we were going to do this. Well then, let's do it."

Through the thin wall that separated the rear of the trailer from the rest of our place, I heard my mom say, "I've already tried that. You have no idea." I could just imagine her standing beside him with her arms crossed and chewing her thumbnail like she always did when she's had it. She raised her own voice toward my door.

"Molly, open the door. Sig is here to see you."

I wanted to get up, but couldn't; the way my body felt, large boulders couldn't pin me down any better. The night before I had lain there stubbornly awake in my bed, wondering, in the event that I was dead by morning, what would it be like? My mother would be home since it was Saturday. She would think that I overslept. The hours would pass: eight o'clock, nine o'clock, nine thirty. She would slide open the pocket door and there I would be, still and stiff.

I also wondered if it were possible to will yourself to die. It seemed that people were able to do that in the old days. They would pine away for someone or something, and there wasn't anything anyone could do for them. Then one day, they just didn't wake up. I recalled reading somewhere that it was called the nocebo effect.

"Molly Genre Ohashi, didn't you hear what I said? Stop being rude to your friend. You shouldn't keep him waiting like this." Then, as an aside, I could hear my mother apologize, "I'm sorry. She doesn't listen to anyone when she's like this. She's having one of her 'gray days.' She's had them, since—well—*forever*."

"Yeah, she's told me about them, but she can't let them incapacitate her like this. What's it been, a week and a half straight already?" I heard Sig ask.

"Uh-huh. I know that, and you know that. She even knows that. But, here we are. When she gets like this, there's not much anyone can do to make her come around. Her dad was the only one who could talk some sense into her and get her going again. But he's not here. I wish I could be more help, but I'm in serious need of a smoke. So, sorry and good luck."

The soft thud that vibrated through the wall told me my mother had shut the front door and gone outside to the patio for her Pall Mall break. It was her third one for the day. I really wished she wouldn't smoke like that. I could only imagine how coated with tar her lungs must be by now.

"Are you decent, Molly?" Sig called again with another rap to the door.

"What? What do you mean?" I replied.

"Decent—you're not going around commando in there, are you?"

"Commando? What are you talking about?"

"Yeah, you know—au naturel. In your birthday suit."

"Are you crazy? No! Of course not. Why are you asking such weird—"

Just then my pocket door clicked and next, it slid open. In walked Sig, folding up some kind of tool and slipping it into his coat pocket.

I should have been more alarmed that he had just picked the lock to my room and entered without my permission, but I couldn't muster enough energy. The most I could manage was to wonder about all the things he carried in his pockets at any given time.

"Huh. Sweet unicorn and princess," Sig said matter-of-factly as he nodded at my headboard, ignoring the fact that he had just broken into my room, where I was lying in bed with my comforter pulled up to my chin.

"Please tell me that you didn't break the lock. My mom will pitch a fit," I said.

"What—that? Nah. It's a simple latch. If you shake it hard enough, it will open. So, are we going to do this green festival thing or not? It's about to start in another hour. And we still have to drive over there and park."

"Oh. I'm sorry, but I'm seriously not up for it, today. There will be other festivals we can go to."

"You've already committed to this one. That nice coordinator lady gave you the primo starfish spot, remember? Weren't you ever taught about keeping your word? It'll be bad karma if you don't. And the next thing you know, you'll feel guilty when you read that another bear, or two, or five hundred out there, treaded water for hours with nothing to hang on to, and saying, 'Goddamnit. I knew I should have gotten up and gone to that green festival.'"

I peered up at him.

"Well, at least you'll be saying that. Not the bears," he corrected.

"I found out why Melody did what she did."

My words crowded my small room. I thought they might overtake and asphyxiate us both.

With an almost imperceptible sigh, he nodded. "Yeah. I figured as much. You were bound to sometime." I waited for him to demand an explanation. Instead he just stood there with his hands in his pockets, attentive yet patient, like a mama wolf waiting for her cubs to settle down.

"Well, aren't you going to ask why she did it?"

"No," he said simply. "Everybody has their own story and their own reasons for doing things."

Astonished, I blinked. "That's it? That's all you're going to say?"

"Yup. Anything more is trivial and irrelevant."

His reply was absolute, leaving me perplexed by his attitude. I thought he understood the significance of my friendship with Melody.

"She wasn't a bad person or evil for doing what she did, you know," I said defensively.

"Whoa. I didn't know her, so I can't make any judgments."

"She just couldn't deal with her life anymore. Maybe it's not the way I would do things, but people cope in different ways."

"Yup. Yup they do." Sig shrugged with his hands still in his jacket pockets.

"Listen, is there something you want to say? Because you're acting like you want to, but won't."

"If there was something I wanted to say, you should know by now that I have no problems saying it."

He was right. He usually didn't hold much back.

"So you really don't want to hear why Melody committed suicide?"

"No, I don't. Really. Unless you need to tell me, but that is up to you. If you are going to talk about her, I would rather hear about who she was rather than what she did."

"Oh."

Moments passed.

"Doesn't it make you wonder?" I asked, my stare fixing involuntarily on the photo collage.

"About what?"

"About the tragic, desperate secrets that people around us—people close to us—are keeping and we have no idea, no clue as to what they are feeling or suffering? Whatever Mel was feeling came down to the point where she couldn't stand it anymore. And what blows me away is, I was there for her. I was her best friend. And she still couldn't confide in me. Why is that?"

Sig stared at the floor. "I don't know. I don't know what to tell you. That's just the way it is," he said. "We all get wrapped up in our own world doing our own thing. It gets so big and complicated sometimes, it blinds us. And sometimes we just can't come out and say what we need to say, to anyone. I mean, where do you even start?"

"I will tell you more about who she was. Just … not now. I can't do it right now."

"Cool. I'll be there whenever you are ready."

"Okay."

The daylight had shifted in my room. I knew that when that little quadrangle-shaped patch of sun appeared on my desk, it was getting past nine o'clock.

"So, are you going to get up and get that bear costume on? Like I said before, you've got commitments. And those bears can't keep treading water."

"I can't Sig. I'm not feeling up to it."

"Why? Because it's a Gray Day? You know, you're going to have them regardless, whether you want them or not, and probably for the rest of your life. But it's what you choose to do during that time you're having one that will change things for you. You can spend it in your bed, staring at the ceiling and feeling like shit, or you can do something for yourself or somebody else, and even though you still feel like shit, you are making a difference to someone, so at least it's not a total waste."

Although I knew what he was saying was true, I couldn't answer.

"Trust me. I know what I'm talking about. All right? So come on already."

I really did not want to get up. My blanket felt heavy, like one of those lead aprons the assistants put on you at the dentist office when they x-ray your teeth. But Sig stood there, arms crossed now, and waiting, as if he were mentally willing me to get up with some kind of Jedi mind trick.

It must have worked, because the next thing I knew, I peeled back my confining blanket and swung my legs over the side of the bed.

"Okay," I conceded.

The place was jam-packed with people wandering among booths that featured info, displays, and demos on everything green, from alternative-fueled cars and urban chicken coops, to backyard solar stills and and locally grown kale, and hand-pressed soap made from goat's milk. Kids squirmed at the ends of their parents' arms, slurping up dripping green-tea ice cream in gluten-free waffle cones. A local band, The Climate Changers, performed an acoustic cover of the song "In the Year 2525." I completed the setting with my polar bear costume, preparing to wave to people and pose for any photo ops parents wanted with their kids. We stood in a corner of the conference room behind a curtained room divider getting ready.

I fidgeted nervously, feeling hyper-charged and very self-conscious. It made me miss Mel more than ever. Whereas it took some convincing to get me into the suit at all and down here to the festival, she loved situations where she drew attention. She would've viewed parading around in a costume as an opportunity to be someone else—either a clown or a star performer basking in the glow of the spotlight. I, on the other hand, wished I wasn't leading the way and worried that I might humiliate myself by tripping over my own feet.

"You ready?" Sig asked as he handed me my head.

"I guess. And you promise to stay close?" I placed the stuffed head over my own and started grappling around to adjust it so I could see out of its crooked eyeholes.

"Trust me, it's hard to lose sight of you."

"And the Wite-Out doesn't look too weird?" I asked, patting the now-dried correction fluid I used to cover up the red sutures on my chest.

"Yeah, yeah. It's fine. No one will notice. They'll just think you drooled a little paint. No problem. Now will you get going? That event coordinator is going to start wondering where you are. She thought we were going to be here an hour ago."

"Okay, okay." And off I went, first dropping our flyers, then our collection can, and next elbowing the noggins of a few small kids who were passing by me. I felt distracted and unfocused. I didn't know how I was going to navigate through the crowds wearing this thing.

But in about fifteen minutes, it began to happen. Unexpectedly, people started staring and pointing me out to their families. Some waved, others smiled and laughed—but good naturedly. They parted the way before me, as if I were a presidential candidate, or stopped to snap a picture of me with their phones. It was … *wonderful*.

In the meantime, I could hear Sig beside me, giving his best spiel about our swim platforms. Whenever he presented the idea, it sounded smart and legitimate. Even when a few festival attendees challenged him with more probing questions, he was able to answer them thoroughly. Most importantly, I was encouraged by the remarks I overheard from festivalgoers regarding our project such as, "What a fabulous idea," or "That makes total sense," or "You guys are great to be doing this." I could hear coins being dropped into the can, people asking if they could write checks, and Sig thanking them.

I couldn't believe that Noni's costume was actually working. Instead of being frightened by its deranged expression, kids clung to my paws and hugged my legs. I lost count of how many times people wanted to take selfies with me. About an hour later, we ran into the event coordinator, who ecstatically told us that we were a hit and that in the exit surveys visitors were voting "The Dead Polar Bear" as one of their favorite attractions at the festival.

Later on, we found a low wall to sit on to eat our lunch in the crowded food court and placed our backs against each other for support. Although we were not on kissing terms, I was perfectly content with feeling Sig's lean back against mine. It was sturdy, strong, and cozy warm. I timed my breaths with his and contemplated the way his muscles tensed or relaxed, and how his rib cage resonated when he spoke in his baritone voice. It would have been heaven to stay there forever, away from sorrow and chaos. Feeling him burp, he never suspected how I felt sitting so close to him. Not Sig. His life consisted of these simple pleasures, and he ate them up as easily as he chowed down on the tofu dogs he got for us or sipped his Thai tea.

After lunch, we stopped to count the money we had collected.

"Between checks and cash, we've made four hundred and thirty-two simoleons, and sixteen cents so far. Where the heck the sixteen cents came from, I have no idea. Probably someone was off-loading their coin purse. Anyway, that's not bad bank, in my book, for only a couple hours of work," Sig said proudly. "Imagine how much more we could pull in if we had one of those Square readers for our phones, and people could use their plastic."

"Four hundred thirty-two dollars! You're kidding, right? Seriously?"

"No kidding. If things pick up in the next few hours, we might make close to a 'K' … and sixteen cents."

"That's incredible. We can really make some headway like this. And then there's tomorrow too. There's no way we would have ever made this much on campus—it would have taken years. Thanks for making me get up out of that bed and down here to do this."

He shrugged. "You got yourself up out of bed. If I recall, I didn't lay a finger on you."

By nine o'clock, the festival had wrapped up for the general public and by nine thirty, it was done for the night. Vendors shut down their booths, covered merchandise with cloth and plastic, and stowed things away in boxes under the tables for the next day. Security kept moving everyone off the floor and out the exits. Tired, we headed to where Mr. Chips was parked in a dark lot four blocks away through a sketchy neighborhood. After having arrived so late, it was the only parking we could find.

I was self-conscious about taking off the bear suit, because I knew there was over ten hours' worth of nervous perspiration trapped inside of it, and there was no way I was going to release all of that in Sig's small car. So I left it on, walking with the stuffed head tucked under my arm.

"I have to admit this actually was kind of fun. I'm glad I came. I really needed this, after the other day. When I get home, I have to remember to send Noni a thank you for making this costume. Oh, and air this thing out, too."

"You seemed like you were doing okay. At least when the rug rats weren't whacking you in the butt."

"Ugh. Don't remind me. Luckily, there were only a few that did that. Most of them were pretty cute, though. Like that little girl that kept hugging my leg and asking me for Christmas presents. But did you catch the other kid with the striped shirt that started freaking out when I said hello to him? I was afraid someone was going to call security on me."

"Could you blame him? After seeing that big white head with the whacked-out teeth, he's probably going to be traumatized for the rest of his life. Every time he sees a polar bear now, he'll—"

"*Gimme all your shit, motherfuckers!*" an angry voice barked at us from behind.

Startled, I lost my hold on the polar bear head. It fell and went rolling to the ground, where it settled with its blank eyes witnessing us getting held up, its mouth wide open in a silent scream. I froze as an electric shock coursed through my body and instantly turned my knees to jelly.

We were exhausted from the long day and had been so engrossed in our conversation that we hadn't paid any attention to anything around us. All that flashed through my head in red capital letters was, "*OH MY GOD. WE'RE ABOUT TO BE MURDERED.*"

"Chill dude. We'll give you whatever you want. Just be cool," Sig said as calmly as he could, although I could hear the tremor in his voice.

"Don't turn around! You got a gun? You better not have a gun. I'll shoot your ass. Where's your wallet, you stupid motherfucker?"

My pulse pounded hard in my ears, while my instincts ordered my body to flee, hide, faint, pee, howl, scream—all at once. But all I could do was shake uncontrollably instead.

I searched the street ahead of us. There was no one else out at this time of night in this neighborhood. The only cars I saw moving were several blocks away. There was no way anyone could know what was going down right now on this quiet, forgotten street.

"Here's my wallet. Take it," Sig said, slowly extracting his wallet from his back pocket and tossing it behind him.

"Hey, what does he have in that can?" Another voice behind us asked.

There are two of them? My heart hammered in double-time staccato.

That same voice continued, "And what about her wallet?"

"Take the can. It's got money in it. Leave her alone. She isn't carrying anything on her at all," Sig tried bravely. He chucked our donation can behind him. I heard it hit the ground with a metallic clang and start rolling.

There was a pause, and then a whoop and laughter.

"Goddamn! All right! This asswipe's been holding out on us. Where did you get all of this money?"

"Fuck that. Do you have any more that you're not telling us about?" growled the second voice.

Out of the corner of my eye, I could see Sig take a halting step forward. I realized with horror that it was because the muzzle of a gun was pointed at the back of his head.

"He doesn't! That's all we have! We're telling you the truth!" I pleaded.

"Shut up, bitch. I'm not talking to you."

The next moment, I was involuntarily launched forward as one of the attackers shoved me roughly from behind. I stumbled in my big furry paws and fell hard on my knees and hands on the gritty sidewalk. The pain was bright and shot through my legs and arms.

"What the hell you're supposed to be anyway? Some dumbass dog?"

Sig sprung toward me. "Hey! Leave her alone! She doesn't have any money. And I don't have any more mon—UNH!"

In the next instant, he collapsed on the ground next to me, struggling to rise to his knees. One of the attackers centered up on him, took aim, and kicked him, catching him under his chin. When he went down, the other attacker started landing kicks to his stomach. Sig coiled up defensively from the pain and onslaught. I screamed and screamed.

Just then, a pair of headlights lit up the scene, and our spotlighted attackers scooped up the can and took off. As they ran down the street, they continued to laugh and whoop as if they had just come from a party, apparently pleased with the night's haul. I heard our hard-earned money rattling in the can, the clamor echoing off building walls until it finally faded away. The car drove past, its driver either failing to notice what had just happened, or not wanting to.

Nauseated with fear, I crawled on my bruised knees over to where Sig remained curled up on his side, his arms crossed with his hands clutching his ribs.

"Oh my God, Sig! Are you okay?"

"As well as can be expected for just getting the shit kicked out of me," he said through gritted teeth. He slowly straightened out and then struggled to sit upright. "I thought you didn't take the Big Man's name in vain."

"What should we do? I'm calling the cops," I said, as I patted about on my suit, trying to locate my phone in my pants pocket.

"And tell them what? Did you get a good look at them? *Any* look at them at all?"

In all the excitement, I realized I hadn't. My only clear memory was of their legs lit up in the headlights, running away.

"Besides, I bet the cops don't even respond in this area. They'd probably get rolled just like us."

Our narrow escape triggered an icy shiver that shook me. "I thought they were going to murder us for sure. They would've if that car hadn't driven by."

"I don't know about *murder*, but they sure know how to put the hurt on someone," Sig said, holding his ribs and wincing.

"Well at least they left this." I reached for Sig's open wallet that was lying on the ground and handed it to him.

He took it, checked its contents, and then stared miserably at it. "Huh. I guess my student ID and Subway sandwich punch card weren't worth stealing."

"So they got your cash and credit cards?

"Cash? Credit cards? What are those?"

A sinking realization made my stomach lurch again. All of our donation money was gone. "And those creeps took the can!"

"Well at least they didn't hurt you in any way."

"But they hurt you and still got all of our donation money too!"

"One thousand thirty–three dollars and seventy-two cents," Sig sighed, defeated. "At least that's what it was the last I counted."

"Now we're going to have to start all over again," I sighed sadly in return. "How are we ever going to do it?"

"Hey, after feeling that gun tap the back of my head, the way I see it, at least we still got that chance."

The sun rippled and flickered overhead, illuminating the immense blue world about me. The ocean's surface acted like a watery lens to the sky above. Paddling and paddling, my wide paws stroked rhythmically through the cold water. I aimed my black nose toward the surface and stroked even harder. Somehow, it didn't feel like I was moving at all.

In fact, the only movement I sensed was the feeling of slipping backward. I was sinking. The shimmering expanse above me grew faint as I drifted downward through the alternating layers of cold and warm currents. Although strange, I wasn't desperate for air; breathing wasn't necessary. But still, it was frustrating that no matter how hard I kicked my legs and clawed at the water, I continued to descend into the gloomy depths of the ocean beneath me.

With no ice floe to cling to above, there was only darkness below.

"Are you sure you're feeling all right today, Poodle? Last night was one helluva night for you and Sig. Were you able to sleep any?" my mom asked when I joined her for breakfast the next morning. Concern strained her voice.

"Yeah, I did except for a weird dream I had where I was a polar bear again. This time I was swimming underwater in the ocean and couldn't reach the surface no matter what I tried. Aside from that, I slept well enough," I said.

"How about your knees—are they still hurting a lot today?" She nodded toward my legs that were bruised and swollen from falling when I was shoved. My left knee bore a fresh scab where it had bled the night before. "I still think we should call the cops."

"My knees are all right. They hurt, but I'm okay. And I've already told you that even though those creeps stole all of our money, we can't call the police because there's no way we can identify them. Neither of us got a look at either of them."

"It's not the money! They almost killed Sig. And they could've killed you. And now they are still running loose out there doing God knows what to some other poor person." My mom's hands trembled. She usually needed a hit of nicotine whenever she was under stress. "I don't know what I would've done if they had done anything to you, Molly."

"It's okay, Mom. We're okay. All right?" I reached out and held her hand to calm her. She patted and stroked mine in return, as gratitude reshaped her troubled smile. Then she got up for another cup of coffee. "Besides, for some reason, despite what happened, I actually feel pretty good today. Seriously."

My mom sat back down, cupping her mug between both hands and sipping the hot brew while eyeing me carefully. "Well, you let me know if you need to talk about any of it, okay?"

"I will, Mom. Don't worry."

She let out a small laugh. "Funny how it's *you* telling *me* not to worry. Usually, it's the other way around."

She was right. At any other time, I would've been a basket case by now. I mean, for all intent and purposes, those guys had held a gun to us. They could've subjected us to any amount of torture or killed us. But I wasn't freaking out about it. In fact, I wasn't freaking out about anything at all for once. I had been through one of the scariest moments in my life—and survived.

Because of this, I was jacked. I was invincible and strong, like some kind of superhero who just discovered her powers. It had been more than a year since I had felt much of anything beyond depressed, let alone something so invigorating. A fresh energy coursed through every fiber of my being, and I was eager to tap into it. It was as if my drab old world had vaporized, leaving behind exotic and exciting. Even my Gray Days were distant now, like an old TV show where I had forgotten most of the plot and almost all of the characters.

Better yet was the fact that although my anxiety about something good being followed by something really bad had been proven once again, it didn't matter, because now, something really, *really*, good would happen since this last bad episode canceled everything out.

Capitalizing on this spirit, I thought Sig and I should get back out and raise more money to make up for the stolen funds. I would certainly do 110 percent better in the bear suit than I did before. If he was up for it, we could possibly squeeze in the last half of the festival.

My thumbs flying on the touchscreen of my phone, I texted him:

> Hey—what are you up to?

> Nothing much.

> How are you feeling?

> Eh. All right. My ribs hurt.

Yeah, my knees are killing me.

I bet.

Any chance you want to return to the festival today and make up some of the $ they stole?

Sorry. Not feeling it today

K. That's understandable. Lol. Wanna hang out instead?

Gonna pass. I'm tired. Maybe tomorrow.

Okey dokey. Maybe I'll email those orgs I found and let them know about our platform. Also, I just might do that crowdsourcing video with the suit on. You talked me into it! J

Yeah, you do that. Let me know how it goes. TTYL

From his replies, Sig really did sound out of it. He, most likely, just wanted to chill and recuperate on his couch while streaming extreme sports. So I got to work on my end instead. First, I forced myself to draft and send a blanket email to four conservation organizations I had found to tell them about our project. It was worth a shot if even only one contacted us. Next, I checked over the bear suit carefully, determined that the holes in the knees needed patching, gave it a good washing, and hung it out to dry. I wanted to make sure it was ready for the very next time we went out to raise money. Feeling more encouraged as I checked off boxes on my list of things to do, I started writing the script for our crowdsourcing video.

I moved from task to task, applying to two part-time jobs online, and then sketching ideas for redecorating my room and the rest of the trailer. I was thrilled to catch my dad on his day off, and we talked on the phone for over an hour. As we chatted, I sculpted a vaquita porpoise out of clay.

For the last part of the day, I decided to cook a chicken dinner complete with homemade mashed potatoes and corn on the cob, and finishing it off with ice cream sundaes for dessert for Mom and me. She savored it. Never had I experienced so much drive before and for once, I actually loved my life. It made me envy anyone who was fortunate enough to feel this way all the time.

The next day, Sig wasn't answering his phone. I figured he was probably sleeping in and didn't want to be disturbed, so I packed up the bear suit, found a new can, and decided to head back to the festival on my own. It was the last day of the event, and I was bound and determined to finish it.

Although I was riding on a cloud, I was still hesitant to be there by myself after dark. So this time, I paid the exorbitant amount to park as close to the conference center as possible, and I knew I could leave within the security of the crowds if I wrapped it up before the sun went down. This resulted in me only being able to put in about three and a half hours total before the festival closed for good. It would have to be enough for now. Nonetheless, I succeeded in doing it all entirely on my own.

By that evening, as I drove home after my solo campaign stint, I knew we were on our way to financially recouping our loss. I was floating with happiness.

Hello? Where are you?

> Aren't you ever going to answer?
> I thought we were going to hang out sometime.
> Fine if you want to be that way.
> <crickets chirping>
> Jk.

> But I can't wait to tell you how the rest of the festival went yesterday. I made $185 all on my own!

> This is Janice, Sig's mom.
> Sig's in the ED at St. Luke's.

I reread Janice's two short lines of text four times and still found the message inconceivable. It had been close to two days since I'd heard anything from Sig. When I texted or called him, he hadn't responded. I figured he was discouraged after being mugged, or perhaps he was just being lazy and noncommittal to our cause. How could it be that things were going so remarkably well after the holdup, and next I was hurrying down the long corridor of a hospital?

The soles of my Converse squeaked against the polished floors as I searched for the emergency department. It was difficult to navigate this building with its mazes of floors, subfloors, and walkways. I passed by nursing stations bustling with staff in scrubs and waiting areas with anxious, tired people staring blankly at aquariums of tropical fish. And it unsettled me even more to read the sign posted in the elevator directed at visitors that read, "Are you experiencing coughing? Sore throat? Diarrhea? If you are not feeling well, you are putting our patients at risk. Please reschedule your visit for another day."

Hospitals grossed me out in general with their pathogens lurking about on surfaces. According to an article I read about hospital-acquired infections, MRSA, C. diff, and staph could be anywhere—on elevator buttons, drinking fountains, and door handles. I tried not to touch anything and gelled at almost every hand-sanitizing station

I encountered, until after a while, my hands were thickly coated with the dried gel.

I found Janice in a corner waiting area made from two walls of glass three stories above the city street below. She was sitting next to yet another aquarium and talking on her cell phone to someone. I overheard her saying, "You don't have to tell me it's been over five years. I *know* it's been over five years … No, I don't understand it either … . What? He's being tested again right now. They said he should be done in about twenty minutes, and then transferred to ICU … . Listen, just promise me you'll be here by tonight, okay?"

When I approached, I could see her eyes were red and puffy from crying. Sig had said that he was feeling okay after the holdup. I wondered if there was some kind of complication in his healing. Maybe one of his ribs had been broken, and he just didn't know it. I've also read where you could develop blood clots from heavy bruising.

Janice waved me over to sit down beside her as she hung up her phone.

"Hi Molly, I didn't realize you were coming down here. I just thought I'd let you know why Sig wasn't returning your texts. I didn't want him to leave you hanging."

"Yes, thanks. Is he okay? I was wondering why he wasn't answering his phone."

"No. No, he isn't okay … In fact, I need to talk to you."

Chapter 8.5

Pat Keegan, Department Store Cashier

My wife warned me that working with the general public wouldn't be easy. As a bank teller, she should know. I thought I had seen it all, after thirty-one years as a service technician working on photocopiers and traveling around to major businesses in the area. I realize now that those businesses were *controlled* environments of suits and conference-room behavior, nothing like the free-for-all that happens out on the economy. Now that I'm semiretired, I just wanted something part-time to keep busy for another two years while I wait for Carol to retire from the bank. So I picked up a job as a cashier.

One of the things about working with the general public that I wasn't aware of before, but my wife quickly filled me in on, was that I should expect to see all kinds. Sure, there are the average Joes that come in, especially with kids in tow: they drop a credit card, grab their stuff, and go. Then there are the punks who try to rip you off. There are also the customers who'll talk your ear off, oblivious to the long line forming behind them, or others that won't say a word. And last there are the ones that are "just a little out there," if you know what I mean, whether they are doing drugs or just unstable.

Take that kid who came in and bought all of those cleaning supplies. She must've had about three economy-sized bottles of bleach, five scrub brushes, sponges, two mop heads, 409, window cleaner—you name it. With unusual purchases, I usually joke around with the customers just to break up the monotony of cashiering. So I said to her, "Uh-oh. Looks like you have a lot of spring cleaning to do."

She just stared at me. If I wasn't mistaken, she was going to cry.

Then she dug around in her purse and pulled out a baggie with some folded cash in it. This kid barely handled the bills, picking them up by their corners only with her fingertips, like she expected them to be slimy or something. When she came up a dollar fifty short, she then rummaged around in her purse and pulled out another baggie with change. She laid out one dollar and fifty cents in the cleanest coins I had ever seen. They looked shiny-brand new, although they were anywhere from ten to twenty years old. Next, she sanitized her hands with hand gel.

"So, is this what you do with all of those cleaners—launder money?" Hoping to cheer her up, I joked some more and gave her a wink to let her know I was kidding.

She didn't say anything, but gathered up her bag of cleaners and walked out of the store like a dismal little zombie. She didn't even look at me when I asked her if she wanted her receipt. I sure hope she wasn't taking those cleaners home to huff or shoot up with them, or make something like a homemade bomb. You just never know anymore with what kids do these days.

My wife was right. Working with the general public, you see all kinds.

CHAPTER NINE

A world without polar bears would be sad indeed and with our warming planet, they may be one of the first species of large mammals lost to this change of climate (Allen 52). Sea ice habitat is vanishing taking with it prime hunting areas for prey like seals. Finding dens for their cubs on the shrinking ice is also becoming more of a challenge. Polar bears are facing extinction from threats that evolution and adaptation have not prepared them for. Change is upon them rapidly, and they have not had a chance to catch up.

The gray steel revealed itself from beneath the layers of dead paint and rust, and as I scrubbed harder, it shone metallic. I couldn't stop. It had to be cleaner. The rust, algae, dirt, and moss were overtaking our home. It was unsettling to contemplate how pollen and germs and bacteria enshrouded us in that cramped box.

Foe sat by, watching with cat-focus intensity. He swatted at my scrub brush whenever it swept past him, as if my sole intent was to play a game of sudsy-water swipe with him. After a few more passes, once his paw got wet, the game was no longer entertaining. He abandoned me, leaving wet footprints behind.

Pain flared up in my hand. I inspected my right palm. It was cracked and bleeding, my skin raw. *No matter.* Although it stung, the bleach in the water would kill any bacteria that could cause an infection there. I could keep going.

"Poodle? What's going on? . . . Where are you? Mol?"

My mother's voice came from somewhere below me. Within a few seconds, I saw the top of her head, and next her gaze, appear along the edge of our Solitaire Edition. It wasn't good for her to climb ladders for any number of reasons. For one thing, she never cared for heights. Another thing was she was a smoker and could easily get winded or dizzy from hypertension and fall off. According to the World Health Organization, over three hundred people died each year from falling off of ladders, and that was in the United States alone. Another 164,000 ended up in hospital emergency rooms.

Hospital emergency room. ERs, or now they called them EDs for Emergency Departments. So many people wound up in EDs where they were put in even greater jeopardy from the threat of HAIs, or hospital-acquired infections ... I scrubbed faster, hoping to finish the roof before she made me come down.

"Molly! Honey! What are you doing up here? Downstairs reeks of bleach and disinfectant. And why is all the furniture out in the driveway? Did something happen?"

"Just a few more minutes, Mom. I'm almost done," I said, while my scrub brush swept soapy arcs across the roof of the trailer.

Alarmed, she scrambled up on top of the roof toward me. I felt the metal buckle under our combined weight. It could collapse at any moment, sending us both plummeting below to be sliced open by jagged metal edges, severing our major arteries, and bleeding out before emergency responders got to us.

"Mom! You're too heavy for both of us to be up here." I scrubbed faster.

"Molly?" She knelt beside me and grabbed my hands. "Molly, stop ... Stop it!" Her strong grip brought my scrubbing to a halt. "What are you doing?"

"This has to be cleaned. It's been like this way too long. We're living under a ton of dirt and rust and moss. And it's falling apart. Soon we won't have any place left. And then where will we be? We'll be homeless and out on the street in the cold and no one will help us and you'll lose your job and we'll starve and—"

She held my hands still and locked eyes with me. "Baby, please. Let's get down off of this roof and go inside, okay? We can talk there and you can tell me what's going on." The gentle, measured tone in her voice tripped off a hazy memory in my head from when I was about eleven years old. I remember that same tone had clouded her voice when she told me that Dad had moved out.

"But I am—"

"Please, Poodle? Come on."

I conceded only because her expression turned strange, and she spoke very carefully, as if she were about to cross a minefield. Usually she would just order me to do something if she got mad enough.

Besides, I wasn't sure of the load-bearing capacity of this old roof. It was best for us to get off of it. I'd just have to make sure to get back up here first thing in the morning to finish cleaning. The metal would start rusting and the algae would start building, and the next thing I'd know, I would have to start all over again.

We climbed down the ladder to the driveway. I stopped at the sofa, armchair, and coffee table that were covered with plastic bags and old sheets to protect them from the pollen, dirt, and bird shit while they sat there. I couldn't manage moving the beds or the dressers outside by myself or otherwise they would've been there, too.

"Hold on. We better get these in," I said.

"They can wait, Mol. Let's get some dinner first. It's late and I'm sure you're hungry."

"No, they can't. It'll only take a few minutes." I knew all too well that they would get covered with dust and acid rain, or worse yet—infested with fleas and bedbugs and roaches.

"Poodle, I'll give you a hand with them, but let's—"

"They have to come in now! I just cleaned them today, but I had to put them out here while the carpet is drying. The night dew is going to make them musty. And then they'll start harboring fungus and mildews. Don't you know that black mildew gets on everything? It'll make us sick. We could develop asthma." I picked up the end of the sofa and started dragging it toward the steps. "Come on. Get the other end."

"Molly! You're going to hurt yourself."

"It's going to rain, and this is going to get ruined. We have to get it in now."

I hoisted the end even higher, but the sofa slipped from my trembling hands and fell back down with a thud. Blood and crashing thoughts of terror filled my head and shook my entire body. I growled and tried lifting the sofa again, but my tired arms were useless. All I could do was stare at that cumbersome piece of furniture as my breath escaped in short bursts. A tremendous weight bore down on me like I was nothing more than an ant under a boot. Tears trickled down my cheeks, and my throat felt thick. My chest hurt—inside, my bruised and battered heart complained of beating.

Mom sat down on the sofa and held her arms out to me. The plastic made a crinkling sound beneath her.

"What is it, baby? Please, come sit down."

"But the sofa—"

"We're sitting on the plastic, and we'll get it in in a minute, okay? So stop worrying about the damn thing and talk to me already! I know something is up because although you might not realize it, you're in one of your cleaning frenzies again. This has got to be the worst one yet. Now what is going on?"

I sank down beside her and let her wrap her arms around me and pull me close. Her clothes smelled of the control buttons she worked on all day.

"Poodle, I know I'm not Daddy. And I know I'm not good at listening and answering your questions or understanding you like he does. But I'm really trying here. I want to understand what is going on. Please don't shut me out, okay?" she said.

"It's not like it was a big surprise. I mean, I should've expected it. I knew things were going along too well. I didn't concentrate hard enough on the opposite."

"What? Wait—don't tell me that you are going back to that old dead end. Remember what Annie said? You have no control over the way things are. No matter if you think positive or negative or opposite of what is. So what is bugging you? Something is making you do all of this, and I want you to tell me right now." Her tone was growing firm.

I tried to focus past the tornado of thoughts swirling in my head. One kept flashing intermittently, over and over, like the strobe lights on an ambulance. Finally, it pushed to the front where it finally came out.

"It's Sig. He's in the hospital."

"Oh my God. From what? The holdup? I thought you said he was okay."

"No. With cancer. It's back."

"Sig has cancer? Sweet Jesus." My mom's mouth opened as she blinked in disbelief. "I'm so sorry."

The sun had set in our secluded driveway, and the shadows cast by the rows of trailers dulled the remaining twilight. The carcass of the fallen tree absorbed even more light with its dark trunk. At least the streetlight around the corner of our trailer shone enough so we weren't in total blackness.

I sorted through the details that Janice had shared with me at the hospital and, one by one, they joined and spilled forth in a torrent of painful truth. I don't know if it was the sense of privacy afforded by the darkness in our driveway or the fact that I had my mom's undivided attention, but I couldn't stop.

I shared Sig's story of how he had cancer from the time he was eleven years old until he was sixteen. Then he went into remission for the past five years. Or at least they thought so.

After we were held up, his ribs hurt, so Janice took him in to be x-rayed and examined. The pain persisted, so they ran an MRI. It was then they spotted a single tumor the size of a pinto bean on his liver. The only thing they could do now was run more tests and possibly start on chemo or radiation therapy again.

When the words ran out, Mom held me close and started rocking me like I was an infant, repeating, "Take it easy, baby. Let it go." I felt her stroke my hair and kiss the top of my head.

"I should have really kept focused when things were going so well. I knew it wasn't going to last."

"But don't you understand? You had nothing to do with it. Things are going to happen whether you are being positive, negative, or stay neutral. This is out of your control, Molly. And you can't go around feeling that you ever had any control of it to begin with, understand?"

I spied the outline of Mr. Martino's crushed trailer whose silhouette was of a beast writhing in the throes of death. It suddenly occurred to me what a lonely journey we were on from start to finish. You were born alone; you died alone. For most people, there was no one who experienced those two most personal events with you, or really, when I thought about it, the vast majority of others.

"SIG DESPAIN" was written in dry-erase marker on the whiteboard outside of room RA 4-315. A familiar name in an unfamiliar setting; it was disturbing. The warning posted on the glass sliding door to his room stated, "Standard Precautions: Sanitize Hands Upon Entering and When Leaving the Room. Gown and Mask If Necessary." I studied the warning and the accompanying illustrations to make sure I wasn't misunderstanding anything, then took a squirt from the automatic gel dispenser, rubbed it in, and fanned my hands to dry. Steadying myself, I slid the door open.

"Hello? Sig? It's me, Molly."

The curtain was drawn so I peered cautiously around it just in case he was sleeping or getting dressed or something much more personal. I had never visited anyone in a hospital room before, and I didn't know what to expect. There've always been stories of bedpans, sponge baths, and shots to the ass with long needles when it came to hospital stays, but I wasn't sure how much of it was fact rather than myth.

Instead, Sig was sitting up in bed, playing a video game with two other guys who were sitting in his room. He was dressed in a hospital gown that was tied in the back and had his long hairy legs sticking out from under the blanket. A tangle of multicolored cables and surgical tubing had been plumbed into his arm, tethering him to some kind of complicated robotic tree topped with clear bags of fluids and an electronic beeping box with a digital readout.

"Oh, hey Mol," Sig nodded at my entrance. He played for a few moments more to get to a point where his avatar could take a break without being attacked. It didn't work. Two zombies jumped him from behind and tore him to pieces.

"Dudes, I'm done." He dropped the controller onto his lap.

Feeling awkward, I stood quietly by, not knowing what to say. I had anticipated that he would be alone. In addition to that, I had never seen Sig in bed, let alone in such a vulnerable situation. He turned to me with those dozy eyes. They had dark rings under them now. He tried a smile. It wasn't his usual beam that lit up and warmed the room around him. This was different. Instead, it was weary and faded quickly like the daylight when a cloud passes in front of the sun.

"What are you doing here? Sorry I didn't text. I was kinda busy," he said. "Oh, by the way, these are my friends, Omar and Jonathan. Guys, this is my friend and lab partner, Molly."

Engrossed in the game, Omar and Jonathan each gave a wave and a "S'up?" but remained intent on the screen. Omar was dressed in street clothes, and Jonathan wore a gown similar to Sig's along with sweatpants and Seahawks slippers.

"Yeah, I hadn't even been admitted for an hour when next thing these clowns show up. Word sure spreads fast. Anyway Omar's here for his usual dialysis. And Jonathan's here for a cleanout."

I must've looked confused. Sig explained, "He's got CF. Cystic fibrosis. Jon's what they call a 'Frequent Flyer.' He's admitted every seven months or so to get his lungs cleared out and treated. He's getting ready to go home in a few more days. And Omar's on dialysis until he can find a donor. We all met during my first stay here about five years ago."

"Six," corrected Omar. His attention remained on the screen.

"We used to terrorize that one nurse … what was her name?" said Sig. "Is she still here?"

"Lisa," said Jonathan. "Nah. She left for another hospital right after you left. Remember how she hated that song, 'Rubber Ducky'? That was hysterical."

"Yeah, and you kept singing it to drive her friggin' nuts," Omar said. "You were the only one who knew all the lyrics and could make the duck sounds."

"Is it okay to visit now? Or should I come back later so you can hang with Omar and Jonathan?" I asked.

"Nah. It's cool. They were just getting ready to leave anyway."

A couple more onscreen explosions later, the game was stopped. Sig's friends placed the controllers on the side table and headed for the door.

"Later, bro," Omar said, stopping to fist bump with Sig on the way out. "It's time for me to be getting on the machine. Later, you," he nodded at me.

"Later, Omar," Sig said. "Hey, thanks for hanging. Catch you tomorrow, Jonathan?"

"Same time, same place, as long as you don't have a treatment. Peace out," Jonathan added.

Now that it was only the two of us with no other distractions, the room was overwhelming. I studied the bed table and the food tray full of cold, untouched food, next to an unopened bag of his ever-present Funyuns. There must have been at least twelve red power outlets lining the wall in a row across the head of his bed. I read the whiteboard with the names and phone numbers of Sig's team of nurses and staff, and the pain measurement scale of one to ten with smiling faces morphing to scowling ones and the words, "Choose the face that best describes how you feel." I stared with wonder at the whirring, clicking, blinking, ever-monitoring machinery that pumped mysterious, off-colored liquids into him while glowing numbers and readouts paraded across their screens. One of his fingers was clothespinned into some kind of clip that made its tip glow bright red, like ET's. By the sofa lay his old, beat-up Converse Chucks, forlorn and out of place here. And oddly enough, scraps of paper, a plastic dosage cup, and cut strips of sterile tape littered the floor of his room, which surprised me, since I always assumed that hospitals were orderly places. I also noticed a sealed snack cup of peaches lying within the folds of his blanket.

"What's the matter?"

"I've never visited anyone in a hospital room before," I said.

"You're shitting me. *Never?*"

"Uh-uh. Never."

Sig shrugged. "Well, there's not much to see, although this room is ten times better than some of the old ones I used to have. At least I have a flat-screen here. And I can play video games. One of my old rooms was so lame, the only thing it had on the walls were some god-awful pictures of decorative gourds. And that room was always freezing."

"But I've seen on the news where celebrities and sports stars visit kids in the hospital. Have you had that happen?"

"Nah. Whenever they come around, they usually spend most of their time with the little kids because they're cuter and there's more possibilities for photo ops. They hardly ever visit the teenagers, especially when they are pressed for time. No. I've seen a lot of balloon-tying amateur clowns—you know the kind that do kids' parties. And people with service dogs. Oh wait, I guess I met a congressman once who came through, but it was because he was trying to get his health-care bill passed. Yeah, pretty boring."

"Oh," I said. Before it got too quiet, I asked, "Why is there a cup of peaches in your blankets? I thought you hated peaches."

"I do. But everyone here keeps trying to make me eat. My mom loves peaches, so I told food service yes when they asked me if I wanted any. But they're for her."

Suddenly, an electronic high-pitched alarm sounded from the pole with all the wires and hoses.

"What is that? Is everything okay?" I asked with apprehension.

Sig turned and tapped a button on the machine. The alarm silenced. "It's nothing. My antibiotics are all done, that's all."

After about fifteen seconds, the alarm went off again and Sig silenced it once more. This time, a young woman in scrubs came in and went directly to check the machine.

"Hey Sig, this says you're finished. Wait, did you shut off the alarm?" she asked him.

"Yeah. I get tired of it beeping."

"Well, I know you know what to do, but just make sure to contact me or Kimiko when that happens, okay?"

"Yeah, sure, Tara."

After removing the empty bag from the tree, she scanned his wristband, went to the computer on the counter, and started typing. Then she left. It was odd how people came and went, in and out of his room, without announcing themselves or knocking. "When do you get to leave?" I asked.

"That's the big question. I don't know. No one knows. They have to check my bone marrow first."

"This isn't from getting mugged, is it? I mean, did that bring it on or make it worse?"

"Nah. In fact, I was only getting x-rayed because the docs were worried that I had broken a rib, and that's when they saw something. Given my record, they followed up with a blood test and MRI, and bingo, they found what they were poking around for. Anyway, maybe you can make a figurine of me now. I think I safely qualify as an endangered species. By the way, remember when we talked with Dr. Pope and she blew us off? Now *this* is a setback. Just thought I'd let you know for comparison's sake."

"Oh."

I felt like breaking down all over again, but forced myself to hold it in. Instead, my fingers automatically busied themselves tidying the stuff on his bed table—I covered up the food, placed his Funyun bag off to the side to keep the rings from being crunched, straightened up his book and papers, and lined up his prescription vials according to their height.

"Molly, what are you doing?"

"Nothing. Leave me alone."

"I really wish you wouldn't," he sighed.

"I have to. Anyway, how are things going?" I asked as I retrieved the dosage cup, tape, and papers off the floor to throw into the waste can.

"Eh. It's okay. My mom is taking it worse. She's after my dad to come back to help out, but he's working. I don't know what she expects. It's not like we don't know the drill."

I couldn't tell whether it was resignation or anger that dulled his voice. And whatever bit of energy he had when Omar and Jonathan were in the room ebbed quickly from him now, leaving him looking tired and worn. Either way, what it told me was that he wasn't being exactly truthful.

"No, what I mean is how are *you* feeling? I thought that you might be … well … um, you know.…"

"What? Depressed? Angry? Scared? Well you're right. I am."

He stared out the window at the bright day outside. His hands curled into fists as the bouncing red line indicating his pulse on the monitor picked up its rhythm. "I see it's finally nice out," he said. "Figures."

Then Sig faced me, his cheeks flush and his eyes blazing. "This wasn't supposed to happen again. I was beyond complete remission. They wrote on my chart 'no evidence of disease.' You know what that means? Nothing showed on any of the hundreds of blood tests or scans or exams they took of me. And now … now, I'm right back to ground zero again.

"Do you know how many more months I'm going to have to spend locked up here in this stupid hospital while they pump poison into my veins and nuke me until I'm bald and puking my guts out again, all the while waiting to see if they've killed 'It' before 'It' kills me? How much am I going to lose this go-around? And how many more late effects? Believe it or not, I used to be a straight-A student, like you, before my first chemo. I had a scholarship to Berkeley for engineering. But this shit seriously screws with your brain. Now I'll be glad just to graduate with an Associates from Sea View. And meanwhile, my parents are buried in hospital bills. That's why my dad's out in the fracking fields. So, you honestly want to know what I'm really feeling right now, Molly? I'm feeling tired. I'm feeling so goddamn fucking tired. I don't know if I can go through all of this again."

It was unnerving to see Sig so angry. The universe as I knew it was out of whack, and I felt unbalanced. I couldn't be sure if it was for his sake or mine, but I took hold of his hand.

"You'll do it. I know you will. If there is anyone I know who can, it's you."

He stared at my hand in his. "Don't be so sure. It now makes total sense why your friend Melody did what she did. She actually is the lucky one who doesn't have to contend with this fucked-up world anymore."

His words electrified me, sending a prickly course racing through my body until the hairs on the back of my neck stood up.

"You can't mean that. You can't."

"Come on. Everyone knows it's true, but nobody wants to admit it. There's not one person on this earth that hasn't felt the same way at one time or another. You think you're getting somewhere, but you're not. Instead you keep losing ground over and over and over again. Spinning your wheels and going nowhere. And for what? Nothing you do makes a goddamn bit of difference. Nothing. We all end up dying anyway."

This couldn't be my friend—my hero—talking. Fearless, laid back, cool, composed. That was the Sig I knew and looked up to.

"But I thought you weren't afraid of dying."

"I'm not. It's all the shitty living in between being born and dying that I don't like."

"Melody was a coward!" I blurted out. "She could have turned to anyone and let someone know what was going on. Instead she was selfish and didn't care about who she hurt with her actions. We were all there for her. She could've stuck it out. She just didn't want to try."

I was shocked at what came out of me, but when it did, oddly I felt a sense of vindicated relief.

"No. Your friend was not a coward," he answered quietly. "She was just tired of treading water with nowhere to go and nothing to hang on to."

"Whoa. I'm beat. Me and Kelly were so backed up on the P-2000 project today. Jeff forgot to adjust the schedule after the SatComm contract was squeezed in at the last minute, and then everyone was running around like chickens without their heads trying to make up for it. Meanwhile, the front office was being audited today, so they couldn't pitch in. Anyway, we kept bouncing back and forth between the workstations all day. And then, Jeff is jumping my case saying that we need to get back on the P-2000 project because he has them breathing down his neck. I tell you, it's been a long day … Hey, you know what sounds good right now?"

"A cigarette?"

"I knew you would say that. No. Believe it or not, I'm trying to quit, if that makes you feel any better."

"You are?" I said. "And what made you finally change your mind, if you don't mind me asking?"

"Well, I did a lot of thinking after what you told me about your friend, Sig. He's fighting so hard just to be well, and here I am, throwing my health away. I guess I haven't been making the wisest choices. That, and it's getting too darned expensive to smoke anymore. Anyway, I thought it would be a treat to have a nice cup of hot chocolate. I picked some up today. You know, the kind with the mini marshmallows in it? How about I make us some?"

"Er, okay."

Mom took the kettle out of the cupboard. I watched as she filled it from the faucet with steaming-hot tap water laden with invisible lead, nitrates, and persistent organic pollutants. And then she took out two hot-chocolate packets from the box and shook them, smacking them on her palm to get the powder and mini marshmallows to settle before opening. I read an article that said hot chocolate could grow fungus inside of it when stored on the shelf too long, and another food blog said that the mini marshmallows were nothing but dehydrated high-fructose corn-syrup pellets.

I inwardly shook myself. Here, my mom was looking forward to her hot chocolate to help her relax while I was fearing it with dread. Why wouldn't these stupid thoughts turn off in my head? Instead, they emphasized everything that was wrong with living. Even an innocent comfort beverage was not so innocent. Sig was right. It really was a fucked-up world.

"Mom? I guess I've been thinking a lot about things, too."

"Oh yeah? Like what?"

"Well like, how Melody and Sig are the most with-it people I know. I mean, Melody was really outgoing and energetic, plus she had a perfect family. And Sig—well, everybody loves Sig. He's smart and savvy and really cool."

"Poodle, are you going somewhere with this?" my mom asked. She stole a glance at her phone.

"It's just that … if Melody had everything going for her and she killed herself, and Sig can do just about anything he wants in life, yet he ends up having a relapse from something that is trying to kill him, what chance does a mediocre person like me have of making it in this world?"

She stopped stirring her chocolate and stared at me, her face an exclamation point in consternation.

"I never thought it was possible, but that has got to beat all of the other impossible questions you have ever asked in your life," she said. "Where did that come from?"

"It's just that, what scares me is I am not confident like them. I'm just this little nobody. And people don't tend to like me, either. I haven't really done anything in this world, or impacted anybody. I haven't done anything significant to leave my mark. Somebody like me could easily be forgotten. It's hard to explain, but it's like, I don't have a place in this world."

My mother rubbed her forehead hard, like she was trying to conjure up a genie for a response. "Geez, Mol. Can't we just drink our hot chocolate in peace?"

"I mean, what have I done? I haven't gone anywhere, changed anything, learned anything. It's all been the same. I haven't influenced anyone or anything. I haven't even changed my own self."

"Of course you wouldn't be forgotten. You'd be remembered by me, and Daddy, and Noni, and your Grandma O. Now can we please drop all of this doom-and-gloom talk already and just drink this before it gets cold? God—I am really trying hard not to want a smoke right about now."

By the way her hands trembled as she lifted her mug to her lips, she was not kidding. More than likely, she had a craving for something stronger than a Pall Mall. I knew I had better quit.

Instead, I stared down at the mini marshmallows, like floes of foam floating around in my cup and melting into their sea of hot, brown water. It was obvious that she had totally missed what I was trying to say. What I was really feeling but couldn't articulate was that I was so insignificant, I couldn't even help my friends when they needed me the most. I was perhaps the most powerless person I knew.

That night, I lay awake, pondering. There had to be something—anything—at least one way I could make some kind of difference. If I couldn't do it for the people I cared about, maybe I could do it for a *thing* I cared about. Suddenly, an epiphany occurred to me that instantly unfolded itself like the opening of an umbrella to a downpour. There was something I could do after all. And I would do it.

I added it all up one more time, just to make sure. First, there was $257 from selling Sig's and my textbooks. He had left his books in my car by accident, but I figured that he had missed so much class already, he wasn't going to need them anyway. And I had missed so many days myself, that I had to withdraw before I flunked. Next, my Grandma O money I had saved so far totaled $175. I opened my dresser drawer and withdrew the card Dad had sent me that contained $50 of emergency Gray Day money for me to buy something that made me happy. Then there was the $185 left from my solo stint at the festival. I had just received a $294 income-tax refund from working at the bakery last year. And last, I scrounged around in the cup on top of the dryer that collected the stray coins that had been left in pockets before wash, on Mom's dresser, and from the penny jar on the kitchen counter, and came up with a surprising $22 in change. All in all, the lump sum totaled $983.

I waited until Mom left for work the next morning, and then I brought out my duffel bag that I had packed the night before with my warmest sweaters and clothes we had gotten from the thrift store. I found my passport and fed Foe. I printed up the detailed note for my mother outlining my planned route and stops along the way, the description of my car, my license plate number, my driver's license number, and my scheduled calling times. After making sure the mechanism for my car's convertible roof was completely latched, I loaded my bag, started the car, and took off.

About an eighth of a mile down the road, I had to turn back around to check the windows and the front door lock on the trailer one last time. In my excitement and nervousness, I had forgotten all about them. When they were secure, once again I headed out, bound for Alaska.

The last time I had felt so empowered was the morning after we had been held up. I imagined this was what explorers, researchers, and investigative journalists must feel as the miles roll away and the road stretches before them like a continuous welcome mat. I was thrilled that I had actually forced myself to do this.

But it was nerve-racking, too. I had never been so far away from home by myself. I had no means of protection, and didn't know what I'd do if anyone started following me. I had heard numerous horror stories of creeps on the road that got fixated on other travelers for no apparent reason, and then started harassing them relentlessly. So I planned on stopping to fill up every time my gas dropped below the halfway mark on the gauge, so I'd have plenty of fuel just in case I had to outrun someone. And I hoped I wouldn't come across any bedbugs in the motels I would be staying in along the way, because I forgot to pack my UV flashlight.

The immensity of the world was an icy wave up the nostrils, and all of my senses launched into overdrive. The volume on my radio was kept low so I could listen for sirens or car horns. My peripheral vision scanned for any deer that might dash out at the last second. I traveled past towns, houses, and outlet malls while other cars constantly passed up my old drop-top. And although I was hardly far from civilization, the wide-open farm fields and rolling hills were like an inland ocean to me, and I was a mere speck making my way across them; the swans and snow geese that dotted the fields reminding me of whitecaps on the swells.

From a road sign, I learned that the border crossing at Peace Arch was forty-five miles away. My stomach flip-flopped over the idea that within the next hour I would be in another country. *By myself.* I was glad it was Canada for my first solo trip anywhere. I couldn't imagine having to negotiate in a country where the language was something other than English. I also read that Canadians were pretty friendly and didn't lock their doors because they had a lower crime rate than we did in the U.S.

Suddenly, up ahead, a long line of red taillights started to appear. Next, blue-and-white strobe lights flashed in my rearview, and as I pulled over, the cop car tore past me. It traveled to the point where the cars were completely stopped ahead, and then it started weaving back and forth through the lanes. In my rearview, I could see other emergency vehicles coming up behind me as well, joining in the assist. Within the next minute, with no exits in sight, I arrived at the end of the line of cars and came to a complete stop.

I hadn't anticipated this.

Chapter 9.5

Eugene Peschack, Cashier at the Gas 'n Go near Twisp, WA

WHEN SHE STOOD IN LINE, I hardly saw her behind the big dude who was wearing the greasy hat and the shirt with the cutoff sleeves. She had wandered around the aisles searching for something, but she never picked anything up.

"Do you have any maps?" she asked when she finally approached the checkout counter. She seemed really flustered.

"Maps? Huh. We haven't sold any in a while. In fact, I'm not sure if we even sell them anymore. Everyone just uses their phones or satnavs. Let me think where we put them," I told her.

It wasn't the first time that someone had come into the Gas 'n Go looking lost. We're nothing more than a wide spot in the road—most people stop for gas or maybe a Pepsi. But maps? Personally I don't know anyone who uses them. Well, except my grandparents.

She said, "I'm not in roaming range; besides I don't have a smartphone. And I don't own a satnav."

"Huh."

I found a box of maps shoved under the counter. Now when I recall, I'm pretty sure I remember hearing Tim, our manager, say to Krystal to stock them on the wire rack by the sunscreen a couple of months ago. Figures that Krystal would hide them here. She's always trying to get out of work.

"Which one do you need?" I asked.

"One for Washington. Oh, and Canada. And would you possibly have any for Alaska, too?"

I rummaged around in the box and pulled out a Washington one and a Canadian one. "These are all we have. Sorry, we don't carry ones for Alaska. Why? Are you trying to get there?" People's travels are interesting. I like to connect the dots in my mind's map as to where they are going. Sometimes, when things are really slow in the store, I stand by the doorway and watch the cars and trucks go by and imagine where they came from and all the places they were headed to and why.

"Yeah, I was headed north on I-5, because I heard that it goes all the way to Alaska. But they closed off the highway by Ferndale because a logging truck lost its load of logs. All three northbound lanes were shut down. A state trooper made us turn around because it was going to take hours to clear. He said we would have to detour. When I told him I was headed for the border he said that I would have to go to the next crossing at Lynden–Aldergrove. So that's what I need to find out—how close I am to that border crossing."

I took out my phone and checked for her. "Nope. Says here Lynden–Aldergrove is one hundred seventy-nine miles in the opposite direction from here … about three hours and thirty-six minutes," I said.

She seemed shocked by what I just told her, and then looked really bummed out. "I got so turned around with the detour," she said. "I just kept driving and driving and looking for the turnoff. I must've missed the sign to Lynden."

"Well, you can still get to the border from here."

"I can?"

"Yeah, just stay here on SR 20 until you hit US 97, and then turn left onto that. That should take you right up to the Oroville–Osoyoos crossing. Oroville is …" I checked my phone again, " … about seventy-seven point three miles from here. About an hour-and-a-half drive, depending how fast you drive."

"Okay, thanks. I really appreciate your help. I better fill up here before I get lost in Canada, too. And would you know of a good place close by to eat? I'm starving."

I consulted my phone and scrolled through its screen. "Here's a place called the Copper Kettle in Tonasket, right up the road, not too far on 97. And it says that it closes at nine thirty."

"Okay. Thanks! I'll take these maps, and I need to fill up my car, please."

As I rang her up, I wondered if she was one of those people who freaked out about technology—I think they call them Luddites, or something like that. But as I watched her walk out to her old beat-up car, actually I thought she was pretty badass to travel anywhere without a smartphone.

Dr. Kristin Munghaven, paleobotanist at the University of Calgary

I NEVER ENJOY EATING ALONE whenever I am away from home. I would sooner eat in my hotel room or in my car with a good read to keep me company. Today, however, that was not an option. While driving to the symposium at Central Washington University, where I was presenting my paper on gnetophyta, my jar of formaldehyde leaked on the seat when I swerved in the rain to avoid a distracted motorist who was not only texting on the phone, but crossing over the double yellow line and coming straight toward me. The seat cushion got soaked from the formaldehyde, and the resulting toxic cloud was completely noxious, so I left my car to air out while I had dinner before arriving at my hotel.

I had just been seated when I spied a shy young woman enter the roadside restaurant I had found by chance. Fortunately, I had already secured a table in the small, understaffed eatery, because within the next five minutes or so, it suddenly filled up from the tour bus out front that had just unloaded a large group of about forty Chinese tourists. When the harried host threw her hands up in despair at the mass of people crowding about her restaurant and said, "Y'all just seat yourselves wherever there's room. We'll try to take your orders as soon as we can," the young woman, standing apart from the crowd, appeared panicky.

I managed to catch her attention and waved her over. Hesitantly, she approached with a question in her eyes and asked, "Excuse me, did you want something?"

"You can sit there if you like," I said, indicating the empty chair across from me. "I can share." I figured a nerdy old scientist like me shouldn't pose much of a threat. And conversation would certainly suffice in the absence of a good read.

"Thanks," she said.

"Hi, I'm Kirsten," I said, as I extended my hand.

"I'm Molly."

She had a solid handshake. Not bad for someone of her generation.

"Well, Molly, apparently you and I and about forty-five other people all had the same idea to invade this restaurant at the same exact time and drive the wait staff crazy. Or shall we say, the same misfortune?"

She nodded. "It sure seems like it. Has the waitress been by yet?"

"No, from what I can tell it's only she and one other server out here on the floor. Looks like we're in for a wait, if we want to eat. I would go somewhere else, but I can't stomach burgers, and the next stop is more than fifty miles away. I don't know if I can hold out for that much longer without eating dinner."

"Me neither. Oh, and thanks for sharing your table with me."

"It's my pleasure. I don't care to eat by myself."

"I usually eat out in my car, but its roof is leaking from all the rain. This is better. Not so cold," she said.

"I typically do the same, but I had some formaldehyde spill in my car. I can't eat in there with that dreadful smell."

"Formaldehyde? Are you preserving something?"

"I use it with copper carbonate as a disinfectant and fungicide to control blight and mildew. You know—on potatoes and on grapes. I also pickle an insect or two from time to time, especially the ones that destroy plants. I just caught a beautiful Halyomorpha halys this morning."

Upon hearing my answer, I noticed she developed that twenty-yard stare that most people had whenever I explained any of my projects. It was likely that I'd lose her completely with what I'd say next, but that was okay. I've gotten used to it when talking to laypeople. If she didn't want to converse, then at the very least she was another warm body across the dinner table from me for company. It would be like old times with my ex.

"I'm a paleobotanist. Just in case you were wondering why on earth anyone would want to work with stink bugs or potato blight."

"So you study prehistoric plants?"

I was impressed. Most people didn't get it. "Well, specifically, I study diseases that affected ancient plants. I've been tracking blight evolutionary mutations to uncover whether their alterations and resulting affects influenced plant cellular evolution. But I must start first with ones we have at hand."

"Wow, so you're an actual researcher! How cool. It's my dream to become a researcher when I graduate."

"Is that so? Why dream? If you believe it can or should be, then make it happen. And what would your focus be?"

"I really want to study polar bears and find ways to keep them from extinction caused by global warming. In fact, I'm on my way to Kaktovik, Alaska, where they are. My lab partner and I have devised a plan to help them survive out in open water, since the ice floes they normally haul out on are disappearing fast."

My jaw just about dropped open with surprise. I didn't expect that to come out of this shy one. As she spoke, her enthusiasm and passion for her polar bear project was reminiscent of me, a half a century ago, before my hair silvered and my arms shriveled and my shoulders hunched. I could tell already that I was going to enjoy this dinner conversation. And by her expression that had relaxed some, I believe it was safe to say that the feeling was mutual.

"Now *that's* what I call fascinating. And do you mind me asking what plan you and your lab partner have worked out?"

"We, well actually Sig—he's also my friend—thought of building swim platforms that act as artificial ice floes anchored out in the long stretches of ocean where polar bears might be found. The platforms would give them a chance to haul out to rest up from their swims. Especially the cubs. We are hoping they would learn where these platforms are from their parents, return to them, and eventually teach their own cubs how to find them," Molly said with her hand gestures doing half of the communicating.

"That's quite an idea. Simple, yet potentially effective. The best ones always are. Have you developed a prototype?"

"No. Not yet. We have the plans all worked out on paper, but we haven't been able to build yet."

"No? Why not? Is it funding?"

"That, and we've had some setbacks … ."

"Oh, don't I know setbacks! Just to let you in on a little secret—research work is full of them. I remember when I was teaching in Spain, I lost two years' worth of specimens in ice-core samples when the power went out. Or that time in Russia, when a lab assistant stole all of my equipment. The good news is you can overcome just about any setback. If you work at it, even if it is just a little bit at a time, you'll get there eventually. So what are you hoping to accomplish up in Kaktovik? Are you studying the bears' swim routes?"

My young friend's bright demeanor dimmed as her confidence changed to uncertainty. Oddly, she reached into her purse and withdrew hand sanitizer and started gelling for no apparent reason.

"I, uh … am not sure yet. I need to see them first, and then figure out what to do next. I was hoping to get some ideas or insight as to how to build the platforms once I saw the bears. Both Sig and I wanted to go, but we didn't have enough money, and then he had a relapse with cancer."

"Oh dear, I'm so sorry to hear about your friend," I said as I politely waved off her offer of sanitizer.

"Thanks … It's been strange doing this without him. Actually, this is my first solo trip to, well, just about anywhere."

"It is? Well, congratulations! Take that step and be bold. In the grand scheme of things, the journey we are on is a singular one, so ultimately you must learn to rely on yourself. We share paths with others only by chance and/or occasion."

"Funny, I thought that same exact thing and came to the same conclusion not too long ago. Well, at least the singular journey part."

The server arrived, and while she placed a basket of breadsticks down and took our orders, I took a moment to study my young dinner companion closely as she perused the menu. I noted the way she gelled again, after she handed the menu back to our server. And the way she kept glancing around the room, particularly if anything or anyone was loud. I have always had the ability to "read" my students, and Molly appeared to be very intelligent, but anxious. I couldn't contain my curiosity much longer and wondered what she was running from.

I decided to put it out there. "So, what's your real reason to see the bears?"

"I want to make a difference and do something worthwhile."

I smiled and said nothing.

She looked as if she had been caught with her hand in the cookie jar. I hoped she would trust me enough to share her real story. Over the years, I discovered that people tend to divulge things to me readily, although I don't know why. Some people say it's my patient manner, others say it's the tone of my voice. Honestly, I believe it comes from a lifetime of work with plants. You see, a plant's sense of trust is actually very simple and involves only two things: whether something is going to obliterate it or leave it alone. People aren't much different. Anyway, my mother used to tell me that I was wasting my time with plants and should have been a cross-examiner in a courtroom, because people will spill their guts out to me, most sooner than later.

Molly fidgeted a little, and then started to crack, just as I had expected.

"I ... I guess I couldn't be around Sig while he's so sick. He's like a hero to me, in a way. I had another friend, my best friend, who was like that, too. But she's gone now. What I'm trying to say is I don't know what to do without them. I feel lost. So I thought if I could save something, or do something entirely on my own, then maybe I wouldn't feel so lost. And maybe Sig could look up to me for once."

"But you are doing something already, and I don't mean just this trip. It sounds to me that you have to learn to trust yourself, that's all."

"But I don't know what I am doing half the time. I'm afraid that I am going to make the wrong decisions. Or make some terrible mistakes."

"You will make them anyway, whether you are very careful or not. Things happen beyond our control. And even when they are in your control, you can't expect to know everything about everything. We wouldn't have science without making mistakes, nor could we grow as individuals without making them either. It's an inherent part of how we learn and evolve."

"It is?"

"I'll say it once again—learn to trust yourself. Give it a try. You'll probably feel a lot better when you do."

She was silent for a few moments as she buttered her bread. I noticed how careful she was to lay the butter knife down across the top of her plate when she was done, instead of placing it on the table.

Then she said, "I'm not sure if I can. I mean, it's going to take some time."

"It will, but stick with it. You'll find that it will never let you down."

"Okay … . I'm glad you shared this table with me, Kristin. I feel better already."

"Anytime, my friend. I'm so glad you came and sat with me."

"So, do you really think I should I continue my trip?"

"Think about it for a moment, and then tell me what *you've* decided."

Molly nibbled her breadstick, lost in thought. Then she turned to me and said, "Yes. I'm going to do it. I am going to Kaktovik to see polar bears."

"That's the spirit! You've made up your mind. Now go do it."

Throughout the rest of our dinner, we continued to talk about our research, friends, and homes, until it was time to leave. We exchanged email addresses, and I gave her my business card and told her to let me know how her project is going. I watched her drive off in her old car and wondered how long it was going to take her to reach her destination so far away. However, if our conversation was any indication, regardless if she did or not, it was clear to me that young Molly was on her way to doing something significant.

Brenda Moody,
tow truck driver at All-Star Towing Company

SHE WAS A STRANGE LITTLE THING, kinda jumpy and excitable. It was surprising to find her way out in the middle of nowhere in that rusted heap. These roads get really dark, and there aren't many gas stations in close range of each other. Even I don't like being called out at night to this area if I don't have to.

When I pulled up behind her car—it looked like some kind of old Sunbeam or something. Man, I haven't seen a car like that in years—anyway, get this, it looked empty. My headlights were shining in through the windows, and I couldn't see anyone in it.

I'm saying to myself, *This is weird.* So I double-checked the location on the call slip I had gotten from the 9-1-1 dispatcher again. He said the situation was a woman stranded in an inoperable vehicle, and was called in as a nonemergency. So then next, I'm saying, *Oh no. I hope she didn't get out and start walking.* That would mean that I couldn't do a thing with her car without her signing the waiver, and I would've driven all the way out here in the middle of the night for nothing.

I decided to check the car, just in case she was lying down or something. I came around to the driver's side and shone my flashlight in. Sure enough, there she was hunkered down—but in the floor well—staring up at me with big eyes.

I bet the only reason she sat up and rolled down the window a few inches to talk to me was on account of I'm a woman. The panic on her face told me she might've started screaming or something if I had been a dude.

I said, "Did you call for a tow truck?"

She seemed kinda relieved and said, "I called 9-1-1. Aren't the police coming?"

"They sent me to come get you. Here's my identification." I held up my designated tow truck driver ID. "Are you okay with that?"

She nodded like a little kid. "Yes. Yes, it's okay."

Later on, after she had watched me chain up and secure her car, and we were driving back to the city, I asked her why she was lying down in the floor well instead of up on the seat. And you know what she told me? She said, "I wasn't sure exactly who was driving by. So I hid so I wouldn't be seen."

"Well, why hide?" I asked. "Wouldn't you have been more comfortable sitting up and listening to the radio or something? If you had your doors locked, it really wouldn't have mattered if anyone saw you."

And she said, "I was scared some kind of serial killer or rapist or human trafficker might spot me sitting in my car on that deserted road, and then smash the windows, unlock the doors, and drag me out."

"You got one busy imagination," I laughed.

Then she said, "If you don't mind me saying so, I was surprised when you drove up. You know, because you're a woman and all."

"You don't feel a woman should drive a tow truck? I'm towing your car home right now, aren't I?" I said.

"No, it's not that. It's just it would be scary being alone on these roads at night. I mean, what if someone, you know, goes crazy and attacks you?"

I laughed again. "Honey," I said, "the only thing I'm worried about on these roads at night are bears. Most of the people who call me are in trouble and need help. The last thing they want to do is attack me. I haven't met one person yet in fifteen years of towing who was that crazy."

"Oh," was all she said.

"So, if you don't mind me asking, where were you headed?"

"I was on my way to Kaktovik, Alaska."

"I haven't heard of that one. Where is it located?"

"Up north, by the Arctic Circle."

"Now what in God's name is up there besides a whole lot of cold?"

"Polar bears. I was going there to see the polar bears. But with my car breaking down, that's not going to happen. So I guess I'm headed nowhere now," she said sadly and sighed. She turned away and stared out the window. For the rest of the drive she wouldn't say any more. It was a quiet ride—the only sounds in the cab were the songs on my playlist playing softly and the windshield-wiper blades.

Now what would a girl like her want with polar bears? Or any bears for that matter? It was hard to tell in the darkness of the cab, but I was almost sure she was quietly sniffling to herself. Like I said before, she was a strange little thing.

CHAPTER TEN

Conclusion

If humans continue to make life rough on the polar bear with the ongoing assault on the environment, our future generations may only know of polar bears through Christmas cards and soda commercials. Like us, the polar bears are the top predators in the food chain. If polar bears are removed from the Arctic Circle ecosystem, the effects are going to be far reaching on many other organisms. Finding ways to survive drastic changes in their environment will not only take stamina, resourcefulness, and adaptability, it will also take courage.

Great strong ending. However, are there questions you could have asked? Good paper overall. Nice work!

A-

It was hard to explain to everyone exactly why I did what I had done. I mean, at the time it was perfectly clear to me what my objectives were when I had set off on my journey, and I thought I had made my intent and destination just as clear to all who I had left behind. But in retrospect, my objectives weren't clear enough for even me to understand, and apparently my intent and destination weren't clear enough for them to believe.

From what I gathered from different perspectives, here's how the whole thing played out. My mom found my note when she got home from work and started frantically calling my phone, except that by then I was out of range since we have a substandard local carrier for phone service. She then started checking all the places where I typically hung out—Sea View College, the library, the Avenue. She even went to Noni's just in case I was there, and that was when Noni got involved in the search.

Next, the two of them returned to our trailer and tore apart my room looking for Sig's address and phone number. Noni was convinced that I had run off with him because he got me pregnant, despite my mother telling her that it wasn't likely since he was in the hospital fighting cancer. However, that didn't dissuade my grandmother, who concocted that his illness was only a cover-up to throw everyone off about the pregnancy.

My mom then recalled the name of the hospital where Sig was admitted and went there to ask him if he knew where I was. Of course he had no clue, so at that point, he and Janice got involved, although my mother, in her panic, failed to tell them about my note. Sig called my phone and left messages and texts, but obviously I didn't receive them because, like I said, our carrier is cheap and by then, I was even farther out of range.

Sig had even tried to leave the hospital to help search for me, but he got in trouble with his mother and his care team, so he had to stay put. His care team threatened to call security on him to make sure he didn't leave. Noni seized the opportunity, while Janice and my mother were getting coffee, to start grilling him, telling him to drop the act and admit to knocking up her innocent granddaughter. That was when Janice stepped in and set things straight with her.

When they couldn't get any other information from Sig, my mom called my dad. At first they are worried about me and my whereabouts, but then they started blaming each other and got into a big argument. After that, I'm surprised my mom didn't try to contact Grandma O in Japan to find out if I was headed there. At that point, Grandma O was about the only person who didn't know what was going on.

Luckily, my mom thought she had to wait forty-eight hours before filing a missing-person's report, otherwise she probably would've done it the moment she found out I was gone. But eventually, she grew too impatient and went to the police station anyway to demand that they start looking for me, only to be told that she could have filed a report at any time and that the waiting period was only myth that was perpetuated by TV and movies.

However, since there weren't any signs of foul play or suspicious activity, and I did leave a very detailed note in my own handwriting outlining exactly where I was going in my own car and why, the police didn't feel it was critical to start an immediate search. Instead, they told my mom to go home and wait for the phone call at the scheduled time I had written down. And then, if she hadn't heard from me by the same time the following day, she could start a case.

I never did get to make that phone call because first, there was such a long wait at the restaurant to be served dinner. Then I had a lengthy conversation with Dr. Kristen Munghaven, a cool paleobotanist with scads of experience who had shared her table with me and talked about all sorts of fascinating things on being a field researcher.

There was no public phone at the restaurant, so contact with my mother had to wait until I checked in at the hotel and called from there. I figured she would have come home from work, read the note, made some dinner for herself, and watched TV while she waited for me to call. Except I didn't make it to the hotel because my car broke down on the side of the road when its radiator gave out, and it had to be towed back home. And I didn't anticipate her freaking out.

By the time the tow truck was in our plan's service range again, I checked my phone and saw the dozens of calls and texts from her, Dad, and Sig. I knew I was going to be in pretty big trouble when I got home. Immediately, I texted Sig to let him know that I was all right, and then I texted my dad, but I hesitated before calling my mom. I knew one of them would contact her to let her know they had heard from me.

She had to pick me up from the tow yard anyway. She didn't say much when she arrived and took out her checkbook to write a check for the tow, until I told her that I had already taken care of it. The drive home was silent, too. Trying to feel her out, I wouldn't venture anything, but she wouldn't say anything either.

Finally, when we were back at home and seated across the kitchen table from each other, each with a mug of her substitute-for-cigarettes hot chocolate with the mini marshmallows in front of us, she spoke. But it wasn't my usual mom. This person was different.

And what she said next would change my life immensely, although I didn't know if she knew that.

"Poodle, I have to ask you something," she started off thoughtfully, as if she were pondering a complex problem. "Is this what it's like for you?"

"Is *what* what it's like for me?"

"You had left me a note, explaining your every step of the way down to the last detail, where you would be and what time you expected to be there. You are a grown adult, capable of carrying on your own life. And yet, I panicked anyway. I imagined all sorts of terrible things had happened. I could see you hurt in an accident somewhere, or having run away from home never to return, or kidnapped and forced to write the letter by some abductor, or ten million other horrible, scary scenarios. I was beside myself with worry. It wasn't until the police told me to go home to wait for your call, and then Sig calling to tell me your car broke down and you were in a tow truck coming home that I could stop worrying. In fact, it gave me a moment to think. And then it finally occurred to me that this must be what my baby feels when she has her Gray Days, or when she has to return home to check the lock on the front door three times, or when she's scrubbing the trailer until her hands bleed because she's upset about her friend.

"Am I right? Is this what it's like for you, Molly? I'm not angry with you. I just want to know. Is this how it feels?" Her eyes filled with tears and she took my hands in hers.

My own eyes got moist as gladness and relief swelled within me. For the first time in my nineteen years, she understood. She finally understood me.

I nodded. "Yes, Mom. It is."

"I still can't believe you did it."

"Yeah ... neither can I. It feels like a dream at this point," I said. After I had caught up on some sleep, Mom dropped me off at the hospital to visit my lab partner. "For all I accomplished, I should have just mooned the train instead."

"How the hell were you going to fly to Kaktovik and rent a snow mobile anyway? That's what I'm waiting to hear." Bemused amazement lit up Sig's face, as if he had just asked, "Why did the chicken cross the road?" and was waiting for a totally random and nonsensical reply, like, "It was the first fifty feet en route to Portugal."

To be honest, I hadn't thought it out that far. The planning effort had been spent on rounding up the cash, writing the note, packing my bag, and working out the scheduled phone calls. I had assumed I could drive straight to Kaktovik, and road signs would point me in the right direction along the way. Just the fact that I would have to travel over an international border into Canada by myself and use my passport for the very first time was overwhelming enough, so I had consulted the online maps only as far as Alaska's southern border. Let's just say, the whole trip was the most impulsive thing I had ever done in my life. And for the duration, it seriously felt was like I was on autopilot.

I shrugged. "I thought I could drive it."

Sig laughed with incredulousness. "You have to cross the Arctic National Wildlife Refuge to get there. And that's only about the size of Texas! I know because I looked it up."

I shrugged again, with my shoulders arching a little higher, hoping that he would get the hint.

"So how far did you get?"

It was hard to admit that I didn't even make it out of the state. My car broke down nine miles out of Tonasket. I had only about fourteen more to make it to the border.

"It doesn't matter anymore. It was an epic failure. I don't know what I was doing. And I ended up burning through the rest of our fund money between the gas and the tow back home. Now we're going to have to start all over again. Well, at least I will."

"Why? Are you saying that just because I'm in the hospital, you wouldn't ask me to—"

"No. I just didn't think that you would ever want to work with me again. Not after what I did."

"After what you did? What are you talking about?"

"I don't know—act like a crazy person? I was completely irrational and unreasonable."

"Well, that's exactly why I would work with you. And if I get the chance to get out of this place, I'd do it all over again. In fact, it took real cojones to do what you did. Except, of course, technically, you don't have any cojones. But you know what I mean."

"You ... feel that way?"

"Yeah, I was totally blown away when your mom came here and told me that you had taken off on your own. I was like, '*All right.* Go Molly!' And then your grandma got all up in my face, accusing me of being the father of our unborn love child, which was a bit surreal. It was all good, though. I know she was just worried about you. Grandmas are like that. But now I'm going to have to borrow a hapa baby from someone six months from now just to scare the shit out of her. Besides all that, do you want to know what the best part was?"

"What?"

"You're back. I'll be totally honest in saying that I felt lost and totally devastated without your hand sanitizer. I am whole once more."

"Shut up," I said. But inside, I was smiling.

It was blue. And quiet. The only sound in that silent world was that of bubbles escaping my nostrils. Light rays fanned out in bright triangles slicing through the wavering cerulean ahead of me. They grew faint as they stretched downward toward the gray-black depths below.

My big paws pushed through the water, as I effortlessly paddled onward. I turned toward the sky. It was a very long way up, the clouds resting beyond the shimmering surface overhead. So many times before I had aimed for them and paddled and paddled but never made it. So many times I had struggled to get to those clouds.

Just when it seemed like it was going to be yet another futile attempt, I started to ascend. The clouds grew sharper in definition, and the surface of the water was now a ceiling of glass above my head. My paws swept the water in strong downward strokes, propelling me upward.

The next thing I knew, my big head broke the surface. Fresh cool air flowed into my lungs. The sun shone in brilliant crescents upon the waves rippling about me, as the water lapped against my nose and splashed into my flared nostrils. I searched about for land, and although I couldn't immediately spot it, I was treading water with the easy confidence that I would happen upon it soon.

A lone yellow duck flew overhead, skimming past the clouds. Its wings weren't flapping furiously like other ducks', but instead were held straight back as it soared like a little rocket on a direct course to some place unknown. Instinctively I knew if I swam in the same direction, I would find some place to haul out. I paddled on.

When I came around, I lay in that limbo state between sleep and consciousness in my bed, and wriggled my toes under the blankets with satisfaction. I had broken the surface once and for all. Waking up completely, I pulled back my blankets and got up. For the rest of the day, that dream replayed in my head.

The very next time I had a chance to visit Sig, a strange man was sitting in his room when I knocked and entered. He was tall and weathered, with grizzled, short hair that was mostly covered with a faded cap. He barely nodded at me when I came in.

"Oh hey, Mol. This is my dad, Chester," Sig said.

It was then I recognized Sig's features stamped on the man's leathery face, as I shook his hand that felt as coarse as bark. Aside from a mumbled "pleased to meet you," he didn't say much else.

Chester Despain returned to staring out the window from his seat on the recliner by Sig's bed. He appeared to be a man who probably had no trouble stating his mind when he wanted to. And according to Sig's stories, that usually was the case. However, I guess he didn't have anything to say right now. At least not to me, at which I was relieved, especially if he was anything like his father, as I recalled Grandpa Despain with a shudder.

"My dad's in from Montana right now, visiting me. I tried texting to let you know, but you must've been driving already."

Montana. Right. I had forgotten that Sig mentioned that his dad worked the fracking fields there in Sidney. I learned this one time when we were talking about what our parents did for a living.

"No worries," I said. "I was just going to hang with you, but it's okay. I can come back tomorrow."

Sig nodded and sighed. "Yeah," was all he said. It felt as if I had come in at a sensitive moment and was now intruding. Then he shrugged as if to say, "Sorry about this," so I took it as a sign for me to leave.

Just then, Sig's mom came in looking hassled and tired. "Oh, hi Molly. How are you doing?" she asked, distractedly.

Now with both of his parents there, I really felt like I was intruding on this little family. "Oh fine, Janice. Uh, I was just getting ready to leave."

"No, it's okay if you want to stay. Sig loves it when you visit."

Sig threw up his hands in embarrassment. "Yeah, thanks Mom. I feel like I'm two again."

But Janice wasn't listening. Instead, she stood in front of Chester and in a low voice she asked, "So have you decided whether or not you are going to stay for a few more days?"

"I've already told you, I can't. I've got a job to do, and I can't just take off whenever I feel like it," Mr. Despain grumbled without facing her, staring out the window instead. "I already lost hours this time around. I've got responsibilities."

"Well that's just fine. With all that is going on, it would be nice if I could rely on you for at least some of it."

"If I don't get back to work, you won't be able to rely on any of it, especially my paycheck."

"I just need some support. This isn't easy. It would be good for your son to get some support from his father, too."

"Well, what the hell do you think I'm doing out there all day?" His stare was directly on her now.

The tension in the room was very uncomfortable. Although I felt bad about abandoning Sig in that standoff, I had to get out of there. "I'll text you later, Sig. Good-bye, Janice … And good-bye, Mr. Despain. It was nice to meet you."

Caught off guard, the somber man raised his hand in a half wave. Sig's mom sat down on the couch and rubbed her cheek, as if contemplating another point to debate with him.

"Text me later," I said quietly to Sig.

"I will. Maybe we can hang tomorrow?" he said.

I stole one last glance toward his parents who sat quietly, not facing each other.

"Yeah, sure."

But we never did get together. I had a sore throat the next day, so I wasn't permitted to visit the hospital in accordance with the sign in the elevator about putting patients at risk. And when I was feeling better the day after that, Sig was already gone. I arrived at his room to find the name "Mario Delacruz" written on the whiteboard by the door and a Hispanic family exiting the room.

By that evening, Sig finally texted.

> Sorry 'bout not seeing you before I left. Things got really crazy. I couldn't find the power cord to my phone, so I couldn't call either.

> What happened? Are you at home?

> Actually I'm in Mt. Sinai, in NY.

> NY!??? WTH?

My doc told us about a clinical trial here that was willing to take me ASAP. One of their patients dropped out at the last minute. I was a match for the trial since I am the right age and in the right stage of treatment.

So when do you get back?

My mom and me moved in with my Aunt Mary. She lives close to the hospital. My dad's back in MT. I'll be starting the trial on Monday.

That's great. But when do you finish?

Don't know yet. They say maybe in 30 to 40 months.

My heart was split in two.

My bed pulled on me, heavily. I tried sitting upright but couldn't fight the sinking of my body into the blankets, like the calving of an iceberg into the ocean. I obeyed its gravity by burrowing under my comforter to shut everything out. The world was a desolate place filled only with uncertainty and good-byes. I so wanted to smother the fiery pain burning in the center of my chest and quiet the rainstorm in my head. I wanted to dissolve.

Sig was gone. It was almost as painful for me as hearing the prognosis of his relapse. I knew I couldn't be selfish. The only thing that tempered this news was the hope that this new treatment would help him be free of cancer once and for all. But why didn't it make me feel any better?

The wet spot grew beneath my cheek as tears soaked into my pillow. *The mung bean plant, dried-up and brown by the window. The war raging between imaginary bugs in the paneling. The figurine of my dad standing on the nightstand. The images of the Mel-and-Mol photo collage on the wall.* I contemplated them all, as I always did on Gray Days. My gaze settled upon the snapshot my mom had taken of me in the bear suit standing next to Sig, who was doubled over with laughter. Dr. Pope was right. I was a worthless creature who was unfit for this world. Even Sig was unfit.

I rolled onto my back and focused on the ceiling instead. My sinuses, inflamed from crying, instantly stuffed up, forcing me to breathe past my chapped lips. I had lost count of the number of times I found myself in this same situation because most of the seventeen years I had walked this planet had been this low-down, bottomed-out miserable. Too many hours … days … months I had spent lying like this in this bed, in this drab, dull room; its paneled walls were the sides of the box that contained me. I knew I didn't want to keep going on like this. I couldn't.

I never wanted to cry again.

My mind sifted wearily, wrestling with the pieces of my life that stubbornly refused to fit. My parents were never getting back together. My best friend was dead. My new best friend was dying of cancer. I would always have depression and freak out over everything. I would be stuck forever in this trailer and never have a real life. I failed at almost everything I attempted.

There didn't appear to be any options. And there wasn't anyone who could help me through this. Exhausted, I was adrift and frightened to be alone.

Among all the thoughts that were colliding in my head, one echoed over and over again, cycling in waves and growing in intensity until it could no longer be ignored. It was the secret whisper that haunted my Gray Days, the one that was off limits and unfathomable because it was so terrifying. But now it forced its way to the front where it dominated, unforgiving and bullying.

I should take myself out of the equation.

Once I permitted this idea to surface, it became more and more compelling for several reasons. I wouldn't have to go through another Gray Day or panic attack ever again. My mom wouldn't have to worry about me and could start a new life for herself. My dad could stop feeling ashamed. I wouldn't have to be despondent, scared, or anxious anymore. I wouldn't have to say good-bye, or miss anyone, or ache for anyone to come back.

A few ways to pull it off came to mind as my determination grew. Thinking that pills would be the easiest and cleanest way to go, I hunted for any that I thought should do the job. Unfortunately, aside from Midol or vitamin C, we had only five aspirin left in our entire trailer.

Still determined, the next cleanest way would be the drive-off-the-cliff option. Especially since I could do it with the top down on my car just like in *Thelma and Louise*. But I remembered I didn't have enough gas to get to the rural mountain passes where it was steep enough. And my car would probably break down again along the way as it climbed the grades.

Although it made me really squeamish, and I knew it would make a huge mess if I didn't do it right, the only option I had left was to slit my wrists. I decided if the razor blade was sharp enough, I could get through it quickly and be done.

Take yourself out of the equation.

I methodically prepared for my death. We didn't have a bathtub, but I figured I could sit in the corner on the floor of my shower and run the water hot. I fished out the box cutter from the odds and ends drawer in our kitchen and checked its edge. I undressed. I placed my clothes in the washing machine, along with all of my other dirty laundry and put them to wash. I wished I could have stuck around to put the load into the dryer, fold them, and put them away so my mom wouldn't have to, but that would take too much time. She would be home soon, and I might lose my nerve if I waited much longer.

I climbed into the warming stream of water, closed the curtain, and sat down in the shower. The plastic floor felt odd beneath my bare bum, and for a fleeting moment I worried about getting athlete's foot on my butt cheeks. This close to the floor, the water splattered in my face. I looked up. From this low angle, I spied a fine line of pink mold I had missed in a corner crevice under the cracked soap dish.

Refocusing, I studied the razor edge of the box cutter, and next, the ropy tendons and blue veins snaking under the skin of my left forearm. Taking a deep breath, I placed the tip of the blade against the inside of my wrist between two tendons and took one more deep breath, readying to drag the unforgiving metal up my arm to the crook of my elbow and then repeat on my right arm. I was going to carry through with this once and for all. I would be the one to say good-bye.

Take yourself out of the equation.

But it wasn't so easy.

As I struggled to concentrate, that afternoon working at the bakery and my mom calling to tell me to come home resurfaced in my memory. It was the afternoon Melody had killed herself. I remembered how, by the tone of my mother's voice, I could tell that something was terribly wrong.

Unwittingly, my mind summoned the important people in my life and stood them before me like a police lineup. Where would they be when they learned what I had done? When the realization of my suicide overwhelmed her comprehension, would Mom be sitting with her cup of hot chocolate with those mini marshmallows or would she be reaching for a drink instead? Would she feel betrayed or confused, especially after she thought she finally understood me? Would Dad feel incomparably guilty for ever having left? He would be lying in that firehouse bunk, over a thousand miles away, alone with no one to turn to as he absorbed the news. And then there was Sig, with all of those lines and wires snaking out of his body, sick to his stomach in that dark, colorless hospital room, staring out the window. Would he feel abandoned?

I recalled Debra Chastings' desperate clutch. I could still feel the spots where each of her fingers had dug into my back, as if she were sliding off into some cold abyss. Spasms of pain and grief shuddered that once happy woman so intensely they had rattled my insides while we stood broken and lost in that room filled with memories of her dead daughter.

The sharp bite of the blade breaking my skin brought me back to the present. I lifted the cutter and was surprised at the bright red blood seeping from the small slit in my wrist. It ran from the wound to the floor and quickly mixed with the hot water; I realized then my own blood was splattering in my face. The steady shower stream continued to drum upon the floor, striking the curtain, dripping off the ends of my hair, mixing with my blood, and running down the drain. I was wasting water.

I was wasting my life.

First cold and next hot, I shut off the faucets and climbed out of that confining little space. Taking a last glance at the box cutter, I tossed it into the wastebasket and grabbed a towel. Neosporin and a tight bandage were immediately applied to the slit to stop the bleeding. And I swabbed my butt cheeks with alcohol before I dressed, just in case athlete's-foot fungus was possible. Although my head was now splitting from the turbulence of emotional exertion—from crying uncontrollably, to psyching myself up, to the touching down—I contemplated my next move with fuzzy tenacity. I had to get out of there.

I got into my rusted car and instead of fleeing to plunge off a mountain cliff somewhere, I sought out the lapping, soothing call of something much bigger. I drove to where the Puget Sound met the shore, knowing the salty waves had come there from their faraway travels to the arctic oceans. I put the top down with no care about the weather to pull the fresh, cool air into my lungs and feel the sun kissing the top of my head.

Closing my eyes for a moment, I savored the cries of seagulls overhead and the faint barking of seals crowding on a buoy in the distance. I heard the hiss of the water as it combed over the sand. The foam rolling in the surf indicated photosynthesis was taking place beneath the water from growing algae. The ocean water was evaporating and soon would come down as rain to soak me and the mattress man once again. The world was full of life and I was part of it. Me and Sig, my dad and my mom, the cedar tree and the polar bears, even the mung beetles. We all had a place on this planet, and we were inextricably linked. If any one of us were removed, there would be a hole left in that fabric that just may never mend.

Holding on to this, I contemplated an alternative that wouldn't shatter those I loved or leave a gaping hole where the cold rain could come in. It was a simple and pure solution that made sense.

I could just get through this.

Somehow, I had managed it before, but never at a conscious level. It just happened, and I had endured whatever things had driven me down. More surprising still, I wound up laughing and loving and crying again. It was a cycle of loss and renewal. I determined then if I was here at this very moment, I had indeed been fit enough all along to survive to this point. I also reasoned that eventually, normalcy would come around as it always did. I wouldn't have to struggle and fight to feel it again. But this time … This time it would be my choice.

Yes, why not? I will get through this.

When I returned home, our driveway seemed oddly wide and expansive, like something was missing. It took a few seconds to register exactly what had happened. The tree and Mr. Martino's crushed trailer had been hauled away. In fact, I had just missed the extraction—when I glanced down the row, I caught the back end of the trailer with temporary taillights attached clearing the corner and disappearing from view.

Inside our own trailer, I surveyed my room. It wasn't a bad place, really. It was my own space, and this was my home that I shared with my mom. With newfound clarity, I scanned the photo collage over my desk until I found the image where Melody and I were only freshmen in high school, mugging for the camera, and wearing our matching hoodies. It was an easier time for both of us, before all the trouble had started for my poor, dear friend. I carefully pulled the photo off the wall, removed the tape from the back of it, and placed it to the side. Then I removed the rest of the photos one by one, until they were all taken down and stacked neatly in a drawer. The wall behind my desk was open now, clear and full of potential.

Embracing that feeling, I went to the hardware store and bought several cans of "oops paint"—the ones that people had ordered at the paint counter and then changed their minds about, so the paint was deeply discounted—along with a roller, pan, and paintbrush. On the way back, I spied an overgrown potted fern sitting by the curbside of someone's house. It had a handwritten cardboard sign marked "FREE" on it. I stopped, and when I was sure that no one was looking, so there wouldn't be any mistaken idea of theft, I added the plant to my supplies in the back seat of my car. With the very last few dollars I had left from the trip, I finished up my shopping at the dollar store by purchasing some photo frames.

In my room, the paint roller traveled over any surface it could reach, laying down swaths of robin's-egg blue, bright manila yellow, and lime green in its wake. It rolled over the paneled walls, the pocket door, the antique crackling on the chest of drawers Noni had gotten for me, and across the scuffed princess and unicorn on my bed's headboard. While the paint dried, I fished the box cutter out of the trash and cut holes in the bottom of the mop bucket, tossed out the dried-up mung bean plant, and used its soil to repot the new plant so it would have more room to grow. I placed three photos: the one of Mel and me, one of Sig and me, and one of my mom and dad when they were still together, into the new frames. I set them, the fern, and the figurine of my dad on my desk by the window. I found a wire coat hanger and rigged it so the louvers could open as wide as possible to let in the additional light offered by the absence of Mr. Martino's trailer, and cracked the windows for fresh air.

Moments later, my mom drove up. I could hear the front door open and the jangle of her keys as she placed them down on the counter.

"Hey Poodle. I'm home. Did you see that Mr. Martino's—What the ... ? Oh shit ... Molly? Molly!"

Noticing the things I had moved out into the living room to make space for painting, she rushed into my room with panic and worry expecting to find me scouring away in some kind of cleaning frenzy again. However, when she saw that I was only painting my transformed space, she looked around at the improvements and broke into a smile. Pleased, she nodded her head and sighed.

"I like it, Mol. I like it a lot."

Two months had gone by. One part of me was beyond excited to see him again. The other part of me was crushed, because our visit together would be only for a brief few hours. We had hardly been able to text or call since he'd left because his mom had to switch to a cheaper plan to save money, and they had to share minutes and data. But when he came into view with that long-strided swagger of his, I nearly tackled him out of happiness.

He grinned. "I'm sorry we couldn't meet at my Aunt Mary's place. She works nights, so she's asleep right now. Besides, her apartment is so small, Mom's got her foldout sofa bed, and I got the tiny twin-size bed in the spare bedroom whenever I'm not in-patient. Get this—that bed is so small, my feet hang off of it even if I sleep on a diagonal. Anyway, we don't have to stay here in the park if you don't want to. We can go get some coffee. There's a place close by so we can walk."

"No worries. I'm just glad to be here. And you're looking … good." His dark curls were gone, replaced by a smooth head covered with a beanie cap. Under the cap, his complexion was splotchy and gray. His black-rimmed glasses were windshield-like now, dominating his gaunt face. When I hugged him, I was surprised at how fragile his lanky frame felt. The chemo and radiation had obviously left their mark on him. "Things going okay with the trial so far?"

"So far so good. But I have to take a shit-ton more pills, and the diet is really strict, which means only whole foods, which means no more Funyuns, which totally sucks. But at least I can get out for short periods of time by myself now, as long as my counts are good. Like today. In fact, I'm supposed to exercise some. Anyway, we won't know if the treatment's successful for another six months or so."

"Oh … And then you'll come back home?"

"Yeah, well, that's the plan right now …" Sig trailed off. Switching gears, he said, "So, anymore polar bear stuff?"

"That's been on hold. Really, nothing since that trip. I've been too busy between school and work lately. Although, I'm contemplating another project."

"Yeah? Now what? Swim noodles for polar bears or neon tankinis to help spot them in open water?"

I laughed, relieved to see that Sig was still his old self. "No, this is completely different. So you know how whales navigate by sound? And you know how noisy the ocean is getting because of all the boat traffic? Well, there should be some kind of big visual signs that can be anchored at the bottom of the ocean pointing the way along the whales' busiest routes. Like road signs with symbols that they could eventually learn to read, in a sense, for direction."

"Why not? If polar bears have to learn where their platforms are, and whales are supposed to be smarter than polar bears, there shouldn't be any problem with that. But hey, speaking of learning new tricks, check you out. How did you get here to the park? Did you rent a car?"

"Airport shuttle."

"Get out of here! I thought you hated mass transit."

"I still do, but I actually survived it."

"I wish I had Mr. Chips here. We could've come pick you up. So where are you staying?"

"Do you remember me mentioning my cousin, Denny? Well, I'm staying with him and his wife and baby. I'm only here for one night, though. And then I'm flying to Colorado from here to visit my dad for a couple of days. Unfortunately, I wasn't able to get much time off. But I wanted to come see you while I still had the nerve to fly."

"I can't get over the fact that you're actually flying. Seriously. You're getting to be a regular Amelia Earhart. I never thought I'd see it."

"Actually, I found out the trick to get me through a flight was these …" I extracted a coiled-up pair of earbuds from my pocket to show him. "I learned if I close my eyes and listen to '80s rock, I could tune the rest of the world out, including a plane ride."

"Wow, you really dig it that much now?" Sig asked, a newfound appreciation in his eyes. "Right on."

"Uh, not really. And I still don't get Tears for Fears, but it reminds me of you, so I find it very calming, and I can relax."

"So I bet you're glad I'm not into screamo, then?" he snorted.

"No kidding. But mostly, I tell myself, 'hey, if I can attempt a trip to the Arctic Circle, I can do anything.'"

"Uh huh. I'm proud of you, Mol ... Oh! Right. That's why I wanted to give you this." He fished around in his coat pocket and withdrew a flat package wrapped in its store bag and tied with a shoelace. His magical coat pockets never failed to intrigue me.

I opened the bag to find a book on the Revolutionary War hero, Molly Pitcher. I must have had a curious expression, because he explained, "It's because of your bravery and courage under fire. Well, at first I got it because you both are named Molly. And then the other stuff on bravery and courage was an added bonus."

I paged through the book that appeared to be written for middle-school-aged kids. It was full of illustrations and anecdotes on Mary Hays, who was better known as Molly Pitcher.

"Sorry it's a kid book, but it was the only information I could find on her that wasn't in a history textbook."

"No, no. This is great. Wait, did you do this ... ?"

A block of text on a page, opposite an illustration showing a sweaty and determined Molly Pitcher on a battlefield, had been circled in bright yellow highlighter. It read:

> Mary Hays, otherwise known as Molly to her friends and those who fought alongside of her, was an intrepid spirit and a fighting force during the Revolutionary War. When her husband was wounded on the battlefield, she put down the pitcher of water she was carrying to the troops and picked up the ramrod he used to load the cannon, taking his place on the front. As the battle raged on, she continued loading for hours, never stopping.

Many soldiers on the battlefield who fought alongside of Molly were astounded by her tenacity and spunk. One story tells how the bottom of Molly's skirt was torn off by a British musket ball in the heat of a battle. According to the account, the musket ball had sailed between her legs, tattering her skirt. Surprisingly, she wasn't injured. When her fellow soldiers asked if she was all right, Molly, unfazed, examined her torn skirt and simply said, "Well, that could have been worse," and went back to her task of loading the cannon.

Sig grinned. "I thought that was the best part. It reminded me of you."

"Who me? Yeah, right."

"Yeah, you. Totally. You might not know this, but you are so like a zombie."

"What!" He still had the ability to throw curveballs I couldn't hit. "How so?"

"Zombies are very resilient. No matter what people do to them—shoot them, blow them up, whatever—they keep coming back. But you're even better, because you are not some fictitious undead, so at least you have a sense of humor."

I blushed under his praise and assessment especially since I knew how much zombies meant to him. "Well, I brought something for you, too." Rummaging around in my purse, I withdrew my gift and handed it to him. "It's a souvenir of our glory days."

"Hey, it's Mr. PB! Sweet! He is one of my favorites," he said as he unwrapped my sculpted polar bear figurine and admired it.

"That way, you won't forget what we've been through."

"How could I forget? The memory of you getting held up in that demented polar bear costume is permanently etched in my brain. Oh, yeah, speaking of which, there's one more thing. Here …"

He produced an envelope from his other coat pocket. It held a thank-you card with a photo of a polar bear and the Polar Bear

World Conservation logo on the front. Inside was printed a form letter, with its fill-in information in bold and a different font:

> Congratulations **Molly Ohashi of SPFB!** You helped save **one** polar bear from extinction. Your generous donation of $ **350** will be used toward vital research and conservation efforts to aid this majestic animal from the growing threat of climate change and warming global temperatures. Wild polar bears and we, at Polar Bear World Conservation, thank you.

"Wait. Where did you get this? I didn't donate any money to Polar Bear World Conservation. There must be some kind of mistake," I said, reading it again.

"I did. On your behalf."

"You did? But where did you get three hundred and fifty dollars?"

"It's nothing. Just my wing-suit money."

I was shocked. "But that was for you to fly! You shouldn't have—"

"Hey, I already had the biggest thrill ride in my life tangling up with you. My old pump can't stand another." He laid his hand over his heart in a feigned attack.

I stared deeply into those dozy eyes of his. Did I say that I love Sig? I do.

I grabbed him in a fierce hug and held on tight. "Thank you. Seriously. This is amazing. And I will be paying you back as soon as I can."

He grinned again. "And did you catch that it has 'SPFB' on it? So that way, your organization will start to get some exposure in those serious science-y circles."

I sighed and smiled. "It's '*SPFPB*.' But I've been thinking about shortening it anyway. Want to go for some coffee now?"

"Sure. It's right down the block from here. But I'll tell you straight up—the place is not much better than our own Mr. Liu's."

"Great. It'll feel just like home then."

In that moment, Sig went pale. Next, he wobbled and swayed, and I stopped to brace him until he could steady himself.

"Whoa. You doing okay?"

"Yeah, it's just one of my new meds bottoms out my blood pressure, that's all."

"Well, here. Use me if you have to." I took his arm and wrapped it around my shoulders. "You can act like I'm your girlfriend. No one would know any different."

"As long as you don't set a date for us to pick out matching bath sheets," he quipped.

As we walked along, I could feel him settle in with his weight resting upon my shoulders. It felt good to be able to help him.

"I'm glad that we're going for coffee. I'm freezing," I said.

"I guess your trip to Alaska didn't do anything for your homeostasis?"

"I didn't make it, remember?"

"Yes, Mol. Sure you did."

With my arm around his waist, I hugged him in gratitude. We walked on.

Chapter 10.5

Marine NOW
Neoteric Options for Water

Dear Ms. Ohashi,

A friend and colleague, Dr. Kristin Munghaven, gave me your name. She suggested I contact you regarding your innovative idea to build swim platforms for polar bears especially in areas of long, open stretches of water where ice floes use to exist.

I took the liberty of running your idea by Marine NOW engineers, oceanographers, and marine biologists who work closely with me to provide solutions to problems of wildlife crises due to climate change. My team felt it was a viable alternative to natural ice floes in the interim.

If possible, I would like to further discuss your idea and how it might be planned, funded, and implemented. Marine NOW is a conservation foundation that can offer research, as well as technical and developmental funding support.

It is through fresh approaches like your swim-platform idea that we may slow down the rapid decimation of polar bears. I look forward to your reply and meeting you.

Your friend in conservation,

Gale

Dr. Gale Mengalor, PhD Marine Sciences
Founder and Director of Marine NOW

Guide for Book Clubs and Classrooms

Topics and Questions for Discussion

1) Courage presents itself in many ways and is different for each individual. With this in mind, compare courage between the various characters: Molly versus Melody, Molly versus Sig, Molly versus her mom, Dr. Pam Pope versus Dr. Kristin Munghaven, Shannon Afton versus Debra Chastings.

2) Think of the perspectives of Molly, Sig, and the other characters' accounts. How do we view ourselves and others? How does our perspective influence our capabilities? How does our perspective of others influence their capabilities?

3) Expectations—what do we expect from ourselves? What do we expect from others? What happens when our actions defy another's expectations of us?

4) When you are forced outside of your comfort zone, how do you handle changes to your perspective, expectations, or courage?

5) Molly is an average, ordinary girl who feels powerless to change things. Do you agree or disagree? How powerless are any of us to enact change?

6) In what ways are Molly and Kristin Munghaven the same or different? Discuss how Molly might or might not be like Dr. Munghaven in the future.

7) Why is Sig's outlook on life so different than Molly's? Is one outlook more practical than the other? Why or why not?

8) At the end of the book, do you agree with Sig's assessment of Molly? Why or why not?

9) What is the significance of Molly's recurring dreams? How about Sig's dream of flying?

10) What symbolism is present in the story?

11) Where do Molly's anxiety and obsessive compulsive disorder stem from?

12) What factors (e.g. individuals, circumstances, identity) shaped Molly's journey?

13) In what ways is Shannon supportive/unsupportive of Molly?

14) What is Molly's new strategy for dealing with future obstacles?

Enhance Your Book Club or Classroom

Research topics to enhance or enrich discussion for your book club or classroom:

1) Current work to save polar bears

   polarbearsinternational.org

   www.worldwildlife.org/species/polar-bear

   www.nwf.org/polarbear/

2) The effects of melting polar ice on the environment and living organisms

3) The effects of social media, bullying, and how they contribute to the suicide rate among teens

4) General anxiety disorder and obsessive compulsive disorder

5) Acute lymphoblastic leukemia (ALL)

About the author

TESS MARSET writes in the fiction genres of gothic suspense, contemporary romance, and short story. This is her first young adult novel. Tess lives in with her family in Edmonds, Washington.

More Stories from Tess Marset

With My Little Eye
(Book One of The Mia Series)
978-1-7333609-0-6

Gothic Suspense, Thriller

Shelf Unbound Award Winner – Best Indie Book 2016 Runner Up

I spy with my little eye…

Mia Labont is going insane. Or is she? After enduring the loss of her beloved father and a devastating miscarriage, she cannot surface from the depths of her depression so much so that her husband, Dan, comes home to find her suffering a breakdown with a gun in her hand.

They are launched into a perilous journey of madness when Mia starts to see grisly images in mirrors and other reflective surfaces. The terrifying appearances become vivid manifestations of a tortured teen, so vivid that Mia cannot discern whether they are supernatural phenomena or illusion.

At the hands of a callous therapist, Mia's condition only grows worse, affecting her marriage and health. Dan must make hard decisions whether to believe his wife or institutionalize her. Yet, continuing inexplicable events unfold that make him doubt even himself.

Mia must untangle a web of clues that will determine destinies while realizing her own abilities, yet Dan is the only one who can save her. Will he reach her in time?

Lest We Fall
(Book Two of The Mia Series)
978-1-7333609-1-3

Gothic Suspense, Thriller

*What if you had a unique skill that you never asked for?
A talent that would endanger the lives of your family...*

With the appearance of a young girl in her mirror, Mia Labont's odyssey into the supernatural continues in this sequel to With My Little Eye. She and husband Dan were settling in to a renewed home life after the birth of their son. But their time of happiness is short lived as the forlorn child in the mirror starts to reveal clues of her imprisonment. Mia is forced to call upon her intuitive powers to solve the mystery surrounding the girl's whereabouts in a race against tragedy. In doing so, she comes face to face with a much darker force that will not only test her resolve, but ultimately, her will to survive.

On Frogs and Princes
978-1-7333609-3-7

Contemporary Romance

When Stazie Royale sets her sights on something, she usually gets it. The pampered daughter of a successful defense attorney for celebrities is used to having her way. However, life begins to change for her one rainy night once she runs over Rey Natal while he is riding his bicycle during a blackout. Trying to come to terms with guilt and depression over a tragedy in his past, independent Rey is more than a challenge for Stazie's willful wiles. Encountering more mishaps, this unlikely pair must get beyond misperceptions to gain awareness for what they each had all along: love and appreciation for what they didn't think was possible. On Frogs and Princes is a story of abandonment, forgiveness, acceptance, and discovering that while all frogs aren't princes, even princesses can have warts.

THE X-MAS TREE

978-1-7333609-2-0

Novella

In this coming-of-age tale, 15-year-old Peter gets his first glimpse at the responsibility and commitment it takes in being a provider. *The X-Mas Tree* is about a father and son's love for each other that is tested by the challenges of progress overshadowing tradition and the transformation of a boy to a man.